# IF I WAS A BOY

*BY*
*ALETA WILLIAMS*

1

**If I Was A Boy**

## Dedications

This book is dedicated to Ricky Frazier. You are your family's heavenly angel. Continue to offer your unconditional love, compassion, protection and guidance in their lives. They miss you tremendously. Thanks, Rick, for supporting me, reading all of my books, and being a standup guy. Even after death #YOUROCK!

To my readers, my husband, and children, your support is the biggest reason that I keep on pushing. God bless you and thank you. I mean that from the bottom of my heart.

## Disclaimer

This is a hood book with a lot of hood shit going down. Drugs, violence, hood glory, and sex, is highly influenced in the storyline. However, Aleta will never leave her readers without delivering an important message. Wisdom is the principal thing; Therefore get wisdom. And in all your getting, get understanding. Proverbs 4:7.

This book is almost 80k words with quite a few characters. There will be no sequel, but I think you may want the F&F Crew to tell their stories of trappin' in the hood and living the bosschick life. I would love for you to email me if that's the case, and please don't forget to leave a review on my website, and other platforms.

# Contents

Spade

NUNU

NUNU

SEN

NUNU

A little while later…

Spade

Lucas aka Lo

SEN

NUNU

SEN

NUNU

Two Days Later.

Jo

NUNU

SEN

Days later

NUNU

GAV

Lucas

Next day

SEN

6 months later

SEN

UNO

Dez

Saturday afternoon, the scorching hot sun beamed down on a full crowd of people. The weather forecasters warned people of the dangerous hot conditions on that day and for the next few days. However, it didn't deter the hundreds of spectators who came to turn up with The Fancy & Fine Crew. This would be their 3rd annual "TURN UP 4 DA HOOD" event. The block party was one of many ways to give back to the hood. The mayor gave her blessings for the girls to do their thing. During the holiday season, they distributed food baskets and gifts for the parents and children of the neighborhood. The first weekend in August, they turned up on Saturday and Sunday. Free food, drinks, and entertainment for all. They solely set up one block for the kids to have fun without being in grown folks business. From sun up to sundown, they turned up. The community had so much love for the way the crew looked out for the hood. If they had haters, which they were sure they did, they stayed in the cut, irrelevant and unnoticed. Everyone gave them their respect. Anybody who came at them wrong would definitely get the business. The chicks were straight shooters and to top it off, all of them could fight.

The crew was made up of four chicks who were born and raised in South-Central Los Angeles. It was JoJo, Lil Momma, Shy, and Nova. When their names were mentioned, you couldn't help but think of 'Boss Bitches.' The dope game contributed to their come up and celebrity- like status.

The events always looked like something you would see in those ghetto movies or read about in the urban magazines. Fancy cars, motorcycles, fine niggas, and bad bitches were gathered everywhere. There was a DJ booth on each block.

Each had a different genre of music that catered to a particular audience. One played oldies but goodies, another deviated between R&B and Rap, and the third played a clean version of music for the kids. Due to everything that was offered, and it being free, the event always hit the girls' pockets for about fifteen grand. They appreciated the donations they received, but even if they didn't get them, it didn't matter. South Central was their life. South Central helped them become very wealthy, all within a matter of years, and for that, the crew would always be grateful.

Four red Yamaha motorcycles bent the block. The crowd parted like the Red Sea. On the back of each was a customized license plate cover bearing a red FF with a money-bag symbol at the end. The Fancy & Fine Crew crazed the crowd as they made their grand entrance. The flamboyant DJ made his announcement as they came into view.

"Put your hands together and give it up for the women of The Fancy & Fine Crew. These bitches are the reason we are out here in this heat, having a good damn time, if I might say so myself." He added as he wiped sweat from his face with a blue washcloth.

The crowd cheered loudly and roared. "Fancy and Fine! Fancy and Fine! Fancy and Fine!" They chanted those words out repeatedly to show their love and appreciation.

Each chick did donuts on their bikes, leaving skid marks in the street. When they stopped, they were lined up perfectly, side by side. Looking at each other as they awaited their cue. The DJ went on. "Y'all are some of the sexiest bitches on these bikes. I'm gay, but you hoes got me wanting to test the other side." DJ Coogie admitted. The crowd laughed, and so did the girls.

The popular song Ruff Ryders Anthem by DMX blasted from the booth, lighting the block the fuck up. The crowd couldn't help but move to the shit as they held red cups in the air. Some even waved their hands from side to side and sang along. Almost everyone's attention was on the crew.

The girls revved up their engines, and in unison, all popped wheelies as they rode down the blocks. The shit was so fly it looked like a show. People were excitedly taking pictures. Some even had camcorders out recording. Those bitches were everything a lot of hood niggas, and bitches wished they could be.

After showing out on their favorite toys, the crew made their way back to the first block. They parked their bikes in a designated area reserved exclusively for them. Pulling their helmets from their head and hanging them on their bikes, they looked one another over to ensure nobody's hair was messed up. They then took off the pink leather vest they wore whenever they rode and placed it on the seats of the two-wheelers.

"Them are some fine ass bitches." Dirt said. "Who they fuck with?" He was questioning his cousin. Tasha asked Dirt to come along. He declined at first. He wasn't trying to hang out in no one else's hood. They both stayed with their granny, so they saw each other a lot. Their granny's air conditioner broke just a few hours after Tasha invited him. On top of that, granny was on one. She had been playing church music all day. He had to get up out of that house. Dirt was from out of town. He had moved to Los Angeles to get away from some sheisty niggas in Mississippi that wanted his head. He figured coming to Cali could save his life. It had only been three weeks, but he was missing home. He planned to go back one day. His mom and baby sister were there. California was cool and all, but Mississippi was home.

Tasha was a ghetto hood rat; she only gave her pussy up to niggas that were dropping bags. Confidence was everything, and for her, it paid off. To say Tasha was ugly ass fuck was an understatement. She looked like a pit bull in a skirt. Her body and what she would do for a little change had niggas ignoring the fact that she could be mistaken for a vicious animal. She was short in stature, rocked a short blond bob, had a nice coke bottle shape, but her facial features were hideous. Tasha was also The Fancy & Fine Crew's personal hairdresser. It was safe to say she was cool with them. They all grew up together, but Tasha was closer with Debra, Jo's sister. Debra wasn't at the event because she took the girls daughters to Disney World.

Tasha eyed the girls with envy as she took a sip from her red cup. She did all of their hair in a silk wrap earlier that morning. Her eyes scanned their fits. All four were dressed in designer sneakers, cute little booty shorts, designer T-Shirts, and enough gold chains and diamond rings to open their own pawnshop. Most didn't know they weren't blood because they looked just alike. Slim-thick, butterscotch complexioned, pointy noses and pouty lips. Nova was the only one who had freckles on her nose and green eyes. There was no denying they were gorgeous women.

"They fuck with some suckas from the valley. Well, Nova. The one drinking the bottle of water, she ain't trying to be tied down. Jojo and Lil Momma I know for sure, mess with two of them. Shy, I think she goes both ways. The niggas are brothers. They out here acting like they "that nigga" because they fuck with them. Well, I guess they are because-" She stopped mid-sentence when four black Maserati whips pulled up. They parked in the reserved parking area close to the girls' bikes. A lot of people had a feeling who were behind the wheels of the foreign whips, but it wasn't until the men stepped out that it was confirmed.

"Okay, we see you." The DJ announced. "If I didn't know any better, I'd say y'all trying to stunt on my bitches. But we know y'all love them fine ass hoes." Ohhhh's and awwwww's came from the crowd. Nova strolled off. She felt like shooting dice.

"Hook me up with her." Dirt told Tasha. He was referring to Nova. Tasha looked him up and down and cut her eyes.

"Hook yourself up. I ain't no matchmaker." She walked off. Dirt didn't have a problem stepping to the fine ass Nova. His cockiness was above the roof. He was a fine nigga with good dick, and game for days. Had he not been who he was, he probably would have been a little intimidated by her status. He wasn't no broke nigga. He was certain he could bag her. Dirt watched Nova as she made her way to where she was going. He didn't give a fuck who was watching him as he watched her. He made it his business to gawk at her thick sexy ass. A few niggas and bitches made it their business to get her attention by calling her name. She spoke but kept about her way.

Nova was a die-hard gambler and dice were her favorite. She loved the adrenaline she got taking niggas money. That was just what she planned to do when she approached the dice game. A few bitches were amongst the crowd, lightweights in comparison. They weren't on her level, but they were about their paper. One of the chicks she didn't recognize, but that wasn't out of the ordinary. As always, the niggas outnumbered the women in craps, but money had no gender. The shit talking was turned all the way up. Nova joined in.

"What we shooting for?" She asked as she squatted. There was a pile of money in the center and Red Head Richard had the dice.

"Whatever you wanna shoot for. It's your world, I'm just wishing for a nut." Another dude who looked like Ezal from the movie Friday answered.

"You going to keep on wishing with that bullshit ass twenty in your hand." Nova shot back. Everyone laughed. Red Head Richard told her to wait until the dice go around, and after that, she could call it.

"200 or better." Nova called out when she got on the dice. Niggas started dropping their bills. "Don't be scared now. Bet." She challenged. She shook the dice and rolled them. "Ah." She popped her fingers as she watched the red dice land. "Bitches rule the world." She had hit another 7. Nova was on a roll. It was always like that when she got in the dice game. As if, the dice only fucked with her. That was how good her luck was.

She smelled his cologne the moment he stood next to her. Looking down at the Gucci sneakers on his feet, she looked up at him. *'Oh'* she thought. Nova peeped him with Tasha. When the crew was at the shop earlier, Tasha had told them she was inviting her cousin. Nova assumed he was the cousin. She didn't do light skin, but she had to admit to herself that baby boy was handsome. His Caesar cut fade had waves so deep a bitch would drown in them. He had peanut butter brown eyes, a cute narrow nose and some kissable ass lips. You could tell that he worked out from time to time by his medium, but muscular arms. He was staring at her, and she knew that he might have been lost in her emerald green eyes, all the while thinking how beautiful she was. She would admit she was very conceited, and she wasn't ashamed of it. Nova turned her head. She didn't want light-skin to get the wrong idea.

"I'm betting with baby." Dirt said, throwing his money in the game. He looked at Nova and winked. She ignored him and continued on her winning streak.

"Somebody bring my fine ass a bottle. That's the least you could do. Niggas ain't good for nothing else." By this time, all but one of the few chicks had left. All except the one, she didn't recognize. She hadn't broken the Jennifer Lopez clone's pockets yet. Nova made a mental note to learn who she was.

"Sis, I got you." Jo said. She walked up with a bottle of Hennessy in her hand. Nova turned it up the moment she got her hands on it.

"Damn, girl! You are full of surprises." Dirt said. The way she was out there taking money, and had him winning in the process, made him desire her that much more. He loved how hood she was. Drinking straight from the bottle and not giving a fuck who saw her. His gut told him that her pretty ass knew how to turn off the hood shit when needed. He didn't know why, but he felt that.

Jojo looked at Dirt and smirked. She thought he was cute, too. She saw the way he was gawking at her girl, though. She wondered if Nova would give him some play. Jojo could feel someone staring at her and when she looked up it was the other female, aside from Nova, that was left in the game.

"Shouldn't you be paying attention to the game? Fuck you looking at me for?" Jo asked. She was already pissed off. Pair that with being tipsy; so she was ready to take her frustration out on somebody. Jojo's nigga, Wiz, pissed her off pulling up in another damn foreign whip. A whip she never knew that he was purchasing. It wouldn't have been an issue had he run it by her, and had he not purchased a brand new Benz a month ago today. He was doing too much. Here she was trying to figure out more ways to get money, and this nigga was doing janky shit to bring attention to them. When she asked him about the whip, he got an attitude, telling her that he had to head out of town to handle some business they had with some cats from the DMV. He also spazzed and told her that she needed to stop tripping over what he does with his money. She was the reason he and his brothers were eating like they were. How in the flip was she just finding out he was leaving to handle business in another state? She was feeling like Wiz was trying to boss up on what she and her sisters built. She wasn't feeling it at all, and she planned on letting him know. His brothers weren't even moving like that. Yeah, they had new rides too, but they were nowhere moving like Wiz. For the most part, they were low-key. Jo never wanted to admit it, but she had a strong feeling Wiz was going to attract some serious attention from the pigs, and she wanted no parts of it. She'd kill him before she allowed that to happen.

The chick Jo had checked rolled her eyes and focused back on the game. The scowl never left her face. Jo stood there a bit longer watching her sister clean house, and Tasha's cute ass cousin benefiting off Nova's winnings. He was still betting on Nova. He was smitten, no doubt.

"Aye, sis. I'm about to take this call." Jo said, as she eased away from the crowd. She smiled at the caller ID. Her boo was right on time.

It was now Red Head Richard, the one chick no one knew, and Nova still in the game. Dirt was still by her side. Nova was getting tired, and she had to pee.

"Aye, this it for me. I'm out." Nova said, standing up. She could barely feel her legs. The sun had gone all the way down. Finally, a little breeze was blowing.

"Good. It's just something about you. But I wasn't going to let you run me off." The J-Lo clone said. She gave Nova the once over and then cut her eyes. Dirt, Red Head, and a few others that were on the sidelines looked at ole girl like she was crazy. Did she know who she was talking to?

"Bitch, who the fuck are you talking to? I will beat your muthafuckin ass and take all the little money you won." Nova's words slurred a little. She was gone off of those large gulps of Henn she drank, but she was functioning.

"Drunk, bitch." The chick fanned her hand. Nova reached down, grabbed the Hennessy bottle, and hit the little bitch over the head, knocking her out cold. She wasn't done with her, though. Nova didn't do disrespect.

"Bitch!" Nova yelled. She kicked the girl in the head two times before Dirt snatched her up and tossed her over his shoulder. "Nigga, you better put me the fuck down!" She yelled, trying to fight him.

"Girl, calm the fuck down. Now, if you kill the bitch, I'm going to be mad as fuck at you. I can't have my woman in

18

jail for life. Too many witnesses. All these muthafuckas out here don't fuck with you like they claim they do. Catch that bitch when she's alone." Dirt said. He was dead ass serious, too. From the short period of time he spent with Nova at the dice game, he became more intrigued than he already was. He made up his mind that he wanted to fuck with her. Being that cocky nigga that he was, he knew she would be in his arms soon. That's if her rowdy ass didn't get locked up first.

Nova was still demanding that he put her down, but he meant what he said. Once they were a distance from the dice game, Dirt placed Nova on her feet near a Porta Potty. He looked behind him and a crowd had formed around ole girl. Paramedics could be heard in the distance.

"Don't ever jump in my damn business." Nova spat. Dirt walked up in her face.

"Don't talk to me crazy, because being the man that I am, I won't talk to you crazy. You're mad right now, so I'm going to let that slide." He let it sink in for a few seconds. When Nova didn't respond with no smart shit, he knew that she heard him. "Don't ever let a bitch bring you out of character to the point that you're jeopardizing your freedom. If it's that serious, catch that hoe when she is slipping. No witnesses, no case. You understand where I'm going with this?" He questioned. After getting no response, he spoke again. "I'm going to make my cousin give me your number, and I'm going to check on you tomorrow. I don't do the police, so I'm about to bounce. Gone over there with your crew." He looked behind her and saw her clique was running toward them.

"If Tasha gives you my number, I'm going to slap her ass. If you call me, I'm going to cuss your ass out. Now bye!" She

19

"I know you love that nigga, but baby, he ain't it. He's a fraud. A real man ain't going to be comfortable bragging about some shit he had no parts of. How the fuck you fall for an ole flossing ass nigga?" Judah expressed. First off, they had just finishing fucking, and she was trying to enjoy the moment. Jo heard him, but she wasn't about to pillow talk about her nigga, to another nigga. Although everything Judah was saying she felt, but that was her business.

"Why every time we're together, you bring up my man? Can we just enjoy our time?" Jo asked. She had never brought up what he did, or whom he did it with. His wife and other flings weren't her business.

Judah was Jo's side nigga. She and Judah first met when her homeboys up north referred her to him. Her connect had been busted and she and her girls were desperately looking for a new supplier. Her Papa gave her the green light to reach out to Cavi, and Cavi sent her to Judah. Once the crew got Papa's approval, they started doing business with the big man from the A. The product was cheaper, and it was a better quality. It was a win all the way around. A couple of years ago, Judah and his boy decided they wanted a vacation. They went to Vegas. Judah had been feeling Jo, but lived in another state. Besides, he had more than a few situations around his way, so he never pressed her line. However, the trip to Vegas changed all that. He hit Jo up, inviting her, and surprisingly she took him up on his offer. She showed up alone; that was a bonus. When they finally linked, she told him that she had her eye on him, but she didn't want to mix business with pleasure. Judah wasn't trying to hear that shit. He knew how to separate the two. Over the course of a few

21

months, he really started feeling Jo. He wanted to see her as much as he could. Their situation came to a halt when Jo got pregnant and told Judah she was getting rid of the baby. Her excuse was that she was only twenty-three with a child already. A hustler who wasn't planning on leaving the game. Plus, he had a kid with his wife and four side kids. In total, he had five children, by four different women. Whether you were a fuck or not, Judah would never condone killing his seed. He wanted all his kids. So, when Jo told him she had an abortion, he choked her out and stopped fucking with her. She had other niggas, too. None of whom she was serious with until she hooked up with Wiz. It was like she fell for his ass overnight. Wiz wasn't hood like the dudes she was used to messing with. He was one of those preppy boys. He got his hands dirty, when necessary, especially if it involved some paper. Wiz had done a few years in the Feds for fraud. He was still doing his thang, and Jo did her own thang. A year into their relationship, he stepped to her on some Bonnie and Clyde type shit. She let him know that it was four the hard way. The four consisted of her and her sisters. Being that he was her dude, she was willing to get with the girls to see where, and if, he and his brothers could be used in the organization. Wiz was the oldest. He was the smartest, too, so they put him in charge of counting both the drugs and the money. His younger brother Dino handled customers who didn't pay or were short. His wrath held no prejudice. Bobby was the middle brother. He handled drops. Either he made them, or he found people he trusted to do them. Papa didn't agree with the girls bringing the men on board, but it was their organization, and they did what they wanted. Everything was going good until Wiz began to floss.

All she wanted to do was enjoy her sex high, but Judah was ruining it. She didn't want to talk about Wiz and his shenanigans. Jo's back was against Judah's chest.

When he spoke responding to her comment, she turned to face him. Judah was so damn fine to her. He was the only nigga she would duck off with for days and didn't care how hard Wiz tripped when she resurfaced. Judah was the color of honey, with cinnamon-colored eyes that sat perfectly underneath a set of long lashes. He had a deep dimple in each one of his cheeks. His wide nose and juicy lips added to his already handsome features. Not only was he fine, but his short bowlegged ass had a big dick, and he knew how to use it.

"We get money out here! We, meaning your crew and my crew. No matter the clout we get from these dirty ass cops, there's always someone out there that wants to do right by their city. Do you think we won't ever come up on the Feds' radar? I ain't counting your paper, but you and your crew doing it big. Y'all pushing more weight than a lot of these niggas out here." Judah shook his head as he sat up in the bed. His gut was telling him Jo's lil fuck boy was going to be her downfall. Maybe his too, being that they worked together. "Why the fuck you let that nigga buy two foreign cars in a one-month span? Baby, that's raising all kinds of red flags. I got a wife, but I fuck with you tough. If I didn't low-key care about you, I would still feel the same way. Get rid of him. He's a bitch, Jo. On all five of my sons. If you don't, I'm walking away. I just don't trust him. I can't risk it."

She bit the bottom of her lip. It was something she did when she was contemplating. She couldn't believe Judah would give her such an ultimatum, but she understood. Judah saw the nervousness in her face, and the way she bit on her lips. He pulled her into his chest and held her. Like he said, he had a wife that he loved wholeheartedly. He even had other baby mommas. But Jo isn't just anybody. She's his Cali bitch he had mad love for. Jo was a hustler, a boss, like him. He wanted her to make it in the game, not sink because of some lame.

"Boom Boom Boom!" There was a loud banging on the door. Both of their hearts dropped. Judah was just warning her about getting caught, and here he was with her. The irony. He knew it was the police. The hard knocks were a dead giveaway. He was pissed. He looked at her, and she looked at him. And then.

"Judah. Bring your muthafuckin ass out this room. Bitch ass nigga, I know you in there. On our son, I'll shoot this bitch up."

And he knew for certain, Sarah wasn't lying. *That bitch had me followed. How the fuck?'* It had been two years he had been creeping with his out-of-town boo. She ain't ever come up with their issues. He was confused.

Jo jumped up from the bed quickly. Happy as fuck it wasn't the police, but annoyed that her sidepiece's main bitch was at the door. She threw on her DKNY sweat suit with the quickness, and then slid on her sneakers. She grabbed her gun off the nightstand on her side of the bed. She looked at Judah.

"Open the door. I will shoot your bitch on God." Jo warned. And she meant it. She didn't give out passes. If a bitch came for her, it wasn't no next time. The bitch her sister knocked out at the block party better be glad she had walked off. It was Judah that saved the girl when he called her phone.

By this time, Judah slid on his jeans and put on his shirt. He looked at Jo. Even when she was mad, she was pretty.

"She ain't even like that. She came for me. Put the gun away. That's my wife." He gave her a look to say he wasn't playing. Yeah, he liked Jo, but Sarah came before all the other baby mommas, and any bitches he played with.

Bam Bam! "I said, open this goddamn door. This is my last warning." Sarah was hot. She was so tired of the nigga and his hoe ways.

Jo stood there with her gun visible, ready to shoot a bitch.

Judah's heart raced. He wasn't trying to go there with her. Sarah was his rider. He didn't want to hurt her; he was just doing him. When the door opened, Sarah punched Judah in the face. He stumbled back and grabbed his nose. The brass knuckles assisted with an already mean left hook. She stunned him, had the nigga groaning.

"Awww, bitch. Sarah, what the fuck?" Judah's nose was leaking. You could hear the pain in his moans. And Sarah didn't give one flying fuck.

Sarah and Jo locked eyes. Both of their faces held a scowl. Their anger didn't stop them from recognizing the other for their good looks. And just being real, they knew the other was a boss in their own right.

"A bitch don't owe me shit. I don't fuck you. I don't have kids with you. This nigga owes me loyalty." Sarah said. She looked up at her husband. "Nigga, let's go before I flip the fuck out." With that, she walked out of the doorway and stood near the balcony. Judah had three seconds. If he took a second longer, she was going to shoot his ass in the leg. He better pray she didn't hit a main artery.

Jo had no time for the bullshit. Sarah wasn't tripping on her. She grabbed her purse, her keys and walked out the door, leaving them to figure it out. She had other things to worry about, like the car she didn't know that was following her.

"Damn. I feel special as fuck. I knew you liked a nigga." Dirt said.

He exited his car and was standing right next to the fine ass gangsta chick that had been curving him for the last three days. All he had to do was slide his cousin Tasha a big face, and she gave up the number. "I'm going to tell her you stole it out of my phone." Tasha told him. He didn't care what she said. He had the number and he was using it.

After a few attempts, Nova finally answered his call and when he told her who he was, she hung up. Dirt had a feeling she would diss him the first couple of times, but he wasn't giving up. The last time he called was the day before, and she didn't pick up. And now she was here, at the M&M soul food joint on Crenshaw. He assumed she was about to have breakfast, like he was. Her little ass didn't know that today was going to be their official date. Dirt was cocky as fuck. He ain't never had to do no extra shit to bag a bitch. He was handsome. Niggas said he looked like the actor Larenz Tate. He was a stockier version and had waves that would have a bitch seasick.

Dirt had a big smile on his face as he stared at Nova's fine ass. She had just put her helmet on her sports bike. Nova had a sleek ponytail pulled to the back. It was bone straight and long, almost reaching her bra strap. Her shit was real, too. He peeped it when she was in the dice game. She wore some red biker shorts with the words DKNY on the side with the matching sports bra showing off her flat stomach, and light tiger stripes indicating she may have been a mother. On her feet were a pair of ankle socks covered by a pair of red and

27

white Nike Air Max sneakers. The Gucci fanny pack around her waist is where she kept her strap.

Any other time, Nova wouldn't even react when she heard a nigga throw a line her way, but when she heard his voice, she couldn't help but to spin around. With an annoyed look on her face, she gave Dirt the once over. He was dressed in a simple pair of black basketball shorts, and a white tank top. He had on long white socks and a pair of black Jordan's. *'Country nigga.'*

Dirt had a goofy ass smile on his face. Despite her annoyance, she couldn't help but take in how fine he was, and the nigga smelled good. That was a plus. She was sure he heard it all the time that he looked just like Larenz Tate. And Nova loved her some Larenz. However, she wasn't trying to entertain right now. She was focusing on her paper. A fuck maybe, but she could sense that if she went there with Dirt, he wouldn't leave her alone.

"Those eyes and freckles. Damn, baby." Dirt said. Nova didn't bother to reply. As she made her way toward the restaurant, Dirt was on her ass. He ran ahead and opened the door for her.

"You know this is a date, right?" He told her as they waited for the waitress to approach. Nova looked back at him and rolled her eyes.

"Yeah, right." She said as she rolled her eyes for a second time.

Dressed in an all-black uniform, Natalie, the waitress, approached the pair. Dirt peeped her name tag sitting on her big ass breast. He saw the way she looked at him with lust-filled eyes. She was cute, but she wasn't Nova.

"What's up, Nova. You have a guest today?" Natalie looked at Dirt and smiled. The bitch's eyes were lingering a little too long. Nova wasn't feeling it, but she wouldn't say anything.

"Nah." She went to say, but Dirt cut in.

"Yeah, for two." Dirt spoke up. He put his hand on the small of Nova's back. He then leaned into her ear. "Stop being so mean. You know you think a nigga handsome. I see the look you just gave Natalie. Baby, I don't want no other woman in Cali but you. Don't be hitting no hoes with bottles and shit. I'm all yours. Now, let's enjoy our first date."

Nova couldn't help but laugh. "Boy, what the fuck ever."

"Follow me." Natalie said, walking off. Dirt lightly tapped Nova on the back. As instructed by Natalie, they followed.

"What the fuck is your problem? Why did you even bring your ass up there?" Shy was furious. Her blue pumps click-clacked against the floor as she paced back and forth in the small hospital room. Regretting that she even fucked with the bitch, and mad at herself for doing so. Although she now knew who Blanca was, she still fucking cared for her. She should have been left her alone. She was a fucking cop bitch. It had been four days since Blanca was hit in the head with the bottle by Nova. Six stitches and a concussion later, and she still didn't feel like she was in the wrong.

"After four days, you are just now coming to see me. You are sitting up here mad at me because I fell in love with you. That bitch attacked me!" Blanca cried. "Why don't you love me as you love them? Why do you always put them first? Why, after all of this time are you still hiding me?" Blanca cried. She was crying so hard her body shook.

Shy took a deep breath. She ran her hands through her honey-blonde individual braids. The entire situation had her stressed the fuck out. Blanca was doing far too much. She knew why the fuck they couldn't be public.

The shit Blanca was starting to pull was running her low.

Shy met Blanca up in Virginia a few years back. She was there visiting her grandmother and her mother. Shy had taken them out to dinner one night, and that's where she ran into Blanca. She was on her way coming from the ladies' room and walked right into her.

"My bad." Shy offered. She went to walk around Blanca, but paused at the comment she made.

"So, you don't think I'm cute? I saw you looking at me." Shy stopped in mid-stride. She looked back at Blanca. *'Damn she fine.'* Hispanic women have always been her thang. Besides her crew, no one knew that Shy was attracted to both males and females. She did her thing with discretion. Being that they were in Virginia, Shy didn't hesitate to go there with Blanca.

"I wasn't looking at you, but if you want me to, I can." Shy said. Shy gave Blanca the once over. She was dressed in high heels, tight-fitting slacks, and a leather jacket zipped up. Her hair was in a ponytail. When she replayed the day that they met back in her head, she could now see it. She had the look of an undercover cop bitch. It was Blanca's boldness and fiery sex appeal that had her blind to whatever it was she needed to see. Now here she was, in love with a jealous ass, spoiled cop bitch. With Shy though, it was peace over hoes, and money over bitches. She didn't even go through this bullshit with the niggas she fucked with. That's why she left her fuck ass baby's daddy. She hated insecure shit.

"Look." Shy started. She walked next to where Blanca was laying in the bed. She wanted Blanca to look into her eyes. She needed her to grasp the seriousness of the situation. Blanca's eyes were red and puffy. Shy wasn't at all moved. She brought the shit on herself.

"Look, B. The moment you are released from this hospital, you need to take your ass back to Virginia. I mean that shit. If I wanted to bring you around my daughter and sisters, you fucked that off."

31

Blanca's eyes widened.

"That's the problem. They aren't your fucking sisters. You are fucking them bitches, I know you are, and if you don't stop, I swear they will be your downfall." Blanca didn't even see it coming. Shy pulled her gun from her jeans and had it against Blanca's head. "Bitch, are you threatening me?" Blanca didn't say a word. She wasn't scared. She was willing to die for what she wanted and what she believed in. Being that she fell in love with a criminal, it broke her heart. She risked her career by doing so, and to know this was how their relationship would end fucked her up.

"I fucking hate you! I hate you! You never cared. You're so fucking stupid."

Shy had the pistol still pressed to her head.

"I asked a question. Are you threatening me?" That's all Shy wanted to know.

"No. Now get out!" Blanca yelled.

Satisfied with Blanca's response, Shy put the gun back in the waist of her jeans. She grabbed her purse off the chair, threw it over her shoulder, and switched out the room. Leaving Blanca, and what they had behind.

'You black hoes always think you get the last word. Ha.' Blanca thought.

"This mutha too gotdamn crowded." Dino complained. With a slight frown on his face, he reached in his jeans and retrieved a wad of money. After counting the required amount for admission to the drive-in movie theater, he pulled forward. He looked over at his girl, his gangsta bitch. That's what he called her. He smirked. Her little fine ass was laid back in her seat with low eyes. She was in her own little world. Lil Momma was too high to give a fuck one way or the other. She heard him complain. She was cool if they stayed and cool with leaving. The only reason why she picked the drive-in on Tuesday night is that they were running back all of her favorite movies. It was 2 for the price of 1. Tonight, Vermont was showing Menace II Society and Poetic Justice. She thought it would be cool to watch a gangsta flick, followed up by a love story. When Dino asked what she wanted to do, that was the first thing that came to mind. But if her nigga didn't want to be there, she didn't either.

"You wanna leave?" She was still looking straight ahead.

She felt Dino massage her thigh, so she looked down at his large hands. Her name was going across in italic writing. Underneath it were the words *"My Gangsta Bitch"* in bold letters. They had gotten matching tattoos a month after dating. Hers was on her right hand. It read "Dino" and underneath was "My Gangsta." Her sisters and his brothers clowned them. They were saying that they were on some sucka for love type shit. They didn't care, though. What they had was real. As long as they understood the bond, and felt each other.

Dino thought Little Momma was a female version of him. From day one, when he saw her get active on some bitch that stepped on her shoes. Ole girl kept walking like it was nothing, so Lil Momma snatched her by her hair, slung her to the ground, and stomped her out. She began screaming a name. A nigga ran in, and before he could get near the fight, Dino hit him in the head with a gun, laying him the fuck out. They both were arrested, but their peeps bailed them out the same night. Dino was the youngest of his brothers. Although they shared the same father, and he had moved with them when he was thirteen, he still felt like an outcast. Born and raised in the Ville, one of the toughest neighborhoods in St. Louis, Missouri, to a mother who thought she could mend her broken heart by having a slew of men in her life. She eventually was hooked on drugs, and shit went downhill from there. Dino ended up staying with his father when his mother called, crying about him killing her man. Dino made a promise to himself. He vowed to kill Stacks if he ever put his hands on him again. One-night Stacks came in high and drunk. And just like he did every time he was loaded, he punched on Dino like he was a man instead of a little ass boy. That night, Stacks fell asleep on the sofa. Dino beat the nigga in the head with a bat; killing him. Afterwards, he waited for his momma to come home. She loved Stacks, but she loved her son more. There was no way she would let him go down for what he did. His father, Montana Santiago, was a dirty politician. One phone call, and it was as if the shit never happened. They didn't know what happened to Stacks. After that incident, Yarny saw a change in her son. He was cold and mean. Constantly in trouble and always disrespecting her whenever he felt like she was in his business. A year later, Yarny called Montana's ass. She told him that he had better tell his wife that his illegitimate son was coming to stay with them, or else. To her surprise, Montana wanted his son to come and live with them. The day Montana came and got Dino was the last time Yarny and her son saw each other. The news reported that her decomposed body was found in an old abandoned warehouse. Dino took it hard initially. Then eventually he pretended she didn't exist, in order to forget about it, he had to forget about her.

Dino didn't share his story with many people, but with Lil Momma, he opened up on their second date. She told him that her mother overdosed, she never even knew her father, and how she was in and out of foster care. She bounced around the system being mistreated until she was placed with Ms. Ann. Ms. Ann was Jo and Debra's biological mother. He felt he found his soulmate. On top of her story, she was a gangstress getting it out of the mud. Dino would forever be grateful to his brother for hooking up with Jo, which led him to Lil Momma. And even more grateful that The Fancy & Fine Crew put him on. He was in charge of punishing those who didn't pay their debt, or simply fucking them up, and most of those times, Lil Momma was right by his side.

From his radio, Dino tuned in to the frequency. The first movie would be starting soon. When he was done, he looked at his girl. Lil Momma was rolling a joint. She looked up at him and smiled. Damn, she loved her man. The way he stared at her with love and admiration gave her butterflies.

"I'm about to go get something to eat."

"I'm going." Lil Momma replied. She finished rolling her joint and placed it in the ashtray for when they came back. Dino didn't smoke, but he drank with her. They had Hennessy in the trunk.

He was going to sip after he ate.

After demolishing their nachos, popcorn, and soda pops, Lil Momma lit her pre-rolled joint. Dino got out of the car and grabbed the Hennessy from the truck. As he was getting back in the van, he spotted a gold old school Chevy Impala. It was about five cars down. He took a few steps closer to make sure he wasn't tripping. By this time, Lil Momma had peeped him from the window. The way he was staring, she already knew something was up. She put the lit joint in the ashtray.

With the quickness, she grabbed her pistol from up under the seat. She slid out of the car and made her way over to where Dino stood.

"What's up?" She asked. Her eyes were searching in the direction he was looking.

"That's Flip." He threw his head toward the Impala. A few weeks ago, Flip was arrested after being caught with two birds he picked up on consignment. When they checked, he had no bail. Being that The Fancy & Fine Crew had connections on the inside, word got out that Flip had flipped. He was willing to give up his ex-best friend, as well as his operations, for a chance to get out. It was hard for the crew to believe that. Flip was a real nigga. He didn't fuck with snitches. He hated them with a passion, or so he claimed. Being that he was out, it was no doubt, he turned snitch.

"Yup, that's him." Lil Momma replied. Pulling her eyes from the car that Flip was in, she looked over at Dino. He knew that look.

"Nigga didn't even bother to switch up his routine." Dino said. After spotting Flip, they left the movies. They parked their car at a shopping center a few miles elsewhere. Dino

36

was the lookout, while Lil momma hot-wired a minivan. They rolled back up to the theater and parked by the exit. The moment they saw Flip pull out, they followed. He went straight to a motel. It was a rundown spot, only a few miles away from where they parked, and close to a freeway.

"Nigga foul, but that's his life." Lil Momma spat. They watched as he got out to pay for the room. They pulled into the lot. Flip got back in the car, and pulled in front of his room. They pulled up and parked close to him, but not on him. They still had the straps on their sides. Both pulled their ski masks over their faces, and in unison hopped out the G-Ride.

Dino snuck up on Flip. Lil Momma got on the bitch who was still sitting in the car.

Pow! Dino fired one to the back of his head. Flip dropped. The bitch could only get out a half of a scream. She was quickly silenced by the Glock 9 Lil Momma shot her with. They jumped back in the car and pulled off like it was nothing. Once they hopped on the freeway, Dino did 90 all the way to his destination.

"Fuck snitches." Lil Momma grumbled. If Flip could snitch on his own people, he deserved to die. He didn't even attempt to get at them about the dope they fronted when he got out. It had to happen. There was no telling when he was going to snitch on them. The chick was just a causality. Wrong place, wrong time.

The couple drove in silence for about thirty-minutes. When they pulled up to the Holiday Inn hotel, Lil Momma smiled.

"My Nigga." She said as she leaned over and kissed her man on the cheek. Whenever her baby was about to beat her pussy up, she would get extra excited. It was normal for them to go fuck, after they finished handling business. Each time they did, Lil Momma was thrilled. While her man was paying for the room, Lil Momma was right by his side. Hand in hand, they made their way into the hotel room. The moment they entered, Lil Momma went straight for the shower. Dino was right behind her. He watched in admiration as she undressed. Lil Momma didn't know it, but she was the only reason he gave a fuck about living.

She was the reason that he looked forward to the next day. When she fully undressed, she turned and looked at her man. Dino was still fully dressed.

"What's the matter?" She asked, placing her hand on his face. Dino placed his hand on her wrist.

"I love you. I love your daughter. I will give my life for you and Kay. I don't wanna live in this world without you. Baby, will you marry me?" Tears fell from Lil Momma's eyes as she watched her man get on one knee. He looked up at her. "If you say yes, you'll have your ring tomorrow. I didn't even know I was going to-"

"Baby, yes. Yes, I will marry you." She leaned down and kissed him. After a long, intense kiss, Dino stood up.

"Thank you, babe." She sang happily.

"You are welcome." He replied, looking at her hungrily.

38

"Now, take off these clothes. I want some dick." She told him.

Dino stripped down and climbed into the steam filled shower. They made love for the first time as an engaged couple.

"Gotdamn, Jo! This pussy is good." Wiz said. He had Jo bent over, gripping her ankles as he deeply stroked her from the back. With his hands on her small waist, he grew harder at the sight in front of him. A beautiful body glistening in sweat, a fat, heart-shaped ass jiggling on his dick, as it disappeared in gushy pussy. "Ohhh, shit. Just like that. Bounce that ass." He groaned, and she did just that.

"Like that?" She said looking back at the fine man behind her.

"Yeah, just like that." He told her. He could feel himself about to nut. Wiz pumped a few more times and then pulled out. Jo knew the routine. When he pulled out with ease, he was trying to avoid coming prematurely. Without being told, she walked over to her California king-size bed and laid flat on her stomach.

SMACK… Wiz hit her on her left ass cheek.

"What you want me to do to this pussy?" He asked her.

"Suck the shit out of it." She purred.

"Assume the position." He demanded, smacking the right ass cheek. Jo got on her knees, eyes closed, bottom lip in her mouth, and anticipating the pleasure. Wiz's mouth watered at the sight of her shaved, pretty, pink pussy.

Wiping the sweat from his forehead, Wiz got on his knees in front of Jo. Spreading her ass cheeks open, he licked between her juicy booty.

"Ahhhh… Wiz." Jo rocked back and forth. Before she got with her man, she didn't know how good it felt to have your ass ate. Wiz continued to tease her with a few more licks. When he had enough of the appetizer, he went for the main course. Wiz devoured her pussy, bringing her back-to-back orgasms. After the third one, Jo tapped out. She laid on her stomach, trying to regain her composure. It was only a matter of seconds before her nigga flipped her over onto her back and slid his 8 inches inside of her.

Wiz always dicked her down, but this night he was giving it to her like he was trying to prove a point.

Wiz gave it to her so good that she laid there with her two fingers in her mouth. He listened to her snore for about thirty minutes.

"So, what happened in DC?" She asked him after the short nap. Jo was in the kitchen, ready to start breakfast. Wiz's heart skipped a beat. It wasn't supposed to be like this. He stared in a daze. When Jo didn't get a response, she turned and looked back at him. "Boo, you hear me?" He looked up at her.

"What you say, baby?"

"I asked what happened in DC." She opened the top cabinet and pulled out the pancake mix.

"Man, this shit is going to be big. These niggas are hungry. The prices I offered them; they can't beat." He rubbed his hands together. "I'm about to take over the game." He smiled big.

"Good morning, y'all. What's up?" Lil Momma said. She and Dino had just come in. They heard Wiz in the kitchen.

"Nothing." Wiz spat dryly. He didn't like Dino. He was envious.

"It sure in the fuck didn't sound that way. You were in here loud, talking about how you were about to take over the city. You ain't got shit to tell me? Goofy ass hater." Dino barked.

"Man, gone with that pussy shit." Wiz fanned him off. "I ain't got to hate on you. You wanna be me. Ole crybaby ass. You be acting like a bitch." As soon as the word bitch left his mouth, Dino stole on him. The punch landed on the side of his face. Wiz fell out of the chair.

Jo and Lil Momma looked at each other and shook their heads. They were brothers, so it wasn't their place to jump in. Wiz did come at him wrong, and as long as they didn't mess up their house, they kept quiet.

"Nigga, don't ever disrespect me like that." Dino warned. He glared at Wiz, daring him to get up. But just like the bitch he knew he was; he didn't move.

"Come on, babe. Let's go out and eat breakfast." Lil momma grabbed his hand. Dino gave Wiz one last stare.

"Man, get your punk ass up. Sitting there looking like a hoe on the floor." He laughed. And just like that, he and his fiancé bounced.

When they got in the car, Dino looked at Lil Momma.

"I don't trust that nigga. It ain't just because I don't like him. That nigga sneaky." Dino always felt like his oldest brother didn't care for him. He didn't give a fuck, though. As long as he respected him. Over the years, Wiz had said some fucked up shit to him, and every time he did, Dino whooped his ass. His other brothers were cool, but sometimes they could be on that hating shit too.

"I feel you. We gotta figure out something. I know Jo feel some kind of way about how the nigga be moving, but she ain't saying shit."

"Why Auntie always talking to us about going to college, and blah blah?" 10-year-old Shay asked. She was in the backyard with her cousins. They were supposed to be practicing their dance routine, but they were tired. Shay was Shy's daughter. She was the calmer out of the four young girls, but she was also the sassiest. She had an opinion about everything.

"You don't wanna go to college, you wanna work at McDonald's?" 9-year-old Kay asked. With one hand on her hip, she stood there with her face balled up. Disgusted. As if, Shay had said the weirdest thing. Kay was Lil Momma's daughter. She was the fighter of the crew. She was also the smartest. Kay's teachers saw a promising future for her. Even at a young age, she was a math genius.

"Hell, no! I don't wanna work at no damn McDonald's. What I look like? McDonald's ain't going to have me fly like this." Shay looked down at her designer sneakers.

"So, if you don't go to college, how are you going to get money?" Kay wanted to know.

"I'm going to be a dope dealer like my momma." Shay said.

Kay's eyes bucked. She looked at Dez, who was Jo's daughter, and then at Nunu who was Nova's daughter.

"You hear this girl?" Kay questioned.

44

"Yup." Dez spoke up. At 9, she had heard her momma and aunts discuss the dope game, and how they were taking over the city for years. She wanted to be just like them.

"Fuck school! I wanna be hood famous with money and fancy clothes, just like my momma." Dez was dead ass, too. She looked at Nunu. "What about you?"

"Hell, yeah. We're going to have all the money." She said, at 8 she was fantasizing about all that she was going to do in the dope game.

"Aye, what y'all doing? You guys are supposed to be practicing. You all got a competition in two days." Debra, their aunt, fussed. She was like a second mother to all of the girls. She stepped up when their mommas weren't around. She loved the shit out of them and would forever have their backs.

The music was blasting from Dez's stereo system. Dez was laying at the foot of her bed, smoking a joint. Kay was sitting at her desk on the laptop, and Nunu was on the floor polishing Shay, aka UNO's toes. Debra ambled into the room. Instantly, her nostrils flared. With one hand still on the doorknob, and the other on her wide hip, her eyes scanned the vicinity. Though Dez was her only blood relative, each of the girls was family. Debra took in Dez, Uno, and Kay after their moms were sent to the Feds 9 years ago for conspiracy to sell drugs. They were also charged with being the masterminds behind their boyfriends' empires. Which, in actuality, their men worked for them. However, it was the niggas flossy ass lifestyles that got them all locked up. It was said that Wiz was an informant. Nova, Nunu's mom was out of town when the Feds got her sisters. That same night, she was murdered; caught up in someone else's beef. The girls took it hard when their mothers left, but thank God for Debra. She made a vow to her sisters that she would keep the girls together and take care of them, as if they were her own. Within a years' time, Debra inherited four girls to see after. She did all she could to push the girls to be better than their parents, and even better than her. She could see by their lifestyle choices that they were headed down the wrong road. Deep down, she knew that she couldn't deter them from the life of a hustler. It was in their blood. But that didn't mean she wasn't going to let them know how she felt about it. Debra entered the room and everyone looked her way once she shut off the music.

"Dez, what did I tell you about smoking without the windows open? That shit is too loud. If you can't respect

47

what I say, don't smoke the shit in my house period." She snapped.

"My bad, Auntie. I apologize." Dez replied. She got up from the bed. Deb was in her early 40s. She felt she could relate to the girls. For the most part, she allowed them to do most things other parents wouldn't allow their kids to do. Smoking and hanging out late at night wasn't a problem, as long as they did it respectfully. Dez knew weed smoke was her aunt's pet peeve, so there was no need to try to defend her fuck-up. Dez put the joint out in the ashtray by her bed.

"That's your last warning." Debra let her know. She walked over to the center of the room. With a smile on her face, she said. "I'm so proud of you all. I know your parents are as well. Y'all will be high school graduates in a couple of days. That's a big fucking deal." She looked at the girls and their faces held a blank expression. "What's the problem? You guys act as if you aren't happy. Muthafuckas were counting you out before you were even born. Even niggas in the hood thought you wouldn't be shit because of the lifestyle your parents lived." She looked over at Kay. "Lil Momma." She said, referring to Kay's mom. "Was the only one who graduated, but y'all broke that curse. All four of my babies are about to walk the stage." She smiled. She was proud.

"Auntie." Uno spoke up.

"What's up?"

"I hate school. I'm only doing it so I can have something to fall back on. And so, you won't put me out." She was too serious. It was true. Deb warned them all that the only way they could stay in her house was if they went to school.

"So, what are you saying?" Debra glared at Uno. She looked just like her mom.

"I'm a hustler. The degree is just for backup. I'm trying to make some real money. We all are." She looked at her cousins, and they nodded their heads.

They all agreed.

"And what the fuck does that mean?" Debra wanted to know.

Dez answered. "It means once we give you your diploma, we're doing what, we feel, is best for us. We should be moving out soon, too." They had been hustling since the start of high school and saving their money. They knew their aunt wouldn't approve, so they formulated a plan. Right after graduation, they were getting their own place. Debra shook her head.

"Y'all got it all figured out. Y'all boosting shit and selling it. Dez thinks she is the weed lady at the school. No telling what else y'all ass is doing. It was nothing for me to find out, so you know it won't take no time for the police to find out. I just don't want y'all to end up in jail. Your mommas. I wanted to be just like them." She smiled, thinking about how her sisters had it going on at one point. "But they told me 'The life' wasn't for me. They made me stay in school. I did just that. And if I didn't, I don't know where you guys would have been now."

Silence…

"I'm not going to stress myself out like my momma did, and end up dying with a broken heart. So, the only thing I'm

49

gonna do is pray for you girls. Pray that you don't be stupid."
With that, Deb walked out the room and slammed the door.
They didn't know it, but tears were running down her face.

**P**apa lifted himself from the hood of the old Chevy Impala
and turned to face his driveway. He squinted his eyes from
the sun to get a better view. A Camel cigarette hung from his
mouth. He watched as the yellow cab pulled up. For an old
man, his eyesight was fairly good. He saw his granddaughter
sitting in the front seat. It was Nunu. He was sure the
grandkids he inherited were with her. Papa pulled the old
dirty rag from his back pocket and used it to wipe his greasy
hands. He made his way over to where the cab stopped. Once
he reached the driver's window, he asked in his southern
drawl.

"What dey owe ya?" Papa took one last pull from the
cigarette, held it from his mouth, and tossed it on the ground.
The African driver looked at his meter. Accent heavy.

"Fifty-five- twenty." He answered.

"Fifty-five dollars?" Papa yelled. His handsome face held a
scowl. Papa looked like an older version of the former
Lakers Player Rick Fox; only he had green eyes. One by one,
the girls exited the car. They were prepared to pay, but since
Papa was already willing, they let him be. "Where the fuck
he pick y'all up from? Better not be from no nigga's house."
Papa asked.

The girls ignored him. They hardly ever paid his blunt, or
rude attitude any mind. No matter how much shit he talked,
he loved each one of them. Even without him ever saying so,
they knew it. The four of them made their way onto the small
porch. Papa resided in a one-story yellow house. He raised

Nunu's mom in that very same house. Nunu and Uno sat on the steps while Dez and Kay sat on some empty crates.

"I ain't given you no fifty-five dollars." Papa reached in his blue khakis. "I ain't giving your slick ass but twenty." He pulled out a wad of money.

"No. No. It's fifty-five-twenty. That's de price." The man argued.

"I don't give a mammy fuck, what you say. You probably ain't even legal. And wanna go by the book. Where your papers at? Let me see 'em. Show me your papers and I might give you thirty."

"No. It's fifty-five you see." The man pointed to the meter.

"I won't give you shit. You better take what I'm giving you." Papa tossed the money in the window. "And get out of my yard before I go get my gun." He strolled off.

"You are a thief!" The man yelled. Papa turned around quickly.

"Fuck you, bitch! You got five seconds to get out my damn yard." He bent down, dug in his sock, and pulled out a .22. The taxi driver's eyes got big as saucers. He hurriedly backed out of the driveway. Papa didn't turn his back until the cab was out of sight. The girls were on the porch laughing. They were all doubled over in laughter, holding their stomachs. Uno even had tears rolling down her face. Papa always gave them a good laugh.

"Ain't a damn thing funny. I wasn't given that ole foreigner no damn fifty-five nothing. Where y'all come from?"

"We're coming from our graduation." Nunu said.

"Oh yeah. Congrats on your graduation. I wasn't feeling too good, sorry I couldn't make it. I got something for you gals. One of y'all go in the kitchen and look by the microwave. In that basket are four cards." Dez got up to do it. She was thirsty anyway.

"So, all y'all going to college?" Papa asked.

"Yeah, just part-time. A community college." Nunu said, not sounding too thrilled.

"If that's what you wanna do, go for it. You smart."

"Really it ain't. I'm doing it for my momma. I made her a promise and I wanna keep it." Nunu said somberly, while looking down at the ground to keep her emotions at bay. It had been 8 years, and it was still hard to talk about her momma. Ever since she could remember, her mom made her promise that she would go to college and become some professional. Nunu didn't recall ever telling her mom what she wanted to do in life, but she did promise her that she would go to college. The front door opened and shut; Dez walked out with a bottle of water and four cards. She read the names aloud and handed them to who they belonged to. The girls thanked Papa with a hug. He had given each one one-thousand dollars. Papa walked to the side of the house. He grabbed a kitchen chair, came back, and sat down, facing the girls. He looked at each one of them before he spoke.

"Nunu, you a good girl for not breaking your promise to your momma. There are two things you need to remember. Never make a promise you don't tend to keep, and never make a promise just to please the next muthafucka. Remember that." Papa was a real one. He crossed his legs.

Papa left Louisiana when he was 17. Him and his two brothers. While his brother picked Cali for the good jobs, Papa sought to hustle. When he left home, he was done working for the white man. He gave enough of himself picking cotton. He didn't care how much they offered to pay; he wasn't working no job. Papa found him a small hustle, which eventually led to a better hustle, and it didn't stop. He even taught his daughter the game. She and her friends fucked up when they allowed love to enter their hearts. He never warned them that a man could be their downfall. He thought by teaching his daughter how to get money, she would automatically know she didn't need a man. He was wrong. His daughter's death ate him up, but he was trying to stay strong for Nunu. He wouldn't fail her like he did his daughter. He would teach her everything he didn't teach Nova.

"So, what you guys going to do to get money?"

"Papa." Nunu started. When he gave her that knowing look, she changed her mind. "Dez got something she wanna say." Kay and Uno giggled.

"Dez, what you wanna tell me?" He reached into his front pocket of his shirt and pulled out his pack of cigarettes. Everyone watched as he placed one in his mouth and lit it. "You ain't saying nothing."

"We wanna be hustlers, just like our parents, and you. But better." Dez said with her chest poked out. "We have a couple of things in mind. But we need a real one to feed us the game. So, here we are."

"Yeah, Papa, we ain't trying to work for the white man." Nunu added. "I'm only going to college because my word is bond, even after death, but I want to be a Queen Pin with bands."

"Just because we are getting our hands dirty, don't mean we don't want nothing legit out of life. We just need help getting us to where we wanna be. And that help will come from fast money." Kay added. Papa smirked. He saw it way before they even mentioned it. All of their mothers were involved in illegal activities. It wasn't the life he wanted the girls to live, especially if their fate would be like their mothers. However, he knew if he didn't support them, and school them, they would be out of the game quicker than they started.

"I ain't going to try to talk you out of it. Ya mind is made up. You all know the life of a hustler. Their fate ain't always like mine. I'm here today because I'm smart. I didn't let pussy knock me off my square. And everyone is suspect."

"We ain't falling in love, either." Uno added her two cents.

"You say that now, but some nigga come along and pop that cherry, and your little asses will get off your square."

"Can you teach us not to work with feelings?" Uno asked.

"I'm going to teach you a lot of shit. But know this, nothing comes for free, not even your papa's wisdom. As of today, you will work for me." He saw the surprised look on their faces. No one knew Papa was still hustling, and he liked it like that.

"Trust, follow me, and listen, you'll eat for a long time."

"I'm not sure if I wanna do this. This credit card shit will get you caught up. I prefer to take my chances selling weed." Kay explained. They sat across the living room. It was after midnight, and Papa had just dropped them back off at home. 7 hours of straight talking, and the last hour they were given their first assignment. Dez stood up. She walked into the center of the room.

"See, you ain't thinking like a hustler. Papa Smurf just basically gave us the blueprint on getting rich without working for nobody. This credit card shit is going to open up the door to much more. It's four of us. If we go into high-end stores and we each get one item for at least four thousand, that's sixteen thousand a day. After we give Papa his cut, we still hit for eight thousand in one day." She stood there with her arms folded.

"Damn." Nunu mumbled. She calculated the numbers in her head.

"Bitches won't be able to tell us shit." Uno added.

"We ain't about to do nothing but stack. We will floss later." Dez explained.

"I got a name for us." Uno said excitedly.

"What, bitch?" Nunu wanted to know. She briefly thought about the crew her mom was from, 'Fancy & Fine.' Her heart ached. She missed her momma so much.

"Bitches Getting Bandz." Uno spat, as she clasped her hands together.

"I like that." Kay finally spoke up. "I'm going to follow your lead. But like Papa said, we need a backup plan, so I'm staying in school. If this shit works, we are going legit. I wanna own shit. I don't wanna do this and the only thing I got to show is material shit." Kay said.

They all agreed.

They may have been young, but they knew what they wanted. Bosses didn't just have nice clothes and money. The real bosses invested their money and had shit with their names on it.

"We got one of the oldest and wisest teachers in the game. We're good. And like he said, we don't do shit on the side without the other knowing, and don't let these fuck niggas knock us off our square."

"I got a play." Nunu whispered to a dude named Break. He was sitting in VIP, pretending to be in tune with the female entertainment. The whole time, he was looking for his next victim. As always, Nunu came through. Although Nunu would never admit it, hooking up with Break was going against The BGB code of conduct. She detested being sneaky, but she fucked up. What she and Break had going on was going to help her get it straight. The pair ate a few times off the plays Nunu orchestrated. Her cousins didn't know the real reason behind Nunu stripping at Club Slick. The girls thought Nunu was dancing because she wanted the experience for when they opened their own club. It was like she was an intern learning the business before they started their own, but that wasn't the case. Nunu had fucked up. Now she had to fix it.

Break gave her a head nod and threw up the number four. He secretly watched her as she walked away. Dressed in close to nothing with her lime green lingerie, Nunu made her way toward their mark. In four minutes, Break would be meeting her in the employee lavatory, so she could put him up on game. On the other side of the club, Nunu passed by Tone and winked. He was the young boss from Atlanta that she was about to score on.

"Hey." He pulled her by the arm, and she carelessly fell into his lap. Tone wrapped his arms around her waist and whispered something in her ear. She giggled and whispered back. He gave her a head nod and tapped her on the ass. When she got up, she looked back at him and blew a kiss. Tone grabbed his dick. He couldn't wait to hit.

"So, you about to trick on that hoe?" His God brother asked. He was sitting next to him with a bottle of Patron in his hand.

"It ain't tricking if you got it." Tone laughed and turned up the bottle of Ace of Spade. Boy Boy chuckled.

"The hoe better be bringing some friends."

"And that she is." Tone confirmed.

Nunu sat on the restroom sink and Break stood between her legs. His hands were planted on both of her thighs.

"Alright." She started. "He's from Atlanta. He and his boy are here on business and trying to have a good time." NuNu explained.

Looking into her captivating green eyes, Break rubbed her thighs. Break loved everything about Nunu. While Nunu tried her hardest to keep her feelings about him in check. She would never admit that she was feeling him on some 'you my nigga' type shit. She and Break rocked how they rocked with no strings attached, and both of them were cool with that.

Break never exposed his hand, though. His feelings were growing for Nunu. He wanted her all to himself, but it wasn't time yet. They both were young, risking their lives everyday chasing a bag, and turned up as they pleased. He didn't have the patience to try to get Nunu to be the girl he would have desired her to be. Which was out of the strip club with her ass at home and never ever risking her life for a bag. He would take care of her. One day, though, when they both had

58

what they wanted in life, he would step to her on some serious type of shit. If they lived to see that day.

"I want you to be safe. Send the 'addy' as soon as you get there. Don't get distracted by the nigga's charm." Break grabbed her by the chin. She took a deep breath as she gawked back at him.

"I saw how you were all up on him, smiling and shit. You were feeling the nigga." Jealousy was evident in his tone. Nunu wasn't lying. She respected what she and Break had too much to play with his intelligence. She thought Tone was cute, and after the thirty minutes she spent with him, they connected on another level. He was funny, a shit talker like her, and flashy. Yeah, she was digging his style, but she wouldn't admit it. Plus, her bag came first, fuck the rest. She learned her lesson.

Instead of responding to Break's assumption, she leaned forward and kissed him on his juicy lips. A light moan escaped her mouth when she tasted his meaty tongue. Break's hands roamed her body, turning the heat up between the two. It didn't take much for Break to have her hot and bothered. She was getting wetter by the second. When she felt his thumb on her clit, he had her gone. Grinding on his fingers, she found his belt buckle and began to undo it. Being that they were in the employee restroom and pressed for time, they had to speed things up. Break helped her by unbuckling his jeans and pulling his pants down.

"Oh, babe." She mumbled against his lip.

His thick penis was at the entrance of her hotbox. Removing her lips from his, she pushed the back of his baldhead toward her left breast. Break hungrily took it into his mouth.

59

Shoving himself inside of her, they both cursed. Shit, she cried. Fuck, he grumbled. Together, they were in ecstasy. Break worked her pussy like only he could, and she gave him the wet wet like only she could. They would never confess it to each other, but neither of them could get enough of the other.

"It's so good. Damn, I love the way you fuck me. Please, don't stop." Nunu cried out from pleasure.

"Babe, one day you're going to be mine. I swear." Break confessed for the very first time-ever. Nunu's heart dropped. She was scared to entertain the idea of having a man after her first heartbreak, but Break's confession had her open at the moment. She tightened her muscles and worked her hot box on his dick. Break couldn't control it. He was about to nut.

"You love this pussy?" Nunu panted.

"Fuck, yeah." He groaned and exploded right inside of her. His head now rested on her forehead. They both gasped, still trying to recover from their intense session. Knowing they had to go, Break pulled out. "Make sure you get the pill. I couldn't help myself. I apologize." He told her, pulling up his pants. He was referring to the morning after pill.

"I will." She assured him. She damn sure didn't want kids. Break grabbed some paper towels. He reached over and turned on the water. Using the hand soap, he put it on the towels and then put them under the water. He handed them to Nunu, so she could clean herself up. He then kissed her on the forehead.

"Be safe. I'll be waiting for your text." He turned to walk out of the restroom. Nunu grabbed him by the shirt. When he looked back, she only stared at him. Her gut was telling her to speak what she felt, but then she didn't want to jinx what they had going on. The feeling was sudden. It was a feeling she never felt before. The warning was so deep. *Stop. This play won't work.* Is what she was feeling.

Instead of telling him how she felt, she replied, "You be safe, too. Come back to me." Break smiled, winked, and departed out of the facility.

As if they needed anything else to add to their wardrobe, Kay, Uno, Dez, and Nunu were spending part of their day at The South Coast Plaza shopping. They claimed they were shopping for an outfit to wear to Uno's event. Normally, they didn't do local night-clubs. Uno was performing, so of course they were about to turn the fuck up. It was going on her $2^{nd}$ year in the rap game, and she had already made a name for herself as one of the hottest underground artist in Cali.

"Hold on." Nunu called out. Her eyes were on one of the two dudes who were headed into the Tom Ford store. She twirled her lollipop in her mouth as she eyed the one who she thought was fine as fuck. The crew peeped what she was on and gave an approving nod. It wasn't nothing new for one of the girls to push up on a piece. They were all single by choice and did whatever the fuck they pleased. Like, Papa taught them, they didn't love them niggas.

"We're definitely going up in here." Uno called out, referring to Saks Fifth Avenue. She didn't do dudes, so she wasn't interested in either one.

"I'm going to see what the other one all about." Kay tossed her hair as she followed behind Nunu. Out of the crew, none of the girls gave no fucks when it came to working with feelings. They had been schooled. Those feelings will get you caught up. Uno was the worst. She'd fuck and leave them quick. Dez was all about her paper. Besides her cousins, she didn't care about anything but money. Secretly, Nunu had slipped up and fell a couple of times. She prayed it never got back to her cousins. Kay made a promise that when she walked away from the hustle; she would open up to the possibility of love whenever that was.

The duo sauntered toward their destination with one thing in mind, adding another handsome ass boss to their roster. Why not?

Dez and Uno strolled into Saks and went straight to the shoe department. They were looking at a pair of designer sneakers when Dez's phone rang. It was Vance.

"The fuck this nigga calling for?" She questioned. Uno didn't even bother to respond. There was always someone ringing their line. It was someone they preferred not to be bothered with. Dez let the phone go to voicemail, and a millisecond later, it rang again. With a frown on her face, she answered. Her body weight shifted to one side. "Yeah?" She wanted to make sure she heard the nigga correctly. "Say it again?"

"Man, stop playing with me. Where Kay at? She said she was with you, but she ain't picking up." Dez put the phone on speaker. Uno needed to hear this fuck shit.

"Vance, bro, last time I checked, my cousin was single and don't owe a nigga no explanation."

"Oh, that's what she said? She ain't let you know we made it official?" The girls burst into a hearty laughter. They knew he was lying. The BGB girls didn't do relationships. "Fuck all that. Where is her ass at?" He sneered.

"Look, I don't even know how you got my number. I don't think she gave it to you, so your pesky ass had to be all up in her phone." Now Dez had his number because Kay called her from his phone once. She stored it just in case she needed it. She knew damn well her cousin wouldn't give out her number without her permission. Vance was on some weak shit.

"Right." Uno chimed in. "Don't call this phone no more looking for my cousin who ain't trying to be found."

"Period." Uno and Dez said in unison.

"That's how y'all get at me?" He questioned. For the most part, Vance was cool. He and Kay messed around for a couple of years. As far as they knew, it was nothing official. However, even if it was, he wasn't about to be calling their phones trying to keep tabs on their girl.

Uno spoke up. "If she wanted to be bothered, she would answer." She snatched the phone out of Dez's hand and ended the call. "Let me find out this bitch doing relationships." Uno said as she picked up a pair of cute Dior sandals.

"Right. We are clowning." Dez said, taking her phone back from Uno. "I want those." She was referring to the sandals Uno was holding. The female sales clerk walked up.

"Can we get these in a size 7 and a 9 please?" Uno then picked up another shoe. She was so busy feeding her addiction. Shoes. She hadn't even noticed the clerk was still standing there until Dez spoke up.

"What you gon' do stare at her all day, or get our shoes? I know you see celebrities all day." They were at an upscale mall where celebrities frequented. The clerk chuckled. Dez didn't even know, she was 'that nigga' and the only reason why she was at this job was to keep her PO off her ass.

"Damn, D." Uno laughed. Her eyes darted to a rude Dez. Uno was always friendly with her fans, even if she wasn't in the mood. After all, they were part of the reason she was one of the hottest underground rappers out of Watts, California. With a warm smile, she gave the clerk her attention. When her eyes landed on the employee, she, too, was stuck. She had never been attracted to studs but the chick in front of her was enticing. It was something about her tom boy swag that had Uno intrigued.

"She may not know it yet, but she's mine." Thought the clerk.

"Let me go get your shoes." She gave Uno the once over and licked her lips. "Who would have ever thought I would run into the famous Uno. It's my lucky day." She smirked and winked before strolling off.

Nunu and Kay sauntered into Tom Ford. The male greeter spoke, and the ladies returned the salutation. The entire time though Nunu's eyes were on the tall, caramel latte complexioned dude with the nice physique, and the two long braids. She thought he had to be bi-racial with his curly hair and slanted eyes. She gave him the once over. Ole boy was dressed in Versace sneakers, white Versace jeans, and a white Versace T-shirt with the gold medusa emblem on the front. He was looking at a pair of black jeans. Although Sen was into what he was doing, he was alert at all times. He saw ole girl and her friends before he went into the store and now, while he was browsing the jeans. It wasn't nothing new to Sen; females stayed flocking to him. And why wouldn't they, he was that nigga. Sen didn't do thirsty females. He saw them as a turn off. The bitches he fucked with may have only dealt with niggas of his caliber, and he respected that. It wasn't nothing wrong with having standards, but nine times out of ten the chick glaring at him was just a bag chaser with no future goals of her own. While Sen was ignoring ole girl, his brother Spade was ready to entertain the friend.

Spade bit his bottom lip as he eyed the 5'8 butterscotch hottie. Her long legs, small hips, and perfect plump ass complimented the black Balenciaga jumper she was wearing. Her pretty toes sat off in a pair of 6-inch Christian Louboutin heels. Her flawless skin only added to her beauty. With a smirk on her face and lust filled eyes, Kay gave him an agreeing head nod to let him know they were on the same page. *'Damn. Baby is a joint'* she thought, staring him down. Spade stood at 6'2. His body was beefy just the way she liked. A man with muscles always made her pussy wet. And he had dark skin, too. She most definitely had to get up on him. Both Spade and Kay were eager to be acquainted, and wasted no time with the introduction.

A few feet away, Sen was about to piss Nunu off. With one hand on her hip and the other holding a red lollipop, she sashayed closer to Sen.

"I'm not sure if you heard me the first time, but I asked if I could have a minute of your time." He didn't like the tone she was using while interrupting his time. He looked up at her and quickly looked away. He noticed her alluring green eyes. *'She fine, but I ain't fucking with her.'*

"I ain't trying to converse. I'm shopping, can't you see?" His baritone sent chills down her spine. He gave her the once over before going back to what he was doing. Her face was pretty, and body was banging, but he wasn't interested. He

66

didn't know what it was, but it was something about her that told him not to entertain her at all. Plus, he didn't trust Cali bitches. Especially since, he believed that was the reason his younger brother was killed.

"That's cool. Put my number in your phone." She said, handing it to him. Sen thought it was amusing. Apparently, ole girl was used to getting what she wanted, but not from him.

"Baby girl, I'm good." He let her down easily. Her left eyebrow raised. He wasn't the first that played hard to get, but it was something about the way he didn't even seem a tad bit interested that had her in her feelings. It was as if he were different, like something she never had. His presence alone spoke highly of him, but even so, Nunu refused to believe that she had butterflies. *'He's just another piece of meat.'* She coached herself. He was a piece of meat that she desperately wanted, but she wouldn't press.

"I'm going to let you keep thinking that. I'll see you again, though. Hopefully, you are in a better mood." She popped her lips and then put the lollipop in her mouth. Not knowing that shit made his dick hard. After giving him one final look, she strolled off. When she made it over to where Kay was, she chuckled at her cousin. Kay was cheesing big time. All up in ole boy's space and he was eating every bit of it up.

"I'm about to go over to Sak's." Nunu tossed out and sounded bothered. Kay looked over at Sen, then back at Nunu. She tossed her head up to say what's up?

"Girl, he is tripping right now. I'll get him next time, and that's a fact." She looked at Spade. "Sup." She spoke. She peeped the Cubans around his neck. The iced-out Joker

"What you trying to eat?" Spade asked Sen. They were standing at the valet waiting on their ride.

"I'm going to the hotel. I need a nap before we go handle that." He replied.

"You're right. Stop at In-n-Out Burger. I have been dying for one since we got here."

"Hell, yeah." Sen replied, walking over to the driver side of the Porsche that they had rented.

Sen and Spade were from Atlanta, Georgia. The organization the brothers ran was so successful that their name alone held weight. The Jank Brothers are what they were called. However, if you didn't know them, you would think Spade and Sen were just average niggas with money.

"You trying to hit the beach before we fly back home?" Spade asked. They hadn't had business in Cali in five years. Their brother, and their God brother, came out to handle a small business situation and ended up dead. Ever since then, their family refused to do business with any niggas from Cali. They weren't sure how their folks were killed, until they found out not one Cali native could eat off their table. The only reason why they were doing business with this particular person was because their father called all the shots, and the nigga only lived in Los Angeles, but Black Sam was from the A. After their folks were killed, Cali left a bad taste in Sen's mouth. Deep in his heart, he knew some bitches set his brothers up. Tone loved hoes, and he made it his business to hook up with a bad bitch wherever he went. He couldn't prove it, but he believed a hoe was the cause of his brother's demise.

Ignoring the greeting of the hotel staff, the brothers made their way to the elevator.

"I don't trust this city any more than I trust that bitch from the mall. What I tell you about hooking up with these out-of-town hoes? Especially in this grimy ass city." Sen grimaced.

"Man, them bitches is it. Them ain't no average hoes. Did you see the bracelet my bitch was wearing?" Spade retorted.

"Your bitch?" Sen chuckled and shook his head. He pressed the button on the elevator. When it opened, they stepped in. Spade used his key card to gain access to the suite.

"I don't trust them." Sen admitted.

"I don't trust the hoe like that either. That's why I invited her here. You can watch my back while I get some." Sen instantly caught a headache. There was no need to argue with Spade; he didn't listen. He always did what he wanted.

Spade was actually his brother on his father's side. Judah Jank had five sons. The two of them were the closest, but they all were a team. Since he was the eldest, he was in charge. Once they made it to the room, they went their separate ways around the large suite. Sen was on his way to the shower. Ironically, on the way to shower the chick he shut down at the mall was on his mind. If he had to rate her, she was definitely a hard TEN. He then wondered how she and her girls got their bag. *'Chasing rich niggas like me.'*

70

Sen concluded. Fucking with that bitch was out of the picture. No out-of-town pussy would get him off his square and leave him dead.

I'd rather be a B-I-T-C-H (I'd rather keep it real with ya)
'Cause that's what you gon' call me when I'm trippin' anyway
You know you can't control me, baby, you need a real one in
ya life Them bitches ain't gon' give it to you right (Ayy)

Why you wanna play with me? You know I'm undefeated
A real hot girl know how to keep a nigga heated.

It was the perfect day in the city of Costa Mesa. The girls left
the mall and had lunch at their favorite restaurant by the
beach. Today Nunu brought out her black foreign
convertible. She drove as Kay sat on the passenger side. Uno
and Dez were in the back seat. They cruised by the tall green
palm trees alongside the highway. The cool breeze brushing
against their faces as their hair blew in the wind had them
feeling themselves. A blunt was in rotation. Heads banged
and bodies rocked to the music. Dez leaned over the front
seat and turned the radio down. She was high and felt like
shooting the shit. She loved a good laugh.

"So, yeah. What was up with those niggas y'all pushed up
on in the mall?"

"Girl, ole boy ready to take me shopping out in New York. I
started to tell him that don't impress me." Kay said.

"Okayyy." They all chimed in.

"I was like…I'm cool with being treated. I really appreciate
the offer, but I got my own. I just want some dick. He was
smiling big. He pulled me into his arms and hugged me tight.

Talking about, he can tell that I'm going to be problems." Kay laughed. You couldn't notice because of her designer sunglasses covering her eyes, but she was high. She looked back at Uno. "Dick big as fuck. You know I put my hand down there." They all laughed.

Kay's the wildest. She held a bachelor's in science, but like her crew, instead of pursuing a career in their field of study, she was an entrepreneur. A hustler. They had one setback that they were aware of. A loss of 200k, but they were working hard to get that back, and more. During their short time in the game, they started a few lucrative businesses. Alone, Kay owned a beauty salon and a dance studio. She was also co-owner of BANDZ Strip Club, and the million-dollar home the girls stayed in. Although she established legit businesses, she still was getting her hands dirty. She and her girls were the plug. They were real-life balling ass boss bitches. They got it from their mommas.

"Nunu, I'm starting to think you got curved." Dez clowned. "You ain't said a word about ole dude."

"Kay told you that shit, I got curved?" She looked at her and rolled her eyes.

"Bitch, he did though. But for what it's worth, I checked his ass when you left." Nunu's head snapped to the side.

"What you say, hoe?" She shook her head.

"I was like you ain't even all that while you trying to play my cousin. I only wanted her to come with me while I pushed up on your boy. He laughed, girl. He was like, I don't give a fuck and walked off. Left me and my boo in the store." Hard

73

laughs filled the car. Even Nunu had to laugh. Ole boy was showing his ass. She prayed she got another opportunity, and when she did, she had a trick for his ass.

Finally looking up from her phone Uno was like, "I bet ten racks that you can't bag ole boy." She challenged Nunu.

Silence.

"Man, fuck that bet. I ain't about to press his fine ass." Nunu's clit tingled just thinking of him. The girls laughed. As they pulled up to the valet, they inhaled the aroma of food. Their stomachs immediately began to growl. After they finished their food, they headed to the warehouse where they shot the shit with other bosses and had a little fun.

Sitting on the plush sofa, Spade was stuffing his face with cold fries as he FaceTimed the girl from the mall. Kay was more than his type. She had the looks, the body, and the confidence he desired. On top of that, she was proud to let him know that she had her own bag. Basically, anything he offered wasn't needed, but appreciated. Kay answered with a smile.

"What's up, boo?" Her voice was angelic.

"I got a pet name already?" He smiled.

"Not until I test the dick. If it's good, I'll call you daddy. I call everybody boo." She teased. Spade took his bottom lip in his mouth and used his right hand to grab his dick.

"You trying to pull up now?" He asked, peeping her background. It looked like they were in the back of a building. From what he could see, there were quite a few people out. Loud music and loud talking filled the air.

"Drop me your location. I just took all these niggas money. My time is done." He raised a brow at her declaration.

"How you do that?"

"Dice game. You shoot?" She asked.

A sting hit his heart, and he was now smiling again. The woman he met today was of a different caliber. To add to her already fine attributes, she gambled. Only if Kay knew he wasn't just a gambler, but a gambling god.

"You know your man shoot." Spade tossed out. She giggled at his comment. Another head got in the phone.

"Who you?" The chick asked. She was a pretty light skinned hottie.

"I'm her man." Spade shot back. The chick pursed her lips.

"You are the second one today that claimed my girl. We don't do relationships, so you niggas lying." Uno let it be known. Spade fell out laughing.

"Y'all females are something else. The right nigga would fix all that." Spade assured them.

"Uno, you ain't shit." Kay retorted.

"Uno, the rapper chick? I knew her little ass looked familiar. That's what's up." Spade was familiar with her by way of IG. He remembered his promoter homie promoting a show she did in their city not long ago. By this time, Uno stepped to the side. Kay flipped her camera on her phone accidentally as Sen walked up. Sen's eyes landed on Nunu. She had a bottle of Hennessy by her as she squatted on the ground shooting dice. Sen shook his head. It wasn't nothing cute to him about females acting like niggas. Sen believed in a woman's place; and that wasn't it. Kay flipped the camera back on her. Sen walked off.

"Uno having a show tonight so I gotta make it quick. Send me your location."

"We might pull-up. I gotta see how good the pussy is first." Spade teased.

"Boy, bye!" Kay hung up. When the location popped up on her cell, she smiled. *'I'm too damn thirsty.'* She chuckled to herself.

*S*pade met Kay in the lobby, and Nunu was right by her side. He couldn't do nothing but chuckle when he saw the duo. Sporting a black Nike shirt, Nike sweats and Nike slides, Spade strolled over to Kay and pulled her in for a hug. Burying his nose into her neck, he complimented her on her perfume. He looked at Nunu.

"What's up, you must really be feeling my brother?" He smirked.

"Not even. I came to have my crazy ass cousin's back. We don't know y'all and just in case you niggas try something, I'm here." She patted her purse. Spade looked at Kay.

"That's right, baby girl. Don't trust nobody." He kissed Kay's forehead. They both gazed into each other's eyes, trying to figure out if the other could feel the butterflies in their stomach. Was something brewing between the two? Quickly, they checked themselves and concluded the strange emotions came from the excitement of the unknown.

In the elevator, Spade was hugging Kay from the back. Nunu popped her gum as she patiently watched the floors of the elevator.

"You know my brother is mean. He may trip about you being here." Spade told her.

"Oh, we don't do disrespect." Kay let him know.

"Nah. I don't think he would do that. He ain't like that, but he will ignore you."

"I didn't come for him. I'll catch up with him another time." She nodded her head to agree with herself. In all honesty, she did come to keep an eye on Kay and to see Sen. Nunu was determined to get him. Her plan was to fuck him and then leave him.

The elevator stopped on the 31$^{st}$ floor and the trio made their exit. Kay's phone vibrated for the 100$^{th}$ time since she pulled up. She hit ignore, once again. Vance was blowing her up.

"That nigga on you tough." Spade said. "Why don't you just turn it off."

"Cause it's my phone." She snapped. He gave her a warning look before pulling his key card out and opening the door.

"Fucking with them lames that's why. And you better watch that smart ass mouth." He mumbled, but the girls heard him. Nunu smirked because she caught the attitude. Kay didn't comment. She was still tripping off how the nigga had the nerve to use his eyes to check her. What made her annoyed was how she didn't say shit back. Spade walked inside and held the door open for the ladies. Kay was the first to enter, then Nunu.

Rap music played at a respectful level. The familiar smell of cherry fragrance lingered in the air. The penthouse was what it was, an upscale, one-bedroom apartment. Nunu mentally noted how they were staying. Either they were niggas with money, scammers with money, or simply scammers. She didn't know yet, but she planned on finding out. Sen was sitting on the sofa on his laptop when they walked in. He looked up and shook his head. His eyes landed directly on Nunu.

"Why are you here?"

"Because my cousin is here. Thank you." She switched over to the loveseat opposite of where he was sitting. Taking her purse off her shoulders, she laid it next to her and then gave it an assuring pat. The entire time, she and Sen never broke their gaze. She was intriguing, gorgeous, and her body was everything. He could see she was about some money by the ice around her neck, wrist, and ankle. The woman in front of him with the mesmerizing green eyes, was a walking explosion, and he wanted nothing but for her to be far away.

"Man, why is she here?" Sen looked at his brother.

"What you mean, why am I here? Didn't I just say why?" Nunu tossed his question back at him.

"You can't understand basic English. And was I talking to you?" He snapped back.

Nunu gave him the bird. Spade could tell his brother was losing his patience by the look on his face.

"Aye, bro. My girl invited her cousin here because she didn't trust me." Spade explained.

"Man, she ain't your girl." Sen spat.

"I don't know why the nigga keeps claiming my cousin. We don't do relationships." Nunu added.

"Be quiet." Sen told Nunu. "Always talking when you ain't being talked to."

"Boy, fuck you! I'm starting to think you are overdue for some pussy, and your ugly ass bitch won't give your mean ass none. Dick probably too little anyway."

"Ain't shit little about me Shawty." Kay stood there with a smile on her face as they went back and forth. She was confident that her cousin was going to snag Spade's mean ass brother.

"You two try not to kill each other. Come on, woman."
Spade said. He took Kay by the hand and led her to the
bedroom upstairs.

The moment they got into the room, Spade hit the blackout
button on the wall. As the curtains shut, he pulled Kay into
him. Gripping her apple bottom, he buried his head into her
neck. Her body melted into him. Inhaling his cologne, she
moaned.

"Can I do whatever I want with you?" His warm breath
tickled her neck.

"Yes. This time I'm all yours." She replied. Spade removed
his head from her neck and looked at her pretty face.

"So, I get two chances to make a first impression?"

"Hell, no. You don't do it right. This time, there will never
be another time." She tilted her head. He couldn't do nothing
but laugh. Then he turned serious.

"I need you to turn that phone off. If it ain't business, I don't
want us interrupted."

"How do you know it ain't business?"

"Like I said. Turn it off. I want all my personal time." He
walked away and sat on the edge of the bed. She had sixty
seconds to do as he asked, or it was a wrap. He didn't do
hardheaded chicks. Shaking her head, Kay went into her
fanny pack and pulled out her phone. After powering it off,
she put it back into the bag.

"I don't know why I'm giving you your way, but it's whatever for now." Spade was the type of person who could sense what was going to happen before it transpired. He lived in Atlanta, and she was in Los Angeles. Spade didn't know how it was going to work, but she intended to be his.

"Thanks, babe." He took his bottom lip into his mouth. "Can you take those clothes off?"

"Yes." Kay first unsnapped her fanny pack and placed it on the table. She really wanted to take her time to seduce him, but she was pressed for time. *Next time,* she thought, undressing in record time.

"Damn, shawty." He said, eying her sexy physique. Spade stood up. He quickly undressed himself. They both stood there naked. Kay was pleased by everything she saw. From the abs, the nicely toned legs, and a big dick that was sticking straight up. She was extremely turned on. Her pussy jumped like a kangaroo at the sight of the king standing before her. She could feel her juices flowing down her leg. She couldn't wait to see what he was going to do to her. Spade made his way toward her. Breaking all his rules, he placed his mouth on hers. She welcomed his minty tongue. After an intense exchange, Kay pulled back.

"Once I give you this pussy, I don't want you tripping." She teased. Niggas was known for that. She knew she had a gold mine between her thighs, and Spade would be hooked, too.

"I'm tripping." He admitted.

She giggled. Spade picked her up, and she wrapped her legs around his waist. They exchanged no words as he gazed into

81

her eyes. He walked her over to the bed and flopped down with her, causing the bed to bounce them up and back down.

"Lay down. Let me get this condom." He told her. She rolled over on the side of him. On her back, she moaned while she played in her puss. She was just about to bring herself to a climax, but he snuck up on her and knocked her hand away.

"Damn, that pussy pretty." His eyes lit up. One day, he was going to feast on that bitch. However, for now, he was going to bless her with some of the best dick she had ever had. He secured the condom on his member. Balancing himself on his knees, he took his hard dick and rubbed it up and down her clit, which resulted in swooshing noises. She was so damn wet. The head of his dick touched her entrance, and she arched her back.

"Stop playing and give it to me." They moaned in pure bliss as he entered her tight wet wet. "Oh myyy goo-" Kay moaned, barely audible. And just like that, Spade had taken her to a place she didn't know existed. He stroked her so deep, with just the right pace, he was hitting every spot, and then some. Back-to-back, she screamed. Her mouth was so dry from being open. She couldn't speak. The feeling was spectacular. Kay's eyes rolled in the back of her head. Spade was driving her insane. Kay had Spade's head gone, too. He had to think about other shit to keep from nutting prematurely. Kay fit him like a glove. The way she rotated her hips, trying her best to give it back to him, made him grow harder inside of her. Normally, he wouldn't even think of saying no sucka shit, but he couldn't help it. Being inside of her, he lost control of his senses.

"I love this shit. Got a nigga ready to die for this pussy, shawty."

"I, I, I, I me, too. Tell me it's all mine. Ohhh." She squealed. If it were left up to Kay, she would fuck him all night and day. She knew damn well this would not be her last time.

Downstairs, Nunu and Sen were barely tolerating each other. Nunu thought Sen was a rude, arrogant, and unnecessarily mean ass nigga. Sen thought she was just simply annoying. Without waiting on an invitation, Nunu switched over to the wet bar and made herself a martini. Sen was so intrigued with how she moved like a professional bartender mixing the drinks. He didn't check her for helping herself to their shit. With her glass in her hand, she walked back to her place on the loveseat and sat. She kicked her feet up and sipped from her glass.

"Mmm. Good." She mumbled.

"Next time, ask if it's cool. You don't stay here." Sen told her.

"Next time, act like you got some damn hospitality. I know your momma raised you better than that. Besides, you don't live here either, nigga." She rolled her eyes.

"Man, whatever." Sen shook his head. Sen couldn't stand a smart mouth ass bitch. His momma's mouth was just as smart. Although his moms and pops have been split up for decades, his pops still complained about his momma's mouth.

Grabbing his ringing cell phone, Sen answered it. Nunu was trying her best to ignore the conversation she knew he was having with a woman. He kept explaining himself. About how he wasn't with no other woman. And how he was in

83

Cali on business. She couldn't even focus on the business she was handling on her own phone. He was annoying her that much. Nunu sat there as long as she could before she had enough.

"Oh, my God!" She complained and stood up. She grabbed her phone and stormed off. "Where's the bathroom?" She yelled. Immediately, Sen hung up the phone.

"You did that shit on purpose." He called out, following behind her.

"What, having to piss? I care nothing about you simping to a bitch. That's weak." She shot over her shoulders.

"Keep talking shit with that potty mouth, and I might put something in it." Sen continued to stomp behind her.

"Ha!" She spat. With no help from Sen, Nunu found the restroom. She went in and went to shut the door, but it was pulled back with too much force for her liking.

"What in the fuck is your problem?" Nunu frowned, looking Sen up and down.

"This door is going to stay open, and I'm going to be watching you." Sen crossed his arms in front of him and stared dead in her eyes. *'She's deadly.'* He thought.

"So, you gotta watch me piss?" Nunu shook her head. "Whatever." She lifted her mini-dress and all he saw were thick thighs and a fat ass. The bitch wasn't even wearing panties. Sen watched as Nunu squatted over the toilet and released her bladder. He even watched how she wiped her pretty fat cat. He was going through a mental battle with his second head. Warning it to calm the fuck down.

As if he wasn't there, Nunu tossed the tissue in the toilet. She took another piece off the roll and used it to flush the toilet. She threw that piece in the toilet and put the seat down. Still with her dress hitched over her bubble butt, she moseyed over to the sink and washed her hands.

"Stop staring." She said, looking at him through the mirror. He was so goddamn fine. Nunu envisioned Sen's head between her legs. Her hands were gripped around his two braids as she fucked the shit out his face. Her center got moist just thinking about it. She wanted the nigga badly, but he was too damn mean. Plus, he was weak over whatever bitch he was simping too. *'Just like him to fuck up a wet dream.'*

"Let me see that phone." Sen barked. He pointed his head toward the sink, where she'd placed her iPhone.

"Nigga, no." Nunu frowned. One step and Sen was next to her snatching her phone off the counter.

"Give me my phone, nigga." She tried to grab it, but his arm was unreachable.

"You've been on this phone a lot. I don't trust you bitches. Now, what's the password?" He demanded.

"I'm not giving you shit. What the hell? Your momma the bitch." Sen's hand went around Nunu's neck. He applied just enough pressure to let her know that he was dead ass serious. Through tight teeth, Sen warned her.

"I will kill you, and whoever tries to ride for you. Ask your nigga about niggas like me."

Nunu's heart thumped rapidly. She didn't think he knew anything about her, or her past, but his statement hit a nerve. A nigga who wasn't scared to go out blazing killed her boo. Nunu fought back the tears that threatened to fall when she thought of Break. Until this day, she blamed herself for his death, and the death of their unborn child. It was the guilt that caused her not to run for her pistol and shoot Sen's ass. Nunu was far from a punk bitch, but the burden of guilt had her acting unusual; not like herself.

Sen felt bad. He could tell by her body language and the sudden change in her facial expression that he hit a nerve. A very sensitive nerve. She appeared to be fighting back tears. Now he had no right to come at her like that. He released her neck.

"I'm sorry."

Wham.

Nunu slapped the shit out of him. Her hand stung from hitting his ass that hard. Sen was unfazed. He deserved it until she proved him wrong.

"I ain't going to ask you again." All he knew was that she had better open the phone. Females were grimy. He wasn't putting shit past any of them. They were just like niggas out here trying to come up.

"41237." Nunu found herself calling out the password. She didn't know why she even cared what he thought, but she wanted to prove she had nothing to hide. Her chest heaved up and down as she watched Sen press in the numbers. The word app was open. He scrolled through the document and was shocked. She had about 10 chapters written.

"You an author or something?" He asked.

"Fuck you! Are you done?" She replied. Sen shook his head no. He went to the text app.

**NUNU:** Girl, this nigga over here simping to a bitch. I'm turned off.

**DEZ:** FK him. Probably a broke ass scammer. I can't believe Kay ass.

**NUNU:** Vance going to kick her little ass. Lol

**DEZ:** And I'll kill him. You hoes better not be late to the show fk'n with lames.

**NUNU:** We ain't. Oh, and guess what? I'm at chapter 10. I need you to test read for me. This book is going to be bomb.

**DEZ:** I know it is. You are talented, cousin. Text when you are leaving and ignore that lame.

Sen smirked at their little back and forth talking about him. He was low-key impressed about old girl writing a book. Sen went to the next text thread.

**GAV:** What's up, Boss lady?

**NUNU:** I'll text you Monday. Thanks for stepping in. Take tomorrow off. I'll see you on Monday.

**GAV:** Thanks, but can I bless that pussy tonight? You know a nigga be feening for you.

**NUNU:** No.

**GAV:** You cold. See you Monday.

Sen shook his head. The last text confirmed the girl was something else. The nigga calling her boss lady is what had him more intrigued. What was it that she did? He would not dare ask.

"You don't even know me, but talking bad about me. I'm far from a lame. A scammer? A fuckin scammer, could never be me." And he left it like that. He wasn't about to even mention he was a boss.

"You a punk ass nigga for putting your hands on me. I swear you lucky I don't trip." Nunu didn't put an ounce of fear in his heart, but he felt bad.

"I apologize. Like I said, I didn't trust you. Still don't, but thanks for showing me."

'Sexy ass!'

Nunu pulled her dress down and headed out the door. He thought she was grimy, and that hurt her feelings. Probably because once upon a time, she was. She set up some niggas before, and even got a few killed. Nunu was halfway out the door when Sen pulled her back and into his arms. Nunu didn't resist. She placed her forehead on his chest. She laid there, taking deep breaths to keep from crying. Sen didn't know why he was holding her, but he didn't want to let her go. She was emotional, and he blamed himself. He kissed her on the top of her head. *'Nigga, you steady doing weird shit.'*

"I apologize. You good?" He spoke softly. Nunu nodded her head yes. Slowly, she pulled away. She looked up at him. Not sure what to say, and before they both realized what they were doing, their lips connected. They shared a deep, electrifying kiss. Sen knew he was going too far with this woman, but his body craved her at the moment. He gave in without a fight. Sen scooped her up effortlessly and placed her on the counter. She immediately wrapped her legs around his waist, never breaking the kiss. She held his face with each of her hands and kissed him as if her life depended on it. She needed him. She needed him to make her feel better. She needed him to take all the guilt away. Sen freed himself and entered her wet box. She gasped. With her eyes closed and her mouth agape, she rocked her hips back and forth, as Sen filled her up with deep strokes. Sen pulled away from her lips and buried his head into her neck. Nunu bit on her bottom lip to keep from moaning too loudly. The only thing that could be heard was heavy breathing and skin clapping. She could feel him pulsating. Nunu tightened her vaginal muscles. A low grunt escaped Sen's mouth as he released. Nunu kept it G. She didn't say a word as her body shook from the powerful orgasm. She laid her head back against the mirror. Sen pulled out of her quickly. Without speaking a word, he fixed his clothes and walked out of the bathroom.

Nunu sat there for a few minutes. It felt like Deja vu. Five years ago was the last time she was fucked that good, and on a bathroom sink. It was that long ago, that Break walked out of the bathroom, and she never got a chance to make love to him again. She felt like this wouldn't be any different. It wasn't like she cared if she ever saw Sen again, but he'd stirred so many emotions in her that she couldn't help but feel some kind of way.

'Nunu, shake it off.'

Nunu jumped from the counter. She looked under the cabinet for a clean towel. When she found the soap, she began to wash in between her legs.

"Nunu. What the fuck is your problem? I can't believe I just did that. Fuck!" She shook her head as she reached for the dry towel.

Sen returned and stood there, staring at her perfect ass. He couldn't lie to himself. That green eyed girl had some of the best pussy ever. Man, how he wished he could take her to the bed and fuck her all night. He could've beat his own ass for going in her raw, though. His gut never lied; she was poisonous. Still, he didn't like hearing how she regretted giving him her body. Especially knowing he wanted more. The entire situation was crazy.

"Aye. We messed up. I ain't trying to have no kids." Nunu turned around to the sound of Sen's voice. He was surprised to see the tears in her eyes. She pulled her dress down and tossed both of the towels that she had used on the floor. She went to brush past him, but he gently grabbed her hand.

"I don't know what happened. On my brother, rest in peace. I ain't never hit a girl raw, not even when I got my first piece of pussy, shawty." She looked up at him.

"I haven't had unprotected sex in five years." She admitted.

"Ok. So, we both clean. What if you get pregnant?"

"I won't. I'll get the Plan B pill. Now if you will excuse me, I need to go get my cousin, we gotta go." She didn't even look at him as she walked out. This time he let her walk off without incident. When she made it into the living room, Kay and Spade were standing there kissing like two lovebirds.

"Hmmm." Nunu cleared her throat. She grabbed her purse off the counter and slid on her heels. "Let's go. I still gotta do my hair." She headed for the door. Kay gave Spade a knowing look, and they both smirked.

Across town, Dez pulled into the back lot of a commercial building. There were two other vehicles there. Killing the engine in her black Audi, she grabbed her key fobs. Purposely leaving her phone behind. She stepped out of the car and shut the door behind her as she glanced over at the white truck. It was parked near the gate just like she instructed. If the bitch she was rolling up on didn't have her money, that truck would be her final ride. Dez's plan was to be in and out. Uno's show was only a few hours away, and she still had to get ready.

Donned in a black Armani sweatshirt and pants, a pair of black Air Max, and a black Nike hat covering her red bob, Dez was dressed down, but still cute. She tapped twice on the steel door. Not even a second later, the door opened.

"What up?" Dez spoke to the tall, chunky Arab. He was one of her workers.

"Sup, boss?" Husky greeted her. He stepped to the side as his eyes scanned the lot for suspicious activity before shutting the door. No words were exchanged. He followed Dez up two flights of stairs. She opened the door that led to a hallway. Husky already told her where the stupid bitch was.

Dez walked a few more steps, and when she got to the door that read Dance Studio; she opened it. She walked into the room. The lights were on. Glass mirrors decorated the wall, and a pole sat dead in the center. There were a few chairs scattered here and there. Mina sat in the center of the room in a brown chair. She was dressed in a tan bodysuit. Her hair was in a ponytail, making it easy to see her tear-stained face, and the two black eyes she had gotten in a previous altercation. Mina's arms were tied behind her back, and her mouth was covered. Dez turned and looked at Husky.

"The fuck happened to her eyes." She asked, walking over to Mina and snatching the tape from her mouth. Mina squealed from the pain.

"Dez, please!" Mina cried out.

"She was like that when I got her." Husky replied. He stood against the door with his arms behind his back.

"Dez, this is so fucked up. We go way back." Mina continued. She was scared. She was hurt. She wasn't grimy, and Dez knew that. It was really fucked up the way Dez was handling her.

Dez shook her head. The black eyes told Dez what she needed to know. Mina was still with Boom. He was known for beating her ass, and for getting her into some shit.

"You know why you're here like this, right?" Dez scolded her as she untied her arms. She wasn't worried about her making a move. In fact, she wished she would, she'd lay her the fuck out.

"Yes, but you know it ain't my fault." Mina explained. "He took the work you fronted me. Along with all the money I was saving, and left. I didn't see him until last night. He came to the job, beat me up and raped me. Said that was his way of saying goodbye. That's on my one and only son. If you

don't believe me, I can show you my papers from the ER."
Tears poured down her face. Mina wasn't lying but the shit
she confessed wasn't none of Dez's concern. All she wanted
was her money.

Mina was a dancer at Bandz. The strip club The BGB Crew
owned. Mina had a fuck nigga by the name of Boom for a
man. Boom was always putting his hands on her, and Mina
never left his sorry ass. She went to jail a few times, busting
fake checks for Boom. And, was almost arrested for stealing
high-end pieces at boutiques. Last month, Mina came to Dez
and the crew about putting her on a hustle. She said that she
wanted to get her, and her kid, far away from California. Far
away from Boom. Dez knew Mina was a hustler. Plus, she
never snitched when she got locked up. She did her time and
remained solid. Dez fronted her 15k worth of different
prescription medications. Mina was to take them to her
connect in Georgia, and bring her money back. The flip
would have made The BGB Crew 30k and Mina 10k on the
back end. She let the nigga Boom fuck that off.

"You dodging my calls makes you look guilty." Dez told her.

"Dez, I know how you get down. You looked out for me too
many times. On my son, I didn't answer because I was
ashamed. I was trying to figure out how I was going to get
you your money back." She stood from the chair and Dez hit
her with a right hook, causing Mina to grab her nose. Blood
gushed out. Mina screamed in pain.

"Bitch, you knew what type of nigga you were dealing with.
You should've guarded my shit with your life." She lifted
her foot and kicked Mina in the gut. Knocking the wind out
of her. Mina flew back and fell over the chair. Dez pulled
her gun from her waist.

94

"You don't have the money. You can't get the money, I know that. It's your fault your son will no longer have a momma."

Mina pleaded through tears. "Please. Don't do this." She scrambled to her knees. Blood continued to spill from her nose. "Don't do it. Let me work it off. You'll be the first person my sister and Boom will suspect if they can't find me."

"Bitch, so. I won't hesitate to murder their asses either."

"Dez." She cried.

Heart cold.

Gun aimed.

Pow Pow…

Dez let off two shots. One to the chest, and the other to the dome of Mina Mills. Without giving one fuck, she headed for the door.

"I don't want her found." Dez said as she was walking out. She was looking for that bum ass nigga Boom next.

Back in the car, Dez pulled out the lot. Killing Mina didn't bother her one bit. She didn't give two fucks about it. When it was regarding business, all feelings and emotions were null and void.

Ring ring ring!

Pressing the green button on her steering wheel, she answered the incoming call.

"What's up, J-Money?"

"I got the info you requested."

"That quick?" Dez was shocked. J-Money always came through, but being that she only had street names, and the city they live in, she didn't think he would find out who Spade, and Sen were so quickly.

"You were right. Both born and raised in Atlanta. The sons of Judah Jank."

"Is that right?" She knew exactly who Judah Jank was. In her opinion, he was the King of the A. She couldn't believe them niggas were his sons. She had been wanting to speak with him about business, but when she consulted with Papa about it, he flat out told her no. He couldn't give her a good enough excuse why not, so she was still interested. She ran it by the girls once. She wanted to distribute in Atlanta, but they weren't going against Papa.

"They're out here doing business with Black Sam." J-Money told her. "Word is they may be investing in a club or something out here."

"Say less. And thanks." The two ended the call. As Dez drove to get ready for the show, all she saw were dollar signs. She was determined to get the girls to agree with going against Papa's advice and proposing a deal with the Jank boyz.

Cruising through the dark streets of Cali. In the city of Los Angeles, where muthafuckas were grimier than any humans on the face of the earth. Spade and his big brother Sen were feeling really good about their next play. They were about to eat good off of Cali thanks to their father, big Judah Jank and the connections he had. Even from the federal prison where he was serving a 50-year bid, Judah was still calling shots. Judah Jank was a self-made King in Atlanta, GA. He was making so much money in his own city. He never considered doing business with outsiders. That was, until he was introduced to his Cali chick. When Judah touched his first 100k at the young age of 22, he knew that he wanted to be in the dope game. Even after death. He thanked God for his boys. There was Sen, Spade, Tone, Jam, and Lucas. Each one of his boys had a part in his empire. He loved his boys more than he loved life. That's why five years later he still was in search of the person who killed his son, Tone. What he didn't know was that Lucas was two steps ahead of them all. He was only 16 when his big brother was gunned down. Now that he was 22, no one could tell him shit. He was making an appearance in Cali on some revenge type shit.

Approaching a red light, Sen looked over at his brother. The nigga had been texting since they left their meeting. Spade could barely pass the blunt back because he was so busy texting.

"What you trying to do?" Sen asked. He looked back at the road and safely made his way through the red light.

Spade replied. "Ole girl said that their homegirl Uno was about to perform. Wanna pull up?" He looked over at his bro. Sen was in deep thought. He always was.

Spade understood how Cali left a bad taste in his mouth; Tone was his brother, too.

Sen believed that it was his fault. He felt that if he would've disregarded his fiancé's feelings and went with his bro, and their god bro, they both would have still been alive. Secretly, he hated himself for not being there for his brothers. He knew deep down that his father blamed him, too. He didn't have to say it, he felt it.

"I know how you feel about partying in the city. We ain't gotta go." Spade said.

Yeah, he wanted to go be up under Kay before he left, but he gave a fuck about his brother's feelings more than he did a bitch he didn't even know.

Sen took a deep breath and let it out. He thought about shawty with the mesmerizing green eyes, tight wet pussy and smart-ass mouth. Truth was, he thought about her multiple times after she left. He found himself wanting to know more about her. Wanting to fuck her a few more times.

"You know I fucked homegirl." Sen admitted. He had a half smile on his face. Spade's smile was big.

"Hell, yeah. I know. I peeped the way you were looking at her when she was leaving out the door. I was waiting for you to stop feeling guilty about cheating on Chanel's spoiled ass. I knew once you passed that you would tell me."

"Fuck you. Put the address in." Sen retorted. They were going to the show.

"Pussy must have been fire. I know her homegirl's was. Gotdamn." Spade shook his head. Their conversation stopped when the GPS spoke the directions. Spade then went on. "I can only imagine how it would feel if I had fucked her raw. Her shit is fire."

Instantly, Sen's heart dropped to the pit of his stomach. He not only broke his own rules, but he screwed the girl bareback. He fucked up wholeheartedly.

Uno sat in the dressing room in front of the mirror. She watched as her stylist flat ironed her 36-inch wig. Tonight, her stylist had her rocking black hair. Uno wasn't feeling it at first. She wasn't used to her natural color anymore, and the song she was performing was titled 'RED HOT.' After a few compliments from her other staff and a FaceTime with Kay, she was sold on the look. Her phone was going off like crazy, but she couldn't respond. Carmen was putting on her lashes, and Go was massaging her feet. That was something he did before every show. It helps her blood flow and keeps her feet from hurting while on stage. Go was Filipino and African American. The two met in community college. From their first encounter, they hit it off. They loved each other's vibe. The glam squad was in conversation when the door flew open and then slammed shut.

"Bitch. Why this nigga Vance outside tripping on Kay?" Dez said.

Uno went to get up, but Dez stopped her. "Nah, she good. Row and Bow right there." Row and Bow were the two security guards that they hired. The pair were brothers.

"I wanna fuck both of them. Damn." Go blurted. He put his hand over his mouth. "Oops."

"You a hoe." Uno laughed, looking at Go.

"Bitch, NO-I-AM-NOT. I just like dick. Them big black muthafuckas can get it." Everyone laughed except Dez. Go annoyed her. Nevertheless, he was Uno's friend so she tried to be cordial. Dez thought he was too flamboyant. In her opinion, he just did too much to be seen. Once she had to tell him about himself. "Muthafuckas know you gay. You ain't gotta be so extra." Go didn't even respond. He knew how Dez was, and he wasn't trying to go there. He would fight a female quick, but she was Uno's girl, and the bitch was fast to up her pistol. Therefore, he let her get away with a lot of shit.

Dez was like. "Why the nigga from the mall here? The one Kay fucked. Girl, I don't know what he did to her, but she asked me to go over and tell him that she was about to wrap up her situation."

"What he say?" Uno asked. She was now looking in the mirror at her makeup. "I look bomb." Uno bragged, and everyone agreed.

"He told me to tell her she got five minutes. He and his brother went to sit at the bar. Girl."

"What, bitch?" Uno laughed. She saw a text on her phone that had her anxious to reply.

Dez was like. "I know Nunu's ass fucked the brother. The hoe has been walking funny all night. She was by the bar,

101

hugging Break's brother. Ole boy was mean mugging her something tough. By the time she noticed he was there, he and his brother were leaving."

"They left?" Uno quizzed.

"Yeah. He wasn't playing when he told her five minutes. The bitch ran after him."

"Noooo…What Vance do?"

"Nothing. She probably lied and said it was business. Your cousins and these out-of-town niggas." Dez shook her head. Low-key, Dez was happy that her cousins were messing with the niggas. It was their way in.

"What do we know about them, though?" Uno was now serious. The BGB Crew were important figures in the city. It was imperative that they knew about whomever they were dealing with.

"Trust me, I did my research. They are official. I'll tell you later." Dez looked at Go and rolled her eyes. After looking at her Rolex, she looked up at Uno. She told her she had to take care of something. In 30 minutes, she would be back.

"Ok." Uno replied.

Uno enjoyed the juice, but she enjoyed texting her new friend Freda. Freda is the fine ass stud she met in Sak's. The one that had her curious as to what it would be like to get down with a stud. Uno was gay, but she had never been attracted to studs. However, Freda had her intrigued. From her looks on down to her cool demeanor. Earlier, Uno invited her to the show, and she texted Uno to let her know she was in the lobby having a drink.

Uno finished her performance and both old and new fans were going wild. 'Keep 'Em' was always a hit. And, her new song 'Red Hot' had them turned up. Before she headed backstage, she took a few pictures with other artists and spent an hour taking pictures with her fans and supporters. She was never too busy to show her people love. Uno was chopping it up with Stylez, a female rapper from Oakland. Dez walked up and whispered in her ear.

"Damn, you just met ole girl today, and you already got her in VIP." She said, referring to Freda.

"Where she at?" Uno asked with a smile and wide eyes as she looked around.

"In line. Damn, let me find out." Dez teased.

Uno cut her conversation with Stylez short. She went to thank Freda for coming. As she was walking away, she gave Dez the bird.

"Thank you again for coming." Uno said.

"I've been a fan, so thanks for the ticket." Freda replied.

Uno, along with two members of her security team, walked with Freda out to her car. Freda smiled the entire time. She thought Uno was fine as fuck. She was a butterscotch complexion with light-brown eyes, the cutest pointed nose, and a beautiful Colgate smile that could brighten the world. She stood 5'3, and to Freda, she had the perfect body. She barely had a mouthful of breasts, but they were just enough for her. Her physique was still deemed A1, small breasts and all. Freda had plenty of females. Each one was a baddy, but Uno was her longtime crush. She had been crushing on her from the moment she saw a video on YouTube. She rated her higher than she rated all the others. She wanted her.

Freda stopped at a royal-blue Benz truck. She leaned against the car and Uno came over and stood directly in front of her. The way Freda was staring at her caused her to be all shy and shit. She had to remind herself that she was UNO THE BOSS BITCH. Even though Freda intrigued her, she couldn't show her hand just yet. In fact, she didn't even know if she wanted to go there with Freda. All Uno knew at that moment was that she was attracted to her big time. A stud had never grabbed her attention before. Freda was the total opposite of the beautiful girls Uno usually messed around with.

Freda was brown skinned with a pretty, but boyish swag. She wore her long hair in five neatly styled cornrows going to the back. The soft baby hairs were molded into s-shaped swirls around the edges. She had sexy brown bedroom eyes that complimented her perfect lashes and well-groomed brows. Her lips were full, succulent, and suckable. When she smiled, she showed that one dimple that made Uno moist. Casually dressed in a simple red Montclair shirt, black jeans, a pair of red and black Jordan's that appeared to be fresh out of the box, she was fly as hell. The Montclair jacket and designer belt set her outfit off right. When Uno met her, she didn't have any jewelry on. Tonight, she was rocking diamond studs and two fat ass Cuban links. One had a diamond encrusted letter F hanging from it. The shorter, but thicker one had the initials K4I. Her Rolex watch was hard to miss. The diamonds in it made sure of that. This bitch was

'Her'. She wasn't for sure, but Uno had a feeling she wasn't able to acquire all that bling, and that fresh ass ride by working at Saks.

A fan walked up asking if she could have a picture with Uno, and of course, she granted her wish. At the same time, Freda's cell vibrated. She looked at it and slightly shook her head before silencing it. She placed it back in her pocket. Uno peeped her move and felt some kind of way about it. She was already feeling territorial.

After hugging her fan and saying goodbye, she focused back on Freda.

"Well, you be safe, ok." Uno said.

"Yeah, it's getting late. You be safe, too. Thanks for the invite, ma." Freda told her. Neither moved from their spot, too busy gawking at the other. Freda could tell that Uno was feeling her. The feeling was mutual, but something was telling her that Uno and that celebrity status were going to be a handful. She was ready for the challenge, though. Freda took a few steps toward Uno and held her hand. Looking into her eyes, she asked.

"When is the next time you are free? I wanna take you out." Uno was about to respond, but the loud mouth Puerto Rican chick cut all that out.

"Baby, I am sorry I missed your show." Lydia walked up, put her arms around Uno's neck, and kissed her on the cheek. Freda snatched her hand from Uno without hesitation.

"You all have a good night." Freda hit the unlock button on her whip and climbed in. As she was closing her door, she heard Uno yell out. "I'm going to call you." She ignored her. Freda wasn't with the shits. She didn't play games with hoes no matter how fine they were. If she did talk to her again, it would be to fuck and leave her. She concluded that was best.

"What the fuck is your problem, Vance? The hoe shit that you doing, is the shit I'm supposed to be doing." Kay hit herself on the chest. She didn't like the way he popped up at Uno's show with the bullshit. Because of that bullshit, Spade walked out on her. Before he could even respond, she stepped over to his bar and made herself a drink.

"Fuck that mean?" He asked.

"All that nagging. I be busy. Shit."

"Really, Kay? You supposed to be my woman, but I can't get a hold of you for hours. How the fuck you think that look?" He yelled. He walked up to her and snatched the drink out of her hand. Vance threw it against the wall, breaking the glass to pieces. Kay didn't even flinch. She was used to the nigga acting like a bitch. Kay picked up the Hennessy bottle and took a large gulp. The shit was comical to her. Kay placed the bottle back down and looked at Vance. He was shaking his head. Although she was pissed that he was tripping on her about not being available when he wanted her, and how she was always disregarding his feelings, she couldn't help but admire how sexy he was. Milk chocolate, with flawless skin, sunken, but beautiful bedroom eyes, and a stocky build. He was a little on the short side, but he made up for that elsewhere. The nigga had a big ass dick. He wasn't too skilled in the bedroom, but that was ok because she knew how to ride that big muthafucka like a cowgirl. Besides, Vance was a beast with the tongue.

107

"I'm horny. Can we fuck and talk later?" Kay licked her lips as she eyed his dick print in his jeans.

"All you do is play games and drink."

"Nigga, I get money! Don't forget that part." She laughed. With the Henny bottle still in her hand, she walked off and made her way upstairs. She needed a hot shower and some fire head. She had to do something because she damn sure wasn't going to give him no pussy by the way he was acting.

"Kay, you are a woman. When you said that you wanted me as your man, I accepted that because I love you. But I need a real woman." Kay was in the process of taking off her pants when Vance made the statement. Yeah, she had feelings for Vance. They had been together for a cool minute, but she wasn't looking to build with him. She was in her feelings when she told him she was ready to settle down. She got like that from time to time. She would feel like she had enough money, a good education, and no reason to hustle anymore. Twenty-six was a good age to start a serious relationship, and maybe even plan a family. Not too long after the thought came, it left. Something would click in her head and the life she thought she wanted, she no longer cared about.

"What if I tell you that I'm not ready? What if I said, after tonight, we should just call it quits for good?" She questioned.

"Damn." Vance had to take a step back. It felt like a blow to his chest and his ego. "Kay, this time if you walk away that's it. I love you, but I can't do this anymore. This back-and-forth shit, I'm cool on that. I'm a good nigga. I won't settle for bullshit."

She walked up on him.

"I understand. I care about you, but I don't wanna string you along. I don't think I will ever stop hustling. This is fun to me. I damn sure ain't ready right now. To be completely honest with you, I may never be ready for a family." She spoke what she felt at the moment.

"Is it because of the nigga you ran after tonight? Keep it real?" Vance wanted to know. He made up his mind he was done with Kay, but he still needed to know.

"He cool. I enjoy his company." She admitted. She would never tell him that Spade gave her butterflies, big orgasms, and feelings she never knew she had. But even so, she wasn't trying to build nothing with him either. She was kinda glad that he was going back to the A. She liked him too much already, and she was scared that a nigga would do her like they did her aunt. Be her downfall. Fuck that, and fuck love.

"Alright, you can stay the night if you like. I'm going to sleep on the couch." Vance didn't want her driving tipsy.

Kay had gotten fully dressed. She didn't feel like the 45-minute drive, but she didn't want to prolong their ending.

"Nah, I'm going to go home." With that, she headed toward the door. They both were silent. As Vance opened up the front door, he said. "I peeped Buck and his boy watching ole boy tonight. You already know how he get down. You be safe."

He was referring to Spade and Sen. They stood out and omitted the presence of some bosses. The only reason he told

Kay about Buck was because he had a feeling she was going to be back around the dude. And despite the situation, he wished her no harm. Buck was a vulture always looking to come up off the next nigga.

"Thanks." Kay replied and just like that, she dipped. When Vance shut the door, he vowed never to fuck with Kay again. He prayed that she found love and got over whatever hurt was hindering her from taking life seriously. Vance wasn't no hustler.

Plenty of professional women wanted him. He was just stuck on Kay from the day she tutored him in college, but not anymore.

The moment Kay got in the car, she called Spade. She couldn't help it. She liked him. He had been on her mind heavy since their initial meeting. Plus, she didn't like how he left tonight.

**Kay:** So, it's like that? You shooting me to voicemail? Ain't responding to my text? Watch this, though.

Kay had called and texted Spade about 5 times total since she left Vance's house. She hated that she hurt Vance; he was a cool guy. Had a legit job as a broker, and he owned several businesses. If she were to ever settle down, she believed he was the type she wanted to settle with. Spade had her feeling something different, though. Over the last few hours, she scratched her head several times. She was trying to figure out what it was about his sexy ass that had her in her feelings. She was really digging his fine bowlegged ass. Although she liked him, she was low-key happy that he would be back in his hometown soon. She wasn't trying to get knocked off her square by a dude. Especially one she didn't even know.

Twenty minutes later, Kay found herself in the parking lot of the Marriott hotel where Spade and his brother stayed while in California. The outdoor light poles lit up the packed lot. Kay drove around the entire area until she finally spotted an empty space that just so happened to be close to the front entrance. BINGO! It was her lucky night.

Kay killed the engine on her big body. She chuckled at what she was on. Tripping over a down south nigga that she only knew for a day, but was just having a mental battle about how she didn't love niggas. Kay picked up her cell and called Nunu. When it came to certain things, she felt Nunu understood her more.

"Hey, girl." Nunu said. She was laid in her bed with the lights on, staring at the picture of Tupac on her wall. Nunu was a die-hard PAC fan. Tupac's music relaxed her. It helped her think clearly. These days she was on some weird shit. She had been fucking a nigga bareback and acting overly emotional about her past. Now she was in a trance thinking about a nigga who had no interest in her. That nigga was Sen.

"So, guess where I'm at?" Kay started.

"At Vance house? Hell, I don't know." Nunu retorted.

"Sitting in the parking lot of Spade's hotel. He came to Uno's show earlier and left because he saw me talking to Vance. I went after him, but the nigga dismissed me. Cold as hell, too."

Nunu frowned.

"I saw they ass."

"You did?"

"Yeah, but I acted like I didn't. You know I fucked his brother."

"I figured that. Was it good?"

"Bomb, but I'm cool." Nunu said, getting in her feelings. Giving it up to Sen so soon was a mistake. "Hold on, this is Uno calling. Let me see what this heifer wants." Kay agreed to wait for her to speak to Uno. A few seconds later, she merged the call. "I got Uno on the line now." Nunu announced.

Kay went on to explain the situation to her other cousin, too. Even though she planned to only tell Nunu because she was more understanding. She knew that Uno's playful ass would probably say something slick.Uno giggled and started to rap.

*"Kay's an addict/ she's addicted/ she's dicknotized/ the way he hit it/ her mind is gone/ the bitch is zoned/ she's feenin'/like a fiend/ she's in a trance/ like he's her man/now, I'll be damn/ she wants the dick again."* Uno and Nunu burst out laughing at the same time. "Girl, if you don't get your ass from over there. I kno' you ain't going out like this. What that nigga do to you?" Uno questioned.

"Whatever. Fuck y'all hoes." She giggled and playfully joked back. Although deep down, she knew she was acting

112

like a sucka. *Why in the hell do I have my ass out here? I gotta shake this shit off. WTF?*

"I'm cool on this bullshit. This is lame as hell. I'll be home in a few." Kay had to check herself.

Right before she hung up in their faces for clowning her, she heard Uno steady cracking jokes. "Girl, he got yo' head gon'." Then she burst out singing the Monica song. "So gone over you… you, you, you!" Kay gave them the click up. She was tripping. She didn't even know Spade. Fucked his fine ass one time, and now she was on some sucka ass hoe shit. She started her truck and pulled away from the visitor parking. Her eyes darted toward the door. Spade and some chick were walking out the door. Kay threw the truck in park. Her heart was threatening to jump from her chest. Here she was riding this nigga's dick backwards, and he was curving her for some light-skinned Barbie looking tramp. Without giving it a second thought, she bounced up out of her truck, leaving the door wide open, rap music blaring loudly. Spade reached for his waist. When he saw it was Kay, he moved his hand. He didn't know what she was on. Her mad face was turned all the way up. Baby girl was tripping, he concluded.

Spade smiled inwardly, but kept a blank expression when Kay's cute ass approached him. He could tell she was pissed.

"What's up?" She said, staring him up and down. She was mad that he was with a bitch, but it still didn't stop her from taking note of how sexy his chocolate-fudge complexioned ass was. In a pair of grey sweats, a white tank, and white sneakers. He smelled good, too. With those juicy ass lips she wanted to lick.

113

"Kay Spade." He called her by the pet name he gave her. "What are you doing here?"

"I texted you. You didn't get it?"

"I ain't respond yet. I'm busy." He looked at the Barbie next to him. She smiled. Kay wasn't no hater. The chick was gorgeous, and her body was banging, but still, the bitch wasn't her.

Kay chuckled. She looked at Barbie. "He gon' call you another time. Go on about your business, ok." Kay gave her a look to say, don't play with me.

"Mike, what is she talking about?" Barbie looked at Spade. The bitch didn't even know his name. Kay chuckled.

"Mike, tell her she's no longer needed. I'll be in the truck. You got one minute." Kay said as she walked off.

She climbed back in her ride. She didn't even bother to look to see what Spade and the chick were doing. She began to count from sixty. By the time she got to forty-eight, Spade climbed in her truck.

"You know I let you get away with that shit because you're my wife, right?" He put his seat back and closed his eyes. He didn't care what no one said. He was making claims to her. She was his, and he trusted her.

"So, I'm your future wife, but you ignore me? You eat? Did the hoe at least feed you?" Kay snapped.

"Kill the attitude. I'm here with you. "She didn't respond. She was trying to not think about him and that bitch fucking.

"Yeah, I'm hungry. I want some pussy first." Spade told her. Spade wasn't crazy. He knew what Kay was thinking. He didn't get the chance to fuck the bitch. He had met her in the bar of the hotel. He got her a few drinks and was walking her to the car. He did get her number and promised to call her. He wasn't the type to explain himself to no bitch, but like he said, Kay was his future wife.

The feeling was strong. The entire ride, neither of them exchanged words. They were in their own thoughts about the other. Neither really understood how they got there, but neither was mad about being there. Kay took Spade to a pizza joint across from Santa Monica Beach. They pulled up to the beach to relax and enjoy their food.

It was later in the night and the temperature cooled down. The sound of the waves crashing against the rocks was soothing, and the crisp clean tan-colored sand stretched for miles. Kay took a bite off her slice of pepperoni pizza and appreciated the scenery.

"I'm out here for a few more days." Spade told her, breaking the silence. He and Sen needed to get the club business situated.

"So, you leaving Tuesday?"

"Yeah. Can I have some of that good pussy? I know you heard me when I said I was horny. And you gon' pull your little ass up to a restaurant. I wanna fuck. I want your pussy, baby." Spade sat up.

115

He put his food on the back seat. "This your truck I'm in?"

Kay finished chewing her pizza.

"Yeah, this my shit. If you ain't notice, you fucking with a boss." She laughed, rolled her eyes, and hoped he knew how serious she was. She wanted to kiss his juicy lips badly, but she held back.

He found out exactly who he was messing with, and it intrigued him even more. Spade put his hand between her legs. Kay leaned over and kissed him. Kay wasted no time sliding over and straddling the man she wanted to fuck her. Spade's hands roamed up her shirt. Breaking their kiss, he tapped her on her nice little booty.

"Take these off." He was referring to her designer leggings. Kay opened the passenger door. She went to climb out, but Spade grabbed her by the arm.

"What the fuck are you doing, shawty?"

"About to take my pants off, so I can give you some." She blinked a few times, trying to figure out his problem.

"You lost your mind? Climb your ass in the backseat and take them off. It's dark out there, and I ain't trying to have you out outside doing that shit."

"There you go." She blushed. Spade was too damn territorial, but she liked it. Once Kay was in the backseat, Spade kicked off his shoes and pulled down his gray sweats. He slid a condom from his pocket. He climbed in the backseat.

116

"Get on your knees and face the window." And she did just that.

Kay moaned when she felt his two fingers slowly slide inside her wet pussy.

"You wet as fuck." His husky voice sent chills down her back.

"Only for you." She teased.

"That's what the fuck I'm talking about."

"Mmmm." Kay moaned when he finally slid his meat inside of her.

"Damn." Spade grunted. He placed both hands on her hips and deep stroked her. Once again, Spade had Kay in another world and vice versa. While the smacking of skin, moans, and groans filled the car, a special kind of connection between the two filled their hearts.

"I'm about to cum." Kay cried out. She tightened her muscles and popped her ass at a faster speed.

"Me, too. Fuck, Shawty!" Spade admitted. In unison, they both released. Kay's head rested on the truck door, and Spade laid on her back.

Heavy breathing.

"You got a nigga fucking in yo' ride. Getting cramps and shit. Who are you?" He asked as he pulled out of Kay.

"Shit, I need to be asking you the same thing. Got me pulling up on you. Ready to shoot a bitch." She admitted. They both laughed.

"So, who is Kay? Can I know now or later?" Spade asked. He knew exactly who she was. He'd shown Black Sam her picture. Black Sam told him that she and her crew were the Bitches Getting Bandz Crew. Both Spade and Sen wanted to know how they got bandz.

"From what I hear, they are into a little bit of everything. Their grandpa is an old-time hustler. Low-key he's still in the game. He's a real stand-up old head. Well respected. Their moms were hustlers, too. Feds got hold of them, though." Black Sam revealed. He wanted to say more, but that wasn't his place; it was their father's.

"So, you think they're out here robbing niggas and getting them setup?" Sen asked. He knew there was a reason he didn't trust that green-eyed, good pussy, sexy ass bitch.

Spade gave Sen an annoying look, but didn't say anything. The question was valid. He only felt some kind of way because he was feeling Kay. He didn't want to hear anything bad about her.

"I can't be sure, but I doubt it. I don't see why they have to. They own plenty of shit. They got the pill game on lock. They move a little coke throughout the city. Aren't you fucking with her?" Black Sam asked.

"Yeah, while I'm here." Spade admitted.

"Nigga sprung." Sen teased. Black Sam laughed.

118

"Well, son, have fun and don't get caught slipping. Pay attention. Now, do she know who you are?"

"Nah." Spade replied. Black Sam nodded his head to say ok.

***

"Who am I, you ask?" Kay and Spade were now holding hands walking along the beach in the cool night air. "Hmmmm… I'm a go-getter, get money bitch, who just so happens to have a degree in science. Who are you?" Kay wasn't offering nothing more.

"A nigga from the hood trying to get rich and stay alive, free, to enjoy that shit." Spade was looking into her eyes when he said what he said.

"I feel you." Kay replied. Spade stopped walking. He pulled Kay into his arms and wrapped his arms around her waist. She looked up at him.

"I like you." He told her. Spade kissed her on the tip of her nose.

"I like you, too." She replied.

Their lips met underneath the moon and stars shining brightly in the cloudless clear sky. Then their tongues slowly entered the mouth of the other. Their tongues moved at a slow pace. Kay let out a low moan while Spade gripped her around the waist and pulled her in closer. He didn't know what it was about her that intrigued him so much, and had him feeling some type of way that he had not felt in a long time. They both felt like teenagers who were falling in love

119

for the first time. It was something that neither had intentionally planned on happening. There was something so comforting about feeling like they were meant to be together. It was as if they were destined to fall in love. On one hand, it felt good. On the other hand, it was scary. However, they both wanted it no matter what the outcome was.

Missing you by Faith Evans and Puffy blared from the speakers of the white G wagon. Nunu was in deep thought as she navigated the grounds of Rose Hills Cemetery. For the last week, she had been moody, emotional, and sad. It didn't hit her until she saw Break's oldest brother, Buck. He reminded her that it was Break's birthday. Tears immediately formed in her eyes and fell without notice. Buck pulled her in for a hug, and the two rocked back and forth. While Buck was thinking, Nunu was crying because she missed his brother. She cried because she had fucked another nigga on her man's birthday. When she saw Sen and his brother walking out of the auditorium, she was happy. Happy that he saw her and Buck sharing a moment. She didn't want him to come over and try to push up on her and cause her to do something else stupid. Like ride his dick until she exploded.

Nunu pulled near the gravesite where her boo was laid to rest. She parked her car and continued to let the music play. When the song went off, she wiped the tears from her eyes, opened her door, and exited the vehicle. She walked to the other side of the truck and grabbed the flowers, balloon, and a bottle of Ace of Spades. It was Break's favorite drink. After shutting the passenger door, she made her way to the grave. It had been five long years, and each time she came to see him, or thought of him, she felt just as guilty as she did the night he was killed. "Why couldn't our ending be different?" She spoke to his headstone. She placed the flowers in the holder and took a seat next to the grave. After popping the bottle on the cognac, she took a hard gulp from the bottle. "Break, why couldn't our ending be different? If I would have told you I didn't feel right about this play, would you have listened?" She asked the same questions each time she came to see him. "Was it my fault? Are you mad I killed our baby?" She took another swig. "Or, was this just how our story was supposed to end?"

Be safe. I'll be waiting for your text." He turned to walk out the restroom. Nunu grabbed him by the shirt. When he looked back, she only stared. Her gut was telling her to speak what she felt, but then she didn't want to jinx what they had going on.

"You be safe, too. Come back to me."

Break smiled, winked, and departed out of the facility.

Ducked in an all-black Ford Taurus, Break watched Nunu exit the back of the club with the two out of town niggas. His blood pressure raised a couple of notches when the tall nigga wearing the glasses felt all over her ass. No, he and Nunu weren't exclusive, nor had they ever talked about being together. To him, that meant nothing. In his mind, she was his. The way his feelings were handling him, he knew that he was going to have to either A: cut Nunu off or B: stake his claims. He wasn't sure if she was ready for all that. And to save face he was weighing more on cutting her off.

"Boy, stop. You starting to make me think you ain't used to pussy." Nunu teased, moving Tone's hands from off her ass. In reality, she didn't even mind him all over her, but she knew Break was watching, and she wanted to respect him. Nah, they weren't in a relationship and have never entertained the idea. Nevertheless, she knew he had love for her, just as she did for him. Countless times, she thought about being his girl, but didn't think he was ready. She really didn't know if she was ready herself. What she knew for sure, was she had strong feelings for Break.

Tone laughed at how Nunu tried to clown him. He got plenty of pussy and didn't have to pay for it. She was green to who he was. He wanted it to stay that way. Which is why he kept his chain tucked, concealing his Joker medallion. Hitting the alarm on the rented black-on-black Range Rover, he looked at his God brother.

"She must not know who I am."

"Who are you?" Nunu challenged.

"A nigga who about to give you some good dick."

"Man, fuck all that. Where your homegirls?" Boy Boy, his God bro asked.

Nunu sighed, hoping the news she was about to deliver wasn't going to fuck up what she was trying to do.

"They got pulled over by the police." She lied. The rest of The BGB Crew had no idea what she was on.

"You ain't scared without your homegirls are you?" Tone asked.

"Nope, but I ain't fucking both of y'all." She snaked her neck.

"I know that. You all mine." Tone opened the back door and Nunu climbed in. Tone got in with her and Boy Boy climbed in the driver's seat. He turned up the music on full blast as he pulled away from the club.

Nunu wasted no time unbuckling Tone's jeans and pulling out his pencil thin dick. She rolled her eyes as she stroked it in an attempt to get it hard. Tone pulled both of her big breasts from her blouse and began to suck on one. "Mmmmm." Nunu moaned. She had to give it to him. He did know how to suck a tittie. His member grew in her hand.

"What you gon' do with this big muthafucka."

"It ain't big, but that's ok. I got you." She replied. By the time she was face to face with his little penis, she had a mouth full of saliva. Nunu took him into her mouth and sucked that muthafucka like it was the biggest dick in the world. She moaned, gagged, and played with his balls.

"I'm going to mess around and keep you." Tone told her. He ain't ever had no head this damn fire.

Nunu was sitting back with a smile on her face. She had literally sucked the soul out of Tone. With his head thrown back against the seat, he was in LaLa land.

"What are we doing here?" Nunu asked. They pulled up into the Marriott by the airport. "I thought you had an Airbnb?" She inquired. She was trying not to seem too alarmed. If Tone was bringing her to a hotel, but staying in an Airbnb, she was sure the money, or whatever he had, wasn't at the hotel. The truck stopped, and Tone looked at her.

"Me and you are staying here. My boy bout to handle something at the pad."

Boy boy looked into the rearview. "Nah. I just got a text. It's a no-go. I'm coming up."

He looked at Nunu. "Don't worry. We got a suite, so you'll have your privacy."

On the way to the room, Nunu's mind was going 106 miles a minute. As they entered the elevator, she had already accepted the fact that this was a failed play. She texted Break her location as they approached the door of the suite. After she fucked and sucked on Tone for close to an hour, she texted Break again, this time from the restroom.

**Nunu**: hotel. Didn't take me to where they sleep.

**Break**: why you been there all this time then?

**Nunu**: trying to figure something out.

**Break**: yeah, ok.

**Break**: have him walk you to the Uber. I'll handle it from there. Ford Taurus. That's me.

"Are you sure you don't wanna stay? I only got one more day in town. We can chill, get some rest, and tomorrow we can hit Rodeo Drive and cop some fly shit."

"Wow, sounds like you are inviting me on a date. You must like me." She blushed.

"You cool, but that head is deadly." Tone kept it G.

"I can't stay. I can try to hook up with you tomorrow, if that's cool." Nunu grabbed her clutch off the bed. She looked at her phone.

"My Uber is pulling up. Are you walking me out?"

"I guess." Tone put on his jeans, shirt, and slid on his sneakers. He grabbed his cell off the dresser and noticed a text from his brother.

**Sen:** You better be focused on money, and not them tramp hoes. Don't get caught up.

**Tone**: Man. I know what I'm doing, and I ain't with no hoe. He slid the phone back in his pocket.

"Your girl tripping?" Nunu asked as they walked out of the room door.

"My punk ass brother." He replied.

Boy boy was sitting on the sofa. When they came out of the room, he overheard Tone complaining about the Warden. That's what they called Sen.

"He texted me, too." Boy boy said, laying back on the sofa.

"I'm walking shawty to the car." Tone let it be known.

"Bet. We are staying here tonight, too. I'm tired." Boy Boy said.

Tone didn't respond. He was tired, too. The Airbnb they rented was like 30 minutes away and neither wanted to risk it. Staying at the hotel wasn't a problem. Shit, he may have to call the other stripper bitch he met at the club to pull up.

Nunu's heart rate increased to an extremely high rate. She didn't know why she was so nervous about this play. She didn't know what he had planned. Blocking out everything Tone was saying, she made her way to the back door of the car. She turned to Tone.

"Can I get a hug?"

"I guess. You could get more than that if you stay." He pulled her into a hug. Nunu licked on his neck. Tone closed his eyes for a second too long. A gun was pressed to the back of his head. Break spoke.

"I ain't got shit to lose. I'm out here starving, and ready to kill the next man if he gets in the way of me eating." He warned. "Man, put your muthafuckin hands down!" He yelled at Tone.

"Get in the car." He demanded.

Nunu eased to the side. Tone did as he was told, and Break got in after him. The gun was now pressed to his temple. Tone was boiling hot when he saw Nunu climb in the driver's seat.

"For your sake, you better know the address to where I will retrieve the jackpot. Otherwise, you'll be a dead man."

Tone read off the address to the house he and his bro were staying in. That's where the money and drugs were. Tone was ashamed. He'd let pussy get him caught up. It was all good, though. He wasn't going out without a fight. If his assailant thought differently, that was on him.

Sometime had gone by before Boy Boy realized his bro hadn't made it back up. His antenna automatically went up. Grabbing his cellphone, he shot Tone a text asking him where he was. He grabbed his burner and secured it on his waist. Boy Boy had put on his sneakers and headed out the door. Tone still hadn't replied. The elevator ride was intense and uneasy. He didn't know if he should alert the other Jank Brothers or pray that everything was good. Deep inside, he knew something was wrong. However, he was too scared to call Sen. He knew there would be grave consequences if something happened to Tone.

"Fuck!" Boy Boy shouted when he made it to the parking lot, and Tone was nowhere in sight. As he paced back and forth a few times, it hit him. He had Tone's location programmed in his iPhone. The moment they landed in Cali, they shared with each other their location, just in case a situation such as this one arose. It came in handy. Sen told them to do it. Boy Boy grabbed his iPhone and scrolled down to Tone's contact. He went to info and when the location popped up, he knew he had to call Sen. The location showed that Tone was at the Airbnb. He tried calling again, but still there was no answer. Boy Boy sped on the highway doing 95 to 100 all the way there. He called Sen a few times, but it kept going to voicemail.

"I got this. Everything good. My bro is fine." He tried to convince himself.

The 30-minute drive was shortened to 24 minutes. When Boy Boy pulled up, he spotted the black Ford. Instantly, his stomach sank to his feet. There was some shady shit going on. Boy Boy snatched his piece from the stash and jumped out the truck, leaving the door wide open.

129

With two duffle bags in each hand, Break was struggling, running down the driveway. By the time he noticed the truck, Boy Boy was already upping his pistol, preparing to let off.

Pow! Pow! Pow!

Break was hit in the arm. The shot caused him to drop the duffle bag. Boy Boy continued to fire. The bullets were coming back to back, in rapid succession. Break didn't stand a chance. The speeding bullets never gave Break the opportunity to reach for his gun. His body was filled with lead. Boy Boy walked up on him. Break's shirt was a hue of red that turned into a deeper burgundy by the seconds. Full of blood. He was gasping for air as blood leaked from his mouth.

"Nigga, we ain't an easy win." Boy Boy aimed at his head, ready to finish the busta off.

POW!

Nunu shot Boy Boy in the back of the head. Her eyes widened, and the contents of her stomach threatened to come up. She was grossed out at the sight of his head exploding. Boy Boy fell, landing right next to Break. Nunu fought the urge to scream. She shook as she looked at the dead corpse. She then looked at Break. Her man was laid on the ground with blood coming from his mouth.

"We gotta get you help." She looked behind her and then back at Break. Her eyes darted toward the house, to where Tone had gone.

"I killed him. Take the money and ...Go." He managed to say. She watched as he coughed. Suddenly, his body jerked. He was convulsing. Just as sudden as it began, it stopped. He was no longer moving at all. He too, was dead.

Nunu picked up the bags and left the scene.

It was by the grace of God that she was still walking the streets today. The detectives questioned her for months before they finally removed her from the list of suspects. That was the main reason she aborted the baby she and Break created that night. She knew for sure she was going to jail. She couldn't risk giving birth to her baby behind bars. She didn't trust the system. They probably would've found a million reasons not to give her kid to one of her cousins. She regretted killing their love child, just as much as she regretted not telling Break she had a bad feeling about the play.

Safely she got away, Nunu sat in a Denny's parking lot. She couldn't stop shaking. She had cried so much, her head felt like it was going to explode. The visions of seeing her man bleeding at the mouth, and taking his last breath, coupled with her taking a man's life, taunted her. "Ahhhhh! This is so wrong. I fucked up!" Nunu cried. She banged on the steering wheel until her hand hurt. Any pain was better than the pain she felt losing Break.

Any moment now, Papa should be pulling up. She called him on the highway, telling him that she was in trouble. He was the only person she thought to call. After all, her crew didn't know what she was on. Papa asked her where she was. She told him that she was next to an exit off the 10 freeway. He told her to drive to Riverside, close to one of his spots. He was right behind her.

About twenty minutes later, she saw his black Charger pull in. She'd told him what kind of car she was in, so he pulled up right next to her. Nunu jumped out of her car. Papa rolled his window down. He demanded that Nunu get back in the car and follow him.

In less than ten minutes, they pulled up to a building. She'd been there a few times when they first got in the game, but it had been a while. It was one of Papa's spots. It was pitch-black inside, but the moment they entered the premises, bright lights lit up the lot. Nunu watched as Papa climbed out of his car. He walked over to her.

"Come on." He went to walk off but stopped. "Grab everything that is yours." Nunu did just that. She followed Papa as he led her toward the black iron doors. He didn't even have to knock. As they stepped foot in front of the doors, they opened. A short Hispanic guy stepped to the side. He greeted Papa as they entered. Nunu followed Papa to his office.

"Sit down and tell me what the fuck you allowed to happen." Taking a seat in a brown leather chair, she told Papa the story. Tears began to fall, but he wasn't concerned.

"Remember Rico? The guy I was dating?" Rico was a dude she started messing with during her first semester of college. Rico is the nigga she gave her virginity to.

"Yeah, that light skinned punk. I remember." Papa said.

"Rico was my first. He was cool, laid back, and getting money. Rico was doing check fraud, bringing in loads of money. He was always telling me what he could do for me and stuff. He took me out to a lot of expensive hotels, and we ate at the finest restaurants. He used to constantly say, "I know you and your crew ballers, but I can upgrade you." There was nothing a nigga could do for me that I couldn't do for myself. I liked him, though, when he wasn't being annoying. He broke up with me because I wasn't submissive enough. I talked to Auntie Deb, and she said, "A man don't want a woman that acts like she doesn't need him." Papa shook his head. This the shit he was talking about when he told the girls not to let a nigga get them off their square. "Papa. I know I messed up. I wanted to prove to him that I was a boss, too. Took him to our house and put some money in the stash right in front of him."

"And the muthafucka got ya." Papa shook his head.

"Yeah. About a month later, he said he wanted to chill. Said he was stressed, and his money was tied up. I offered to get us a room, but he said he just wanted to chill with me at the house. I woke up the next day around 4pm. I think he drugged me. When I realized he was gone, the first thing I did was call him to see if he felt better. I was surprised when the number wasn't in service. I fucked up."

"So, he stole the money, and you didn't tell the others?" She nodded to say yes. Papa shook his head.

"How much?"

"One-hundred thousand."

"I be fuck! The nigga fucked you stupid. How the fuck you going to let a nigga know where you kept that much money? And why in the fuck do you got all your money in one spot?"

Silence…

"Never-mind that. What's done, is done. Tell me how we are here now?"

"I started dancing; told them I was dancing so that way when we open our club, I would have the experience. They knew I always wanted to dance and loved making money, so they didn't question it. Ran into a nigga that seen me at the club. Break, Buck's brother. I don't know if you know them. But he asked me if I was still with the lame Rico, and I told him no. I let him know he robbed me, and I was looking for him. Break and his brother Buck was known to rob niggas. A few months after seeing Break around, I got at him on some "let's get money shit.""

"Robbing niggas, huh." Papa chuckled.

"Yes."

"Hustle is a hustle." Papa didn't scold her like she thought. She continued.

"Almost a year went by. Me and Break did what we did, and we ate decent off of it. Tonight, it was some niggas from the A at the club. Reminded me of Rico the way he flossed. He told me about a lot within the thirty minutes I was with him. I got at Break and put him on him. We were supposed to go back to his Airbnb, but we ended up at a hotel. I had him walk me to what he thought was my Uber and Break was right there. Break put the gun to his head and forced him to get in the car. We made him take us to the Airbnb. I waited outside. I heard shots. Break came running out with two bags." She looked at the bags she brought in. "Out of nowhere, bullets started flying from another direction. It was the dude we robbed people. He killed Break, and I killed him." She said somberly. Papa got up and went over to grab one of the bags Nunu had. He looked in it. It was filled with money. He pulled out the stacks of money and set it on the table.

"I'm glad you are alive. But you fucked up. What happened is between us. Do not tell no one. You're my granddaughter, so I gotta protect you. I failed your momma." His throat cracked, but he checked himself.

"Thank you, Papa."

"This money goes back to the stash."

"I know."

"You'll continue to work at the club for another few months. I'll have Row and Bow there to watch you. Anyone asks you; you don't know shit. The police may question everyone at the club. If they know you left with him, they will be on you. No talking. You have a lawyer."

"Ok."

Nunu felt better now that she shared with Papa what was going on. Papa didn't tell his granddaughter because he didn't want her to worry or ever repeat it. Later he found out that the boys she robbed and killed were Judah Jank's boys. He wanted her to take her secret to her grave. There was no way he was going to lose Nunu like he did her momma. He didn't step on folks' toes. He did him peacefully. He was a calm man. Make no mistake about it, for his granddaughter

"If my Papa knew I was up here five years later still crying over you, he'd cuss my ass out." She laughed. Nunu stood up from the ground as she slipped her hands in her Nike coat. "I gotta stop feeling guilty. Charge the shit to the game and live my life. I think losing you and the baby back-to-back is what fucked me up. I'm still here. I gotta live." Nunu felt good saying that. She didn't know what came over her, but it was like all of a sudden, she was releasing herself from the past and ready for the future; whatever that was. "Thank you for everything. Kiss our baby for me." With that, she walked away with plans to never return. Nunu hopped in her Benz and went to see Debra.

Thanks to the girls and her crazy work ethic, Debra had everything she wanted, and more. However, no matter what she had, she refused to move out of the hood.

It was close to noon when Nunu pulled up to the two-story, four-car garage home. A few years back, some of the hottest female contractors out of San Diego, California remodeled it. Debra's house looks like it belongs on the cover of one of those Home Magazines. The inside was decorated extremely nicely. Her color theme was a dark purple and white. Nunu was both surprised and happy to see that Dez and Uno's cars were in the driveway. Being that they took up the parking in the driveway, she was made to park on the street. She wondered if Kay would be pulling up.

Dez saw Nunu when she pulled up on the home surveillance, so she met Nunu at the door.

The aroma of good food invaded Nunu's nose. She had a small breakfast before she left the house. She wasn't really hungry, but Debra's cooking she would never turn down. Her aunt could cook her ass off.

"So y'all hoes wasn't going to tell me that y'all were coming over here?"

Nunu and Dez hugged. Nunu walked in the house and locked the door behind her.

"She texted last week, inviting us over for Sunday's brunch. Did you forget?" Dez replied.

Nunu removed her Nike jacket and hung it on the coat rack. Ignoring Dez's question, she made her way to the dining room. Most of the food was placed on the table. It all looked so delicious. Freshly baked croissants, roasted pork loin chops, blackened catfish, crab cakes, bacon and eggs, ham and cheese omelets, French toast, and fresh fruit. Nunu knew that wasn't even half of it. Heading to the kitchen, Nunu stopped at the mimosa table. She grabbed a flute and sipped it on the way. Whenever Debra cooked, she always set up the mimosa bar. All the ladies loved to drink.

"Heyyy." Nunu spoke as she walked toward her. Debra came over and gave her a big hug.

"I'm glad you came." Debra told her. She didn't see the girls much. She understood; they were all living their life. Whenever she saw them, she treasured the moment. She worried about how the girls were living. She would always stress her concern to Papa about The BGB Crew. She didn't want them to end up like their mothers. Every time, Papa would tell her the same thing. "Ain't no sense in worrying, it won't change a thing. Pray, and be there for them." And that's what she did, but she still found herself worrying. She even addressed her concern to the girls mothers. They, too, told her to pray for them.

Debra went to break her and Nunu's embrace, but Nunu didn't let her go. Debra rubbed her back. Of all the girls, Nunu was the most sensitive.

"I love you, Auntie. Thanks for everything." Nunu said.

"I love you too, and you are welcome." Nunu pulled away.

Dez announced Kay's arrival as she went to let her in. Uno was supposed to be cutting fruit, but she was texting on the phone. Nunu took it upon herself to remove the fish from the skillet.

"I'm about to fuck this food up." Kay announced. She entered the kitchen with a big smile on her face. Dressed in leggings, an oversized shirt, and a pair of signature Dior heels.

"Someone is glowing. She must got some new dick." Debra called Kay out. The girls burst into a hearty laughter while Uno and Dez told on Kay. They told about how she was sprung and falling for her new fling.

"I knew it! I could tell, shiiiid his dick must be bigger than any dick you ever had because your little ass even walking funny." Debra clowned. She was tipsy, and it showed. More laughter.

139

Nunu gave Deb a high five because she too peeped how her girl was walking. Debra may not have been cool with how they got their money, but she was someone they could talk to. Someone who understood them on a woman's level; that only a woman could.

"Nunu fucked the brother, and she likes him." Kay teased. She licked her tongue at Nunu, who shook her head. She was going to get her ass back.

"When was the last time you girls talked to your mothers?" Debra asked the girls. She was packing their to-go-plates.

Uno said yesterday, Kay told her earlier that day, and Dez said it had been a month. Dez hadn't told anyone, but she was annoyed by her mother. She was tired of hearing her mouth complaining about the game. The game is how she ate. She didn't want to hear anyone constantly telling her to get out the game.

"Nunu, do you feel like dropping your papa this plate off?" Debra was already putting it in the bag.

"Yeah, I will." She answered. Nunu was pouring herself a shot of tequila before she left.

"I'm going to Black Out later." Kay announced. They were walking out the door. The Black Out was the place where they shot pool, gambled, and hung out with the locals. "Cez wanna holler at me about some business." That was the owner.

"It's a beautiful day." Debra said. The sun was out and there wasn't a cloud in the sky.

140

"And we started it with a beautiful person. One of my favorites." Nunu smiled.

"Yeeessss." The others said in unison. Everyone gave Debra a hug before heading to their respective vehicles.

"Well, none of y'all said y'all was turning up with me later, but I don't care. I'll call you and let you know what Cez talking about." Kay said. Since her cousins didn't care to pick up on her invite, she would probably invite Spade to chill.

Once Kay was in the car, Uno looked at Dez and then Nunu. "Let's pop up on her ass. I bet she gon' be with that nigga Spade. Let me find out she's in love."

Debra laughed.

"FYI." She announced, getting their attention. "Ain't nothing wrong with enjoying another person's company, or being attracted to them. It's ok to fall in love." Debra was serious. She had her little boo, and she loved his freaky ass. She couldn't wait to fly out to see him the following weekend. Debra's boo lived in Arizona.

"I'm cool on love." Uno said.

"That makes two of us." Dez added. Nunu said nothing. She tried it and was done with it. There was no need to mention it.

Before Kay pulled off, she yelled. "I'm living, whatever happens!" Before any of her cousins could respond, she turned the radio up to the max volume and pulled off.

It was close to 9pm when Kay pulled into the parking lot of the Black Out. The Black Out was a hole in the wall that a lot of hustlers, gangstas, and regular Joes frequented. The muthafucka stayed cracking. The old building was 5,100 square feet. The parking lot was half the size of a baseball field. Many of the old heads and members of car clubs chilled in the parking lot. Cez the owner sold food himself, but on Sundays, he allowed different food vendors to come out and make their money. The Black Out was one of the only spots in the hood that the police didn't pull up to try to shut down. The hood respected Cez. His background wasn't squeaky clean, but his character spoke volumes.

Kay parked her whip and climbed out. She was rocking some tight-fitting money green leather shorts, with a matching half top, a clear hobo bag, and some clear 8-inch designer heels. Kay slid her holster on her side that housed her Glock 9. She wouldn't be turned away, so she didn't have to hide her shit like the other patrons, whom she was sure had their piece on them. "What's up? One of BGB's finest. Kay is in the mothafuckin' house!" Floated in the air as she made her way in the spot. She spoke to a few, but mostly threw her head up as a greeting. Blues was playing, which wasn't a shock since the crowd was diverse and the owner was pushing seventy-five years old.

Boom saw Kay when she pulled up. He was sitting in an all-black Silverado truck. He'd been in the parking lot since 3 o'clock that afternoon. He was on one. He may have treated his baby momma like shit, but in his own way he gave a fuck about her. It had been a couple of days, and he hadn't heard from her. They hadn't spoken since the night he jumped on and raped her. He went to her house and was shocked when he saw her family there. The worried look on their faces told him something was wrong before he even asked.

"My sister has been missing. I swear to God if something happened to her because of your thieving ass, you are dead. I will pay somebody myself-" Trish's words were cut off when Boom smacked her in the face, causing her to fly damn near across the room. Ignoring the screams coming from his son, he stormed out of the apartment. Boom had been searching high and low for his baby momma. He was far from stupid. The BGB bitches were the reason behind her disappearance.

"Take something from me, I take something from you." He said, as he watched Kay disappear into the building. Boom was going to take the chicks out one by one if he could. He knew what he was planning; he had to do that shit right. Because if he didn't, he would be a dead man. The BGB girls had a lot of connects, and the money to have him killed. He looked down at his phone, at the picture of his baby momma and their son. The picture was taken the day she brought him home from the hospital. It brought tears to his eyes. His girl was a good person. Dez and the rest of them knew that she wasn't no grimy bitch. They knew that she wouldn't steal from them. They knew he did it, so they should have come for him, not her. Who in the fuck did they think they were? They left his child motherless and left him with a broken heart. Those bitches were gonna pay.

"I want you to sit in my seat." Cez told Kay. She'd just walked into his small office and was about to sit in the chair in front of his desk. Cez's office was cluttered with papers, and he had shit all over the desk. The bookshelf was stocked with books, but you could still see the dust was thick as hell on it. Kay was borderline OCD, and she was not feeling the junk.

"Naw, I'm good." She said to the seventy- something year old. Cez was about 5'6, thin built, and the color of coffee. His light-brown eyes and curly gray hair are what made him standout. He was very handsome for his age, and he could dress his ass off. Whenever you saw him, he was dressed in white. Tonight, Cez wore a white linen suit and white loafers. He smelled good, too.

"I'm going to sit right here and let you sit in your spot." Kay told him and took a seat on the black chair that sat across from his.

Cez smiled as he watched her. She crossed her legs like the lady she was, but the pistol that hung from her holster told you she was gangsta as they came. Cez took his seat, pulled a cigar from his box, and offered one to Kay.

"Yeah, I'll take one." She got up and took the expensive cigar. She placed it in her mouth and Cez lit it. Then, taking a seat back in her spot, she began.

"So, you need 20k to save the spot. I'm not trying to be in your business, but how you don't have the money and this place is always packed?" She used her hands for emphasis. Cez sat back in the seat.

"Don't tell your grandfather about this." He was referring to Papa.

"You owe my papa or something?" Kay asked, taking the cigar from her mouth.

"Nah, but what I look like asking his granddaughter to help me, and not him? He's an OG like me." She nodded her head to say she understood. "I owe because my lady has a gambling problem. The dumb bitch got in debt with Black Sam and some more people. Left me with ten thousand in the account. This spot, I put in her name. Had some legal issues, so I signed it over to her. I didn't bother taking it out of her name after it cleared up. I knew she liked to bet on horses and casino hop, but the last 10 years she ain't ever fucked off nothing we had to feed her addiction."

"You still with her?" Kay asked.

"Hell, no. I kicked that bitch out and sent her country ass back down there with her kids. I swear fo' God I wanted to murder her ass, but I didn't think I would get away with it." Cez spat. He was pissed every time he thought about what she did. He purchased the Black Out over 40 years ago. He turned the Black Out into something special, and now this shit. Kay pulled her cell from her bag. She dialed Dez, who picked up on the first ring. After asking her to hold, she called Uno. Once Uno was on the line, she called Nunu, but she never picked up. As long as the three of them agreed, they could put the other up on game later.

"Aye." Kay started. "I'm in the office with Cez. He needs 20k to keep the place. I wanna loan it to him." All three agreed on it.

"I don't know how long it will take me to pay y'all back. I bring in about five thousand a month here, but I still got bills."

"We will give you a year to pay it back. Until then, the deed is ours." Dez said. They chopped it up a few more seconds

146

before Kay told the girls she would call back if she needed them.

"I appreciate you. I have another problem."

"What?" Kay said. Her tone was laced with annoyance. He should have told everything at once.

"I'm asking for the money, but I don't know if Black Sam is willing to give me the deed, or my spot back. He gave me until Friday, and here it is Sunday."

"Call him." Kay said. Just as the words escaped her mouth, a knock was on the door.

"That's probably him. I asked him to come." Cez got up to answer the door.

Kay was already standing. One thing Papa taught her was to always stand when a potential business partner entered the room, and make sure to look them in the eyes.

"Sam, I invited you. I don't know these other niggas." Cez looked at the two dudes who were with him.

"This family." Sam replied.

"I don't know them, man."

Cez was blocking the door so Kay couldn't see either Sam, or the dudes he was trying to bring in. Kay wasn't tripping about Sam bringing anyone else. Far as they knew, his guests were probably tied to the money Cez's woman fucked off.

On the other hand, they could've been there to make sure he had protection. Cez may have been cool, but plenty knew he wasn't a saint, and the old head was quick to pull his pistol if he felt the need. Kay witnessed him pistol-whipping some nigga for slapping his own bitch. He didn't care that he hit her, he just didn't want the shit going down at his place.

"Cez, it's cool. They may be his business partners, like I'm yours. I'm sure Sam ain't here in our city, on no underhanded shit." She walked over so she could be seen. Hastily, Cez moved from the door. Black Sam chuckled at Kay's comment. He knew she was trying to call him out on being from Atlanta. He didn't give a fuck though. He knew all about The BGB Crew, their mothers, and their grandfather. He admired their hustle. But he wouldn't tolerate disrespect.

Right off the bat, Spade heard the voice and knew it was her. So, this was the reason she curved him earlier. Bitch. She was tied up when they were supposed to link. This was the reason she wasn't answering his call. She was really handling business.

Black Sam entered the room, and Spade followed. The smell of her floral perfume hardened his dick. When he laid eyes on her, he was impressed. The way she was standing there like the boss bitch that she was had him ready to snatch her ass up, take her to Black Sam's truck, and fuck the shit out of her. The pair gawked at each other. Sen walked in and Kay put her focus on him. Cez then shut the door. Kay looked at Black Sam.

"You guys walked in this man's shit, and no one speaks? No introductions?" She asked. Kay was in boss mode all the way.

"My bad. The tension got thick all of a sudden." Said Black Sam. He stood to the side, looking like a short knock off version of Omar Epps.

Black Sam introduced the guys to Cez. Even though he learned that Spade was messing with Kay, he introduced her to his nephews, too.

Spade was pissed off at how Kay acted like she wasn't just fucking him doggy style the day before. He didn't say shit, though. He let her handle her business. Sen was amused. He only read about chicks like her in those urban books. He would never admit it, but he would love to see Nunu on her gangsta shit. He wondered where she was.

"Alright. So, Black Sam, I'm offering 20k to get the deed to my peeps spot."

"I told him Friday. So, that won't work."

"It gotta work." Kay spat.

"And why is that?" Black Sam questioned.

"The same reason why he allowed you, on several occasions, to do business in this parking lot. Black Sam, we, the hustlers in the city, is cool with you. You've been doing business in our city without being taxed. You owe us."

"I don't owe you shit." Sam spat. The little bitch was pissing him off.

Kay stood up.

149

"So, what you saying? You really think you are going to keep this man's building? Nah." She shook her head. "I got 25 for you. I ain't going no higher. Take it or leave it, but you need to leave that deed too."

Black Sam got ready to jump up, but Spade stopped him by lightly touching his chest. He looked at Kay.

"Baby girl, you can't go around threatening people to get what you want."

"Baby boy. This is my city. I will die for respect here. I'll never let an outsider do us." Her stare was cold.

Cez stood up. It was his turn. He looked at Black Sam.

"I know business is business. This here building is my life. I'm ready to die for it."

Sen wanted to say something, but he watched it play out. Besides, it was his brother's business.

"Look." Spade spoke up. "The money, that 20k we accept, but I need y'all to add an extra 10k because her mouth slick, and this is business." He made sure to stare at Kay when he said it.

"25." Kay stood firm on her last offer.

"Nah, I got the other 5." Cez said. "Now give me the deed and let's start the paperwork." Cez didn't want any problems, he only wanted his building back.

Kay was pissed and so was Black Sam. He was an old nigga who didn't take threats lightly. If it weren't for his nephew, he was for sure he would have slapped the shit out of the smart mouth bitch. The way he was feeling, he probably would have killed her. He knew Kay wasn't wearing that strap for nothing. While they went over the details of the loan, Kay called Dez back to ask her to bring the money. Dez refused. She told her tomorrow. After a few more words, she made sure their cousin was good, and they ended the call.

"Sam and Spade." Kay looked at them both. "Cez will have the money first thing tomorrow morning." She then looked at Cez. "I'll tell you where to meet me. I will also have the paperwork drawn up for you guys to handle once the money is in their hands." Cez gave a head nod.

"Thank you." Cez said, meaning every word.

"We good?" She looked at Spade, and then to Sam. Sam replied with a nod of the head. It wasn't his money anyway, so it was whatever, but he still wasn't feeling her threats.

"I'm cool with that." Spade replied. Gawking at Kay, he was bothered, and she could feel it.

"Well, if that's it. I wanna thank you. I'm out." She walked out the door. Although Spade had the urge to go behind Kay, he stayed behind with the guys to conclude business.

They all were in Atlanta at Spade's spot when Cez's chick made the bet. Outside of distributing narcotics, Spade was a major loan shark who owned his own gambling spot. This particular night he was throwing a tournament when Cez's woman wanted in. It wasn't the first time she joined one of

Thinking about the way Spade was glaring at her, Kay lashed out as if someone were there talking to her.

"I don't give a fuck." Kay shrugged. In one hand, she was holding a pool stick, the other she used to take the double shot of Patron. Slamming the shot glass back on the bar, she looked toward the door and smiled when she saw Nunu.

Nunu strutted in, wearing a hot pink spandex dress that barely covered her ass. Her hair was in a bone straight wrap, with a part in the middle. In her hand was a tan Chanel clutch that was more than likely housing her Glock. Nunu spotted Kay and walked her way.

Kay signaled for the bartender.

"Let me get four more shots." She told him.

As the bartender set the two glasses in front of her and filled them with double shots of tequila, Nunu approached. She placed her clutch on the counter. Already knowing what it was, she took one of the shot glasses. Kay held hers in the air, and Nunu matched her gesture. They toasted to success, new ventures and to The BGB Crew. Both girls took the shot to the head and placed the glasses back on the bar.

"I'm glad you came." Kay said. Nunu gave an agreeing head nod. Later, she would tell her about what went down in the office. Nunu's eyes landed on the dude walking up.

Kay smiled. She felt his presence. She could smell his cologne. He wrapped his arms around her body. Instantly, she melted into his arms. His minty breath tickled as he whispered into her ear.

"Why you so hard to catch up with?" The deep baritone asked.

Her eyebrows raised. She turned to make sure it was CB whispering and not Spade. Although she was slightly disappointed that CB was invading her space, she was still pleased to see his sexy black ass. CB put you in the mind of 50 Cent. He could be an asshole like him, too. Kay turned around to face CB. He went to pull her into his arms because he liked holding her, but Kay played it off. Instead, she grabbed each of his hands into hers. With a smile on her face, she gave him the once over. In a simple black T-shirt, jeans and no jewelry, CB still had a sex appeal that could grab most women's attention at first glance.

"I didn't know you were coming to town."

"I'm here until next week. You leaving with me?" He asked.

Kay took a deep breath. She could feel her heart rate quicken. She didn't know why she was nervous about Spade gawking at her, but she was. She didn't know if she should let go of CB's hands or not. The red shirt was coming her way. '*Got dammit.*' She thought. '*This nigga is about to act a fool.*' She and Spade didn't even know each other. From the first day he was putting claims on her as he fucked the shit out of her. He had her wanting to spend every minute with him. He was claiming her as his future, and secretly, she wanted to be just that. The reality was, he was leaving soon, going back to his life, and she was staying in Cali to live hers. Spade walked right up on her. The look he gave her was so evil. It scared her and made her pussy tingle. Ignoring everyone but her, he walked up on the side of her and spat in her ear.

"Let's go." The nigga she was entertaining didn't matter. All that mattered was she let the goofy nigga's hand go and left with him.

Kay was her own boss. She did what the hell she wanted to do. She didn't love these niggas, and she damn sure wasn't taking demands from none. There wasn't a ring on her finger. There wasn't a man on earth that could claim her. She looked up at Spade. His lips twitched and trembled with rage. He was enraged and Kay knew it. She could even tell that he was trying to ignore CB who had been ice grilling him since he walked up.

Gently, Kay slid her hand from CB. Looking into his eyes, she said, "I'll try to catch up with you before you go."

CB laughed to mask his anger.

"You feeling this fuck nigga?" CB quizzed.

Spade immediately released a right hook to the side of CB's face, which caused him to stumble. CB couldn't even gain his composure well enough before Spade hit him with a left hook. Kay went to grab Spade, but Nunu pulled her back. They may have been tripping over her, but it wasn't her fight.

By this time, a crowd had formed. Both Kay and Nunu could see the pair going blow for blow. Spade was slightly shorter, but he was throwing hammers. CB had some hidden strength. He charged at Spade knocking him back in the

155

crowd where he went crashing into the bar. Kay lost sight of the duo.

Sen burst through the crowd with a pistol in his hand. He ran over to where his brother was and went stupid. Kay and Nunu's eyes bucked as he pistol whipped CB. They were fucking him up. Kay was digging the hell out of Spade, but she couldn't allow them to dog CB out like that. She went to run their way.

Pow! Pow!

Shots were fired. Everyone was screaming, trying to duck and get on.

"Get the fuck out my spot." The voice over the speaker was Cez.

Boc! Boc! Boc!

This time it was a different gun. Kay and Nunu ducked for cover. They were on the side of the bar. Out of habit, they pulled their guns out.

"Let's go." Spade snatched the gun from Kay's hand and grabbed her by the arm with the other. Before Nunu knew what was going on, she was snatched up by the arm. Her gun was in the same hand. She couldn't do shit but curse.

"Let's get the fuck on!" Sen barked.

Spade looked at Nunu as he ran, pulling Kay with him. Nunu put up a fight. Sen had to pick her little ass up and throw her over his shoulder. Without incident, they made their way to the back exit. Cez opened the door to let them out. Black Sam was already waiting in the truck.

"I'm not going with y'all, let me go!" Kay yelled. She yanked her arm from Spade.

"And put me the fuck down!" Nunu yelled. Sen obeyed her wishes. What she didn't know was he was following his brother's lead. He didn't care if she stayed in the club or not. Spade wanted to make sure the bitches were safe. When the shots went off, he was ready to bounce. He wasn't trying to go to jail. Spade was the one that said, "I gotta go get Kay." He thought it was a stupid idea, but not as stupid as stepping to her because she was talking to another nigga. He didn't even know the bitch. He was his brother's keeper, which meant he would forever have his back.

Spade walked in Kay's face.

"When I said let's go, it wasn't a muthafuckin question. Now you either jump in the car with us, or I'm going with you, but we are leaving together. So, hurry the fuck up!" He yelled. "I'm standing over here with a nigga's blood on me and you wanna act stupid."

"Who you talking to?" Nunu snapped.

"Shut the fuck up." Sen was ready to spazz on her.

Sam roared his engine. He wasn't trying to be around much longer. A fucking shoot out just went down, and they wanted to argue with bitches.

157

"That's my car." Kay said. She strutted toward the black Escalade. The trio followed closely behind.

Kay popped the locks on her ride. Sen and Nunu climbed in the backseat. Kay in the driver, and Spade in the passenger. The moment the truck started; E-40 blared through the "15" inch subwoofers thumping hard from the back. Everyone felt the bass that sent vibrations through their bodies. "Ayeee!" She sang out as she bounced her shoulders to the music.

"I'll bring you to get your car tomorrow." Kay said, temporarily turning the radio down. She was looking at Nunu in the rear-view mirror. Nunu matched her gaze and gave her a reverse nod.

"Go to my hotel." Spade ordered.

"You didn't have to do that shit back there." Kay popped back. As long as she pulled off, he didn't even have to respond.

**Across town ....**

Frowning her face, Uno looked around her. She knew for damn sure this wasn't Freda's pad. She looked in her phone at their text messages to make sure she was at the right address. Uno pulled up closer to the white buildings to read the numbers on the building, and sure enough, she was at the correct address. Uno left the car running. She was deciding if she should call Freda to confirm she was at the correct location.

Ring!

Her phone rang. With a fake smile on her face, she answered.

"Hello."

"Is that you in that red bitch?" Freda asked, referring to Uno's G-Wagon.

'So, this is her pad. What the fuck.' Uno thought.

"Yeah." She answered, trying not to sound annoyed.

"I'm going to open the gate. Pull in. I'm coming down." Freda hung up the phone.

Uno sat there. She didn't know if she wanted to pull in that janky ass parking lot, or go into that ugly ass building. She contemplated turning the fuck around. Yeah, there was a security gate, but even that looked like some trap shit. The gate opened. Uno exhaled, rolled her eyes, and slowly pulled into the parking lot. She thought about how Freda was pushing a big body Benz truck when she pulled up to her show. She speculated about the jewelry she had on, and she looked fly in her designer wear. *'She was a fraud. I did meet the bitch working in a department store.'* Uno thought. She wanted to back out and go on about her business, but she didn't want to appear snobbish.Uno made a sharp right and there was Freda standing next to the same big body she came to the show in.

'Damn, she is sexy.' Uno thought.

Freda had on a black sweatshirt that read BANG on the front in red. She paired it with some black jeans and red

Balenciaga's on her feet. The cap to the back made her look that much sexier.

'I'm straight, coming to see a stud.' Uno shook her head.

Uno parked her whip and killed her engine. After reapplying her lip-gloss and spraying on Victoria's Secret pomegranate and lotus fragranced body mist, she pulled her gun from her console and placed it in the back of her waist. Tonight Uno was dressed in a pair of 7 of All Man Kind jeans, a white wife beater, and a pair of white Gucci sandals with a matching belt. Her hair was in five braids going to the back. After sending her cousins her location, Uno climbed out of her ride.

Freda had taken a call while Uno was preparing to get out of the car. She wrapped it up once Uno exited the vehicle. With a big smile on her face, she strolled over to Uno pulling her in for a hug.

"Hi, how are you cutie?" Freda asked.

Uno blushed.

"I'm good. You smell good." Uno told her.

"Thanks." Freda pulled away. She smiled at how shy Uno was acting. Freda pecked her on her lips shocking the shit out of Uno.

"Let's go up." She took her by the hand.

"You strapped huh, Ma." Freda smirked. She felt the gun when she hugged her. Uno was so caught off-guard by her gesture, she forgot all about her piece.

"I don't leave home without it."

Freda opened the door of the commercial building. Uno inhaled deeply as the smell of a vanilla fragrance welcomed them. Freda held the door open, allowing Uno to enter first. The lights came on, displaying an all-red room. A desk, a few chairs, and pictures of hip-hop artists were on the wall. Freda continued to hold Uno as she led her up a circular stairway.

"You live here?" Uno had to ask.

"You might as well say I do. I'm here more than I'm home. This is my place of business. I run a magazine company. Ball or Fall."

"Get out?" Uno's mouth opened with excitement. Ball or Fall was one of the most talked about new magazines that was out. They hadn't been in the game for more than a year, and people were talking about it all over social media.

"Yeah. I'm the baby daddy." She spoke proudly of the success.

Upstairs was even nicer than downstairs. In the middle of the red and black room was a huge office that you could see right through. From a distance, she could tell it was decorated in a vintage theme. She assumed that was her office.

"This is dope." Freda smiled at Uno's excitement.

161

Decked in an all-black Gap sweat suit, matching hat, and some white Nike Air Max sneakers, Dez grabbed her gun from the center console and climbed out of her ride. The night's chill kissed her in the face, reminding her that it was fall. It was the end of the month, and Dez came to make sure they would have enough product to start the month off properly. Her eyes scanned the rundown neighborhood. A few teenagers were hanging out, as well as Linda and Ronnie, two crackheads who lived in the same building the business was in. The couple was arguing loud as fuck, as usual.

It infuriated Dez because she didn't like attention where she did business. As she walked up on them, she noticed Ronnie holding an Olde English 800 bottle like he was ready to pop Linda. She shook her head. She remembered as a teen witnessing the pair doing the same shit. That was before they let the product they once sold get the best of them. Dez walked near the curbside where they were standing.

Since Ronnie was the one with the bottle, she glared at him.

"What the fuck I tell you two about bringing that bullshit around here? Get the fuck on." She barked. "Dez, in case you forgot, this is our block. We pay rent here." Linda snapped. Linda was a big woman. Standing at 6 '2 and weighing over 300 pounds, she had been fighting all of her life. She wasn't an easy win. That's why Ronnie had the bottle, and he would use it, too. He was about 5'6 and 140lbs at the most, he was no match for Linda. She always got the best of him.

"Bitch, who you talking to like that? I'll lay your big ass out." Dez threatened, as she removed her gun from her waist. Ronnie peeped it, and spoke up to defuse the situation.

"Dez, you ain't gotta do all that. Linda, let's go."

"No, fuck her!" Linda yelled. "Put the gun down, and I bet I'll beat that ass. Cutthroat ass bitch. You ain't nothing like your momma. We heard about what you did to Mina. God-"

*Wham! Bam! Bam!* Dez knocked Linda in the head with her gun. She stumbled back, close to falling, but caught herself.

"Bitch, don't ever speak up on my business." Linda held her head.

Ronnie ran and jumped in front of his woman, trying to stop Dez from hitting her again.

"That ain't right. Come on, Linda." Ronnie grabbed his woman by the arm.

By this time, a few folks had come outside. Some were looking out of their windows. When they saw it was Dez, people started whispering.

"Bitch, you gon' pay for this. Watch! You think you are bad. I know you did something to my niece." Linda said, still holding her head. Dez went running after her again, but two of her workers had run out of the house and held her back.

"Come on before the police come." Blue said. Dez stood there for a second. She wanted to kill that bitch for talking all that shit. "Come on, boo." Blue ushered her. Reluctantly, Dez walked off. It wasn't over. She was going to get that big bitch.

"Calm down, boss lady." Blue said to Dez. They stood in the living room of the trap. Dez was in a daze. Her eyebrows were in a frown, and she hadn't spoken two words since they walked in two minutes prior. She was wondering who the fuck was running their mouth about her being responsible for whatever happened to Mina. She played back the event and thought about Mina telling her about how if something happened to her, her sister and Boom would suspect her. That must've been the case. Dez concluded she would have to visit Trish. She wanted to see where her head was before she off the bitch like she promised her sister she would.

Yeah, they all grew up together. They played double dutch, had cheer competitions, and even slept over at each other's houses while growing up, but business was business, and Dez strongly believed that she needed to make an example out of Mina. She wasn't giving out any passes. She felt like if you signed up for the job, you were signing over your life. In the game, you were sacrificing jail or death. Since Mina wanted a way out and her fuck nigga got in the way of that, she had to pay the price.

Unfortunately, it was with her life. She knew that if she were in the same fucked up situation, the next wouldn't give her no passes, either. She respected that.

Dez looked over at Blue. She was sitting on the flowered sofa rolling a blunt. When she felt Dez's eyes on her, she looked up.

165

"You heard anything about what Linda's fat, funky ass was talking about?"

"Nah. That was my first time hearing it." Blue was honest.

Dez saw the questions in her eyes, wanting to know if it was true, but felt she owed no one an explanation. Dez walked off toward the kitchen and stood at the door. Two chicks by the name of Sasha and Chubby were over the stove. Masks covered their mouth and nose as they stood there whipping up the coke. They waved. Dez chucked her head up and walked off. She made her way to the first room down the hall. None of the three rooms had doors on them, so she walked right in. Lydia, Uno's little bitch, sat at the table. She weighed and packaged the product as it dried.

"What it look like, Lydia?" Dez wanted to know.

"Like your homegirl takes me for a game." She said, rolling her eyes.

"Look, bitch. I ain't got time for the bullshit." Dez spat.

"Well, someone is in a bad mood." Lydia cut her eyes. She put a brick on the scale. As she did her thang, she ran the numbers by Dez who was pleased. She walked off to the next room. Jew was standing by the door as another female worker counted the money.

"Aye, Dez. I need to talk to you." Jew told her.

Dez told the other worker to go into the living room. Once she did, she asked Jew.

166

"What's up?"

"Word going around that you're responsible for Mina's disappearance. That bitch Trish was saying it. I had to pop her ass in the mouth. I was bout to dog walk her ass, but the police came."

"When was this?"

"A few hours ago. You gotta handle that. Her lips too loose." Jew and Dez gawked at each other, Dez cut her eyes in the direction she sent her worker. She wasn't confirming shit, she didn't trust anyone. Dez called for the other worker to come back. She waited for the two duffle bags filled with money and left.

# Part Two

"Damn, shawty. What the fuck is on your mind? I know ain't no nigga got you over here taking shots like that?" Lucas questioned as he looked at the chick next to him. She was already at the bar when he walked in and copped a seat. Lucas took in the sight of the hole in the wall and wondered how the fuck they were still in business. They had some dusty ass strippers and broke niggas watching them dance. However, he couldn't help but keep track of how many shots the girl had taken. "Seven shots in an hour, ma? Either they are watered down, or your ass got a lot on ya mind." Lucas turned up his water bottle and waited for the chick to respond.

Trish wasn't in the mood to be bothered, but even over the semi loud music, his voice sounded familiar. Trish wasn't up for conversations. She was stressed the fuck out. Her sister had been missing over a month, and although nothing was confirmed, she knew she was dead. She would never go a day without coming home or contacting her. Tears spilled from her eyes as she thought of her big sister. Mina was so fucking amazing. She did what she did for the fuck nigga she was deeply in love with, but that didn't take away from how dope she was. Humble, loyal, caring, and compassionate. Those words described her big sister. She didn't deserve what happened to her. A few weeks before, she magically disappeared off the face of the earth. Mina told her sister what happened.

"I got some work from Dez on credit. I was supposed to take it to the A and flip it, but Boom stole it. I don't know what in the fuck I am going to do." Mina confessed. They were in the living room sipping on wine and eating cheese like they did every Sunday night.

"Did you let Dez know?" Mina asked. She shook her head thinking how her sister was always letting Boom get her into some shit.

"I don't want to say anything until I get the money." Mina said. The look in her eyes, Trish could tell that she was nervous and afraid. Trish took a deep breath.

"Well, just tell them. They know you. They know you wouldn't do no shit like that." Mina shook her head to disagree.

"I hope so. I will figure it out. If we gotta skip town until I come up with the money, then that's what we are going to do." Mina took a gulp from her wine glass. "If anything happens to me, just know The BGB are responsible."

"We will figure it out together." Mina didn't know it, but her sister had her back more than she could ever imagine. Trish ended up working for an old college friend's escort company. The long hours paid off. The night that her sister came up missing, Trish was going to surprise her with ten thousand. She never found out how much her sister owed, but she wasn't going to stop hustling until either they skipped town, or her sister had enough to pay her debt. It was too late. Her sister was gone, and she was left to raise her nephew.

Trish shook her head at the guy's question. Only if he knew that she just lost the only person who ever cared for her, he would understand why she was getting so wasted. She didn't wish the pain she was feeling on anyone.

Trish burst into a sob and buried her face in her hands. The bartender approached, she looked at Trish sympathetically. Silently, she prayed that Mina turned up safe. Once upon a time, Mina used to work at Club Slick. She remembers her saying she had the job to help pay her sister's tuition in college. Mina was cool as fuck. She hoped the girl wasn't dead.

"The owner will see you now." Says the bartender. Lucas gave her a reverse nod and stood. She walked from around the bar. With her head, she summoned him to follow.

"Keep your head up, shawty." Lucas whispered in Trish's ear. With puffy eyes, her head shot up. When their eyes met, they both were shocked to see the other.

Dez saw red as she gripped her steering wheel. Dipping in and out of traffic, her mind was on overdrive thinking about how she wanted to murder the muthafuckas that had her name out there. Bitches and niggas knew not to speak up on shit The BGB Crew did, unless they were about that life. Trish, that nerdy ass college hoe, wasn't with the business. Dez smashed on her brakes, as she almost ran a red light. Within seconds, blue and red lights were flashing behind her. *'Fuck.'* She cursed as she was debating if she wanted to pullover or not. Yeah, she was legal, as far as having the proper paperwork needed to drive, but cops were dirtier than a bitch, especially in L.A. In the backseat, she had two duffle bags filled with money. She had a feeling the shit wasn't going to go well. When the light turned green, Dez followed the instructions of the female officer who demanded that she pull over.

Any other person would've taken being pulled over by a cop and being let off with a warning as a sign to chill the fuck out. However, not Dez, she still needed to handle some shit. It was three o'clock in the morning, and she headed to Mina's house to send a warning. If her cousins had known she was out on a mission alone they would've tried to fight her. They didn't take each other's lives lightly. When one had an issue, so did the rest. Dez knew that, too. She'd kill behind them, and she knew they'd do the same for her. This particular situation, she didn't even bring up to them. She handled it as she saw fit. Capered in all black matching the Mustang she stole, Dez slowly turned the corner. It was three in the morning and just like she thought, the neighborhood was a complete ghost town. Her Glock 9 in one hand, the other on the steering wheel. Dez's eyes focused on the white duplex. All she came to do was send a message. She took it personally and handled the job herself.

"Boca! Boca! Boca!"

Dez let off 10 rounds. Bullets riddled the door and windows. If anyone was in the living room, that was Trish's fault. The bitch shouldn't have been running her mouth.

"Stupid, bitch!" Dez shouted, as she sped off.

Dez sat in the visiting area at the table she and her mom would be hanging out at. Her mother's favorite snacks were on the table, which included hot wings, kettle corn, hot tamales, butterfingers, and a subway sandwich. To drink, she had four bottles of water. Water was Jo's favorite drink other than cognac. Dez was just like her. With her legs crossed, Dez looked at the large clock on the wall. It was a quarter to one, which meant the visitors had four hours to chill with their loved ones. Dez glanced around at the families. From the elderly on down to newborns were out. Guilt washed over her as she thought about how it had been months since she saw her mom. Not that Dez didn't love her mom, but they bumped heads a lot. Her mother wanted her out of the game, and she wasn't trying to hear what she was talking about. At twenty-five she felt that she had been grown, been feeding herself and all she needed was her mother to have her back like Papa Smurf had her crew's backs back in the day.

The former street queen commanded attention when she walked into the room. Everyone stopped what he or she was doing to look up at the woman escorted out. Even in her gray sweatshirt, plain white sneakers, Jo looked good. She didn't look a day over thirty-five, and she was well over forty. Her light complexion was flawless. There were not wrinkles or bags under her eyes. Her long thick mane was in a ponytail that touched the middle of her back. Jo already had a nice body, but the prison workout enhanced it. Jo looked at her beautiful baby girl and smiled.

Dez's smile was big as the Pacific Ocean when she saw her mother. It was at that moment that she realized how much she missed her mommy. Dez shot up from the table and walked toward her mom. The women embraced each other. Dez's head lay on her mom just as Jo held her tightly and rocked back and forth. She'd been gone for a long time. It ate her up every day. She didn't wish her fate on anyone. Especially not her daughter and nieces. She didn't understand why they didn't take what happened to their parents and pick a route to be successful, a legit route. A route that wouldn't only get them paid but keep them free. Jo wasn't into praying, but she begged Allah every day to protect her daughter and nieces. Dez was stubborn, bullheaded, and like her was determined to succeed at whatever she did. Jo would never speak on it, but she saw the ending for her daughter a long time ago. Dez was in too deep.

The pair chopped it while eating their snacks.

"So, what is it that you come to talk about?" Jo asked. She wiped her hands on a napkin and then looked up at Dez. Dez was her twin. Not only did she look like her, but she was making the wrong choices in life like her, too.

"Ma. I need you to hear me out." Jo only gave her a look to say, don't come at me with no bullshit. "Momma." Dez whined.

"What, little girl?"

"Kay and Nunu been messing with two of Judah Jank's sons. What you know about him? I know he was out during your time."

Her heart dropped at the mention of his name. It always did. After all these years, she still considered Judah to be the best man that ever came into her life. They weren't exclusive, but he gave a fuck about her. She wished that she would've taken heed to his warning and not been defensive. Things would've been so much different.

Judah Jank wasn't just her connect, but her secret lover. Although Judah cut her off, she would always have love for him. She would always love him.

Snapping back to the current, Jo looked up at Dez. She could see the greed for the hustle in her eyes. Dez was in love with the game, as she once was. Deep down she knew there was no talking her into walking away, but that didn't mean that she wouldn't try.

"Walk away while you can." She whispered.

"No. Can you please tell me what you know about him? I think I wanna do business with him."

Jo sat back in her seat. She crossed her arms. Dez had her burning up inside from being so fucking hard head.

"I know a lot about him. He's a good friend. Paid me and the girls lawyers. When the FEDS took everything, it was him and Papa who made sure we were straight."

Dez was shocked. She had no idea her mom and Judah were cool.

"Wow. I didn't know."

"He's a very private man. Our business was just that." Jo leaned forward, resting her arms on her knees. "He will never do business with you or The BGB. I will make sure of that." She spat. Jo was dead ass. She would never contribute to her daughter's demise.

Dez shook her head with disappointment.

"You can try all you want, but I'll never stop until the clock drop or until I feel like it. You'll never have to worry about me asking for your help again."

"Good. You ready to bounce now?" Jo stood up. She didn't give a fuck about her temper tantrum. Dez was being a stupid ass bitch right now.

"No, I'm not leaving. I'm visiting my momma. Just because you don't wanna look out for me, don't mean I love you any less. You not helping won't stop no show." Dez retorted.

Jo smirked. The shit Dez was talking had her ready to knock her ass out. She wasn't going to hit her though.

"I'm going to head out, baby girl. I'll call you soon." With that, Jo walked away.

Dez hunched her shoulders. If her mother wanted to cut their visit short, that was on her. She wasn't going to beg her to stay.

Dez had a 911 message from the crew to meet up at the warehouse. After the visit with her moms, all she wanted to do was find a bar, have a few stiff ones, and figure out how she was going to prove to her mother that she wasn't going to slip like her. There was no nigga in the picture to bring her down, and she planned to keep it that way. She was going to show her mother that she and her crew were going to do it better. Unlike The Fancy & Fine Crew, The BGB Crew got every dollar out of the mud. There were no hand outs. Papa's wisdom wasn't even 100% free.

The sun was still shining when Dez made it back to L.A. She pulled into the parking lot and Nunu, Kay, and Uno's vehicles were there. The two black Cadillac trucks belonged to Row & Bow, their security. Dez grabbed her phone and climbed out of her car. When she approached the iron door, Bow greeted her and let her inside. Dez entered the building and made her way down the hall to the meeting room.

The others saw Dez on the camera when she pulled up. Every girl was in her respectable seat around the round table. A glass filled with cognac was in front of them. There was even a glass waiting for Dez when she sat down. Everyone was quiet in their thoughts and feelings about the situation they came to address.

When Dez entered the room, right off the bat she could feel the tension in the air. Nunu was the only one who looked at her, but her expression was blank. Taking a calming breath, Dez walked over to her seat. She reached for the liquor-filled glass and downed it. All eyes were now on her.

"What's up? Y'all act like there's a problem?" Dez said.

Kay spoke. "A very big problem if the shit we heard is true."

"And what the fuck you hear?" Dez snapped.

"Did you kill Mina?" Kay fired back.

Dez chuckled. She grabbed the bottle of Hennessy and refilled her glass. She looked at each girl and gulped the glass.

"Since when we giving out passes? She owed a debt she couldn't pay."

"That's fucked up, Dez. You know that girl got a son." Uno snapped. She shook her head. Mina was their childhood friend. She was cool as fuck.

"Why didn't you come to us before you handled her?" Nunu asked.

"Right." Kay added. Decisions like that, they made together. Dez should've come to them, especially since Mina was their childhood friend whom neither felt was flawed.

"Did she come to us when Boom stole or did she try to hide?"

"Wait. What you say?" Uno wanted to make sure she heard her right.

"Boom stole our shit. She went in hiding. She claimed she was trying to figure out how to make the money back. That bitch was lying and even if she wasn't, she's suspect. Should not have been hiding."

"That's some cold shit." Uno stood up. "You know she ain't even like that. She probably was scared. You didn't have to kill that girl. What about her fucking son? You know what it's like not to have a momma."

Dez drank the remainder of her drink and set the glass down.

"My momma, your momma, all of our mommas knew the game was dirty before they signed up. When our parents joined the game, they risked leaving us. We dealt with it and now her child must." She shrugged.

Uno shook her head and walked out. Dez was wrong, and she didn't want to be around her.

"Dez, people talking." Nunu said.

"I know. That's why I gave her punk ass sister a warning."

"Bitch, you shot that house up?" Kay asked. She'd heard about that, too.

"Yeah. Next time, I'm killing her." Dez warned.

Neither of the girls responded. Although they felt that it was wrong for what Dez did being that they had a long history with Mina. They understood it was part of the game and just like everyone else, you have to deal with the consequences. But fuck.

There was a moment of silence before Dez spoke.

"Is that it about this situation?"

"Where's Boom? We need to find him. He knows what's up, I'm sure. We can't sleep on him."

"When I see him, it's over." Dez said. Each girl gave an agreeing head nod.

"Alright, now that's over. Did you two know that y'all fucked Judah Jank's sons?"

"Spade a Jank?" Kay asked.

"Yes. Set up an appointment and let's talk business with them."

"I haven't talked to him. Did you run it by Papa? I know he said before, no."

"We don't need answering from no one. We can hold our own. Fucking with them, we will be millionaires in no time."

"Y'all handle that. I'm going to stick with the prescriptions." Nunu stated.

"What you think, Kay?"

"I don't even talk to him, but I may try to reach out."

Dez was cool with Kay claiming to reach out to Spade. If it didn't work, she would hit up Black Sam and see what's up.

Uno was pissed when she left the warehouse. To know that Dez killed Mina over some fucking money didn't sit well with her. Mina was their childhood friend. She may have been in love with a grimy nigga, but it never changed the fact of how solid she was. Her being solid is the reason the girls didn't hesitate to put her on when she came at them for help. Dez must've forgotten about the time she checked a bitch for trying to move work in their club. Mina had caught her in the dressing room, distributing pills and collecting money. She checked her and took her shit. She could've kept the pills for herself, but she gave them to Dez when she let her know what was up. Dez whooped on old girl breaking her nose and knocking out a tooth. One day, Mina was coming out of the grocery store, headed to her car when the chick rolled up with two Compton niggas pushing their line. She and the sister fought. One of the brothers put a gun to her head, threatening to kill her if she didn't call Dez and have her pull-up. Per a mutual associate, Mina stood her ground. She told the nigga she wasn't calling nobody, and she took the pills and the bitch's money. Old boy was ready to pistol whoop her until the mutual friend and his partner stepped in. It was small shit, Mina could've folded. However, she didn't. She had their backs. It angered Uno how Dez handled the situation and now she was beginning to feel like Dez was getting big headed.

"She had a fucking son!" Uno yelled. She banged her fist on the steering wheel. She knew firsthand how it felt not to have a mother in her life. It wasn't a good feeling. No matter how good the person who stood in the gap of your parent treated you, it was nothing like having a mother, your mother. "That ain't right. She was wrong." Uno shook her head. The thought sickened her. In deep thought, she drove through the city without a destination. *'Maybe it's time for me to walk away from this shit. I'm not obligated to stay.'* Over the last year, Uno was gearing closer and closer to washing her hands of the hustle and focusing on her career. If she did go that route, she knew that if she allowed Dez to continue to manage her, she wouldn't leave.

Uno pulled up to her clothing store. The attendant saw her red G Wagon and removed the cones in front of the store, allowing her to claim her spot. Besides being co-owner of Bandz Strip Club the Pretty One Boutique was Uno's only other business. She was thinking about opening a recording studio in the near future.

"Hey, lady." Uno greeted her store manager. She smiled when a lady and her daughter walked her way. She could see the excitement in their eyes. They were happy to see her.

"That's one of my favorite dresses." Uno complimented the yellow maxi dress the lady was holding. She looked at the dress and agreed.

"Can I take a picture with you?" She asked.

"Of course." Uno replied. Uno ended up socializing and taking pictures with the customers. When she looked up it was closing. Uno was helping her manager lock up when her cellphone rang. She smiled when she saw that it was Freda. Since the night at the spot, Freda and Uno had kicked it a few times. Freda was cool. Uno was finding herself liking her more and more. Uno was low-key salty about how Freda hadn't tried to step to her in no other way. She wanted her pussy ate. However, she was always stealing kisses from her and calling her cute. Uno didn't know what the deal was. She wasn't pressed for no woman though. Maybe that was the reason she was salty, she was used to females begging her to be with them, wanting to fuck, or willing to do anything for her time.

"What's up?" Is how Uno greeted the caller.

"How are you doing, sweetie?"

"I'm good closing up the shop."

"Come see me. Come straight here, too. Did you eat?" Freda demanded and asked, all in one breath.

"Actually, I am about to go have dinner. I can try to come after." Uno invited her store manager and salesclerk out for the night. The girls were cool, and they went hard for her, they deserved it.

"Alright. Get at me when you can." Freda responded.

"Ok." They hung up. Uno stood there in her thoughts about Freda. She was so nonchalant. She didn't like that. Maybe she was going to have to test her, had to see how Freda really felt about her.

**Uno:** Hey, I just finished dinner. Went home and handled a few things. Are you up?" Uno texted.

Uno was sitting on her couch, drinking a glass of wine. She'd been back from dinner for over two hours. Her plan was to come home, shower, change clothes and hookup with Freda, but Lydia called telling her she wanted some pussy. Uno hadn't talked with her in a cool minute. She was tired of Lydia acting like they were in a relationship. Granted, they've been messing with each other for quite some time, but just like any other chick Uno fucked with she wasn't claiming none of them. She was single and doing her. Lydia led herself to believe it was more because Uno dealt with her out in public, spent weekends with her, and even posted them out on FB at times. What Lydia didn't get was that Uno did what she wanted and the fact that Lydia was a pretty bitch with the best head to date, she fucked with her a little harder.

So, when Lydia called and said she wanted some and the way Uno was feeling, she took her up on her offer. Right after they fucked Lydia started tripping. Asking too many fucking questions, complaining about how Uno wasn't treating her right. She didn't have time for that needy shit. When was the bitch going to ask her about her day, what she wanted, or even how her career was going? Freda showed interest in all that mattered. That was another attribute she liked about her.

Uno's phone vibrated. It was a text from Freda. She'd sent Uno her location and told her to pull up. Uno didn't respond back immediately. She was contemplating on if she wanted to go or not. Uno wasn't familiar with the location Freda shot her. She didn't know if she was alone or with a bunch of people.

Uno shot her a text back asking what she had going on wherever she was.

As she was waiting on Freda to respond, she changed from her leggings and T-shirt to something more casual.

She'd already taken a shower after coming back from messing with Lydia. However, she applied more oil to her body and a jasmine fragranced body spray. Uno slid on her black skinny leg Dolce & Gabbana jeans with a white crop top and a thin black & white jacket. She paired her black thigh high stiletto boots and belt to set the outfit off exactly right.

She shot Freda a text back, letting her know she was on her way. When Freda replied with a simple ok, Uno smirked. She caught on to how Freda didn't bother to answer her question.

Uno grabbed her keys and purse. The gun was still in there from earlier. She sprayed herself with her favorite Ralph Lauren perfume and left out of the room, making sure she locked her door.

Uno could hear Dez and Kay talking in the living room as she was coming down the stairs. She rolled her eyes in the top of her head. That was something she hated about living with her cousins. Although they lived in a mansion, there was a possibility they still ran into each other on a daily basis. Uno was not trying to see Dez. She wouldn't stay mad at her forever, but the shit she pulled with Mina left a bad taste in her mouth.

She didn't bother to look at either of the girls. She headed out the door, ignoring Kay when she asked her where she was going.

Uno shot Freda a text, letting her know she was pulling up. And just like the gentleman she was, Freda was waiting out front for her. Uno couldn't help but smile. She took her bottom lip into her mouth as she checked Freda out. Her Tom Boy swag was such a fucking turn on. Freda's mane was wild and curly. She wore a black thermal with a white short sleeve Burberry T-shirt over it. Her Burberry belt held up a pair of stone washed jeans. On her feet were a pair of high-top Burberry sneakers.

Uno parked behind a black BMW truck. She threw her wagon in gear. By the time, Uno gathered her things; Freda was by her car door. She lightly tapped on the window and Uno hit the locks. Freda told her whenever they were together, she didn't want her opening any doors. Being that she said when they were together, she didn't think that when she pulled up wherever Freda was, she was to wait in the car for her to open it. She let her slide the first night they chilled, but the next time she tried, she demanded that she got back in the car. Uno looked at her like she was crazy. At first, she thought she was tripping about something. Therefore, when Freda re-opened her door for her without saying a word, she climbed back into her car. She went to grab her door to shut it, but Freda stopped her. "Kill the attitude. You are a lady and whenever you are in my presence you don't open doors or pay for shit." Freda then politely shut her door. With a smile on her face, she reopened Uno's door and was greeted by her beautiful smile. "Thank you." Uno said, stepping out the car. That day, Freda earned two extra points with her. Uno was smiling tough.

"You smell and look good as always." Freda complimented Uno. Holding her door open as she climbed out of the car, Freda thought about all the things she wanted to do to the gorgeous chick in front of her. Unlike with the other chicks, Freda saw potential in Uno. She wasn't just a cute bitch who thought her looks were going to get her by in life. Uno was about her bag. And from what she heard from the streets the chick wasn't just rapping about being a boss, she was really a boss. She learned Uno was out there every day risking her freedom to make sure she didn't go without. There was no doubt that she rocked with Uno's hustling mentality, but once she took it there with her some things would have to change.

"Thank you. You look sexy yourself." Uno tossed back. She stood by the door, waiting on Freda to instruct her on where to go.

"Can I have hug?" Freda asked.

"Of course." Uno walked into Freda's awaiting arms. She took in Freda's cologne. She smelled good. The way she held her in her arms felt even better. When Freda planted a kiss on her neck, a light moan escaped her mouth.

Every house on the block was massive. The one they were at was about the size of the mansion she shared with her cousins. However, the backyard was twice as big. When the pair made it to the backyard, Uno then found out that Freda invited her to come hang at a mutual friend's book release party. It was all the way live. Some of the city's favorite Indie entertainers were in the building. Uno had gotten the invite but never thought about going. Based on the author being a Crip she thought it was going to be some type of hood function. She was wrong. Brandy had it setup with style.

The duo stopped at one of the three open bars and got themselves a drink. Uno wanted to walk around and check out the party. She ran into a few fans and friends that she chopped it up with. Freda made a mental note of how Uno didn't bother to introduce her to anyone she conversed with.

"Alright, that's enough hugging and shit, you can speak without all the extras." Freda whispered in Uno's ear. She had just hugged one bitch and the hoe had the nerve to rub all over her back. On top of that, Uno didn't even seem like she was bothered. In Freda's opinion, she had been giving out too many hugs.

"That's what I do." Uno shot back. She took the last swallow from her Hennessy cup and sat it on an empty table.

"Noted." Freda responded. Uno peeped Freda's slight attitude, but she didn't care. She was doing her since Freda was too chicken to make a pass at her.

While Freda was staring a hole through Uno, Uno was staring at the famous Instagram model walking up. Brazilian Doll was even more gorgeous in person. The closer she got, the harder Uno's heart began to thump. Consciously, she didn't understand why, but when Brazilian Doll tapped Freda on the shoulder it confirmed why. Brazilian Doll walked on the side of Freda and when Freda saw who she was, her eyes lit up. It wasn't the same way she lit up when Uno pulled up, but she could tell that it was something between the two.

"Hey, babe." Brazilian Doll greeted; her accent was heavy. Uno gave her the once over. Dressed in a simple silk halter dress and stiletto heels, the bitch was still bad. The former volleyball player still had the body of a sexy ass athlete. Toned with the perfect ass and a pair of C-cups that sat up perfectly.

"How are you, stranger?" Freda spoke.

"I missed you and I'm sorry." Brazilian Doll admitted. She poked out her lips, and Freda just shook her head. She knew exactly what the fuck she was doing.

Freda wanted badly to put her in her place, but she wasn't the one to have folks all in their business.

"Call me tomorrow and we can talk." Freda told her.

"You promise?" She asked. Brazilian Doll knew Freda didn't just say shit to be saying it. If she told her to hit her up the next day, that's what she meant. And Brazilian Doll knew that. She only wanted to prolong their encounter. For one, she wanted to get up under Pretty Uno's skin. She knew who that rapper was, and she knew what she liked. She wouldn't be walking around the party with her for nothing.

"How about this." Uno spoke up. The sudden outburst caused Freda to turn and look at her. "You two can talk now. I am about to go mingle. I may call you or not." Uno told Freda. Freda gawked at her. That tough girl shit didn't move her. Freda was far from stupid. She knew Uno wanted her. She also knew that she was a stuck-up spoiled chick who thought everything would go her way. Well, tonight, she was going to give her what she wanted.

"Alright, Uno. If I'm still here when you leave, let me know, so I can walk you to your car."

"I'm straight." Uno turned and sashayed off. *'Fuck that bitch.'* She said to herself and never looked back.

191

"It is what it is." Kay mumbled to herself for the millionth time since she left California to come to Georgia. With thoughts of what transpired the last time she saw Spade on her mind, she rolled her bags toward the rental car company she would be using. "How in the fuck can I be feeling a nigga so much?" She shook her head at her damn self. She and Spade weren't even dealing with each other for a full week, and here she was catching flights to settle beef. The crazy part about it, when she was popping up, Spade had no idea she was coming. She didn't even know if he wanted to see her after the way she acted the night the shooting took place at Cez's spot.

That night when they left Cez's spot, it was her Spade, Nunu, and Sen in her car. Kay was pissed off on how Spade and his brother jumped on her friend. That shit wasn't even called for in her opinion. On top of that, he demanded that she took him and his mean ass brother to their hotel. No matter how pissed she was she was still feeling his sexy ass, and she didn't want him to flip more than he already had. They pulled up to the hotel. Kay parked at the entrance.

"What you parking here for? Pull in visitor parking and come up, we need to talk." Spade said.

"Nah. I was just bringing you back like you asked me. We ain't got nothing to talk about." Kay snapped back.

While Kay and Spade were going back and forth, Sen had his hand between Nunu's thighs massaging her pussy. And she was letting him. Sen didn't know what had come over him. Maybe it was the large of amount of Hennessy he consumed, but he wanted to fuck her. He believed that she would let him.

"Look, I ain't coming up. We ain't got shit to talk about, Spade. You ain't my man." Kay spat. Spade wanted to choke her ass up, but he wasn't in the business to press no bitch. Kay wanted to fall back on him, then he would fall back on her punk ass too.

"Baby girl, I'm going to give you that. Have a nice fucking life." With that, he climbed out the car and slammed the fuck out of her door. Kay's heart felt a sting. She didn't expect him to give up that easily, but he had.

"Comeback." Sen mouthed to Nunu and she nodded her head that she would. When Sen got out the car. Kay didn't even wait for Nunu to get out and get in the front seat, she pulled off.

"Fuck." She hit her hand on the steering wheel. The way she got at Spade, she didn't do nothing but hurt her own feelings. Deep down, she wanted to go back and hear him out, but she was too stubborn. That was a month ago, and now she was catching flights to see her man.

Kay pulled up into the W in Bankhead and waited for valet to assist her. There were two cars in front of her. While she waited, she thought it was a good time to let Spade know that she was out there.

*Kay: This is Kay. I'm out here at the W in Buckhead. Can I see you in a couple of hours? Please.* She held her breath once she hit send on her cellphone. The moment the text

"Gotdamn, Jess. You ain't playing with the dick." Spade growled. He and Jess were in her living room. Her man was out of town. She was sucking his dick so gotdamn good he was ready to scream like a bitch. His mouth was dry from being opened.

Jess's eyes never left his. The ugly faces Spade was making turned her on even more. Spade's hand was planted on the top of her head. She was topping him to where he could feel the back of her throat. Spit dripped from the sides of her mouth. She gagged making more spit. Jess took his dick from her mouth and began teasing him by slapping it all over her face. She put it back in her saliva-filled mouth and quickly removed it. Jerking his dick, she gave his balls the attention they deserved. With the noises Spade was making, she knew she was doing a good job. Mmmmm... she moaned, and she licked and sucked all over his balls. Sucking Spade's dick was one of her favorite hobbies. She knew he loved head just as much as she loved giving it to him, so she would do it until he came. She didn't care if he wasn't hers, and she had a man of her own. She loved Spade.

"Put it back in your mouth. Make me bust, girl." Spade demanded. His voice was raspy, and he sounded so sexy to her. Jess did as she was instructed. She sucked him until he came. He shot it all over her face.

"Damn, you make a nigga feel good." He admitted looking at her. She smiled. Some of his semen got in her mouth. Jess licked her lips. "Go clean your face. I want some pussy." He told her.

195

Spade was butt naked, laid back on Jess's bed when she came out of the bathroom. He felt her presence, but he was tripping off the text he received. He didn't know if he wanted to respond. He chose to read it later. It had been a month since she acted like one of the bitches who thought they had a dick. He concluded that she was the type that only wanted a nigga for dick and to occupy her time when she felt like she wanted to be bothered. Spade didn't fuck with bitches like that. "Ohhh." His mouth formed into an O. "That's why she's out here." He now remembered. His pops hit him up a couple of weeks ago telling him that if he was ever presented with a proposition from any member of The BGB Crew to turn it down. He learned that his dad and Kay's aunt were messing around back in their days. Her folks got at his pops for a favor, and the favor was to not do business with her daughter or nieces. Judah's promise would never be broken. She had his word. *'Slick bitch'* he thought now even madder at her. She only hit him up because she wanted something.

Jess made her way to the side of the bed. When Spade looked up and saw her standing there with her almost perfect body, his dick hardened. Jess was pretty. She was one of those high yellow chicks with pretty hair and a nice body. Standing at an even 5ft, shaped like a coke bottle she turned niggas heads. The only flaw she had was her missing left breast and the scar it left from being removed. The 27-year-old was diagnosed with breast cancer last year. Spade paid her well, so she had the money to get her breast replaced, but she didn't want to. Jess said her seeing the scar every day was her inspiration. She was a survivor of one of the worst diseases given to a woman. There was no way she would cover her badge of honor.

Spade licked his lips as he took her all in. She pushed her hair behind her ears.

196

"Climb on this dick, shawty." He sat his phone on the nightstand. Fuck Kay.

"I thought you'd never ask." Once on top, she rode him like a stallion.

**Part 2**

*Character Take Over*

Spade had me fucked all the way up. It had been two hours since I texted his ass letting him know that I was in the A. I had to call Uno and Nunu on three-way to let them know what he did. I didn't call Dez because she had been asking me damn near every other day had I got at Spade about the business she wanted to do with him. If she knew I was coming to Atlanta, her ass would try to come with me. I wasn't out here on business. I was out here to apologize to the man I couldn't stop thinking about. I did not know what Spade did to me, but deep down I was looking forward to being that future he kept claiming me to be. When he didn't respond to my text, I wanted to say fuck him and do me. I knew a couple of people that I went to college with who relocated to Atlanta. I could easily hit them up and still enjoy my three days. First, I wanted to get my cousins opinion on what I should do.

"First off, bitch. How in the hell did you up and leave to go to Atlanta and not tell nobody?" Nunu fussed.

"She told me." Uno replied.

"Why you didn't tell me? How you know I didn't want to come? Plus, I need to watch your back."

"No, you just wanted to go so you can go and fuck on his brother again. Bitch, stop fronting." Uno teased and I laughed.

"I ain't got to lie to kick it. If I wanted the dick, I know how to fly out and get it like Kay did."

"Ohhhh…" Uno clowned.

"Fuck you. Should I pull up to his spot or not?" I asked. I walked over to the bar and made myself a cup of Hennessy and tonic water.

"If you went to Atlanta to see him pull up. Like I told you before, if you like him then act like it. You did act like a bitch that night." Nunu replied. She had told me that after we pulled off. She said that she could sense that Spade was feeling me, and she knew I was feeling him too so even if he did make me mad, I should have still heard him out. That night when she said it, I wasn't trying to hear the bullshit but as the days passed by, and I had calmed down, I understood what she was saying. I put the cup to my mouth and took a gulp.

"Uno, what you think?"

"I think go. If he acts funny, then leave that nigga where he at." She paused for a moment. "That down south dick got you crazy. I cannot believe you took your ass down there, fa real. I thought you were bullshitting."

"He didn't reply to my text. That ain't acting funny?" I wanted to know ignoring Uno's last comment. By now, I was in the room looking through the clothes I hung up in the closet when I got there.

"Not really. Funny acting is if he diss you for another bitch." Uno retorted.

The phone got quiet. I had already made up my mind that I was going to show up at his gambling spot. However, I was thinking about how the shit was going to turn out.

"I'm going." I said.

"Good. Be sure to send us your location. Anything go down, hit up Juice." Juice was Papa's friend's nephew. I had forgotten he lived in the A. Juice was a sexy nigga. We fucked a few times in the past, but it wasn't nothing like that with us.

"I will." I replied. "Uno." I said.

"Yeah?"

"Have you talked to Freda?" Uno told us how Freda tried to play her for that model bitch. I knew she was mad and felt some kind of way. She wasn't used to females curving her. Plus, I could tell that she liked the girl by how she talked about her all the time.

"Girl, she texted me while we were on the phone. I pulled a Spade and didn't even reply back to her ugly ass."

"Ahhhhhhhhh." Nunu burst out. "You stupid. That girl is not ugly. You just mad, hoe. You found someone to play you at your own game."

"I ain't mad about shit. I'm Uno. Kay, let us know what happened. I got another call coming in."

"Who Freda?" Nunu asked.

"Girl, she hung up." I said when I looked at my phone, and it was just us two on the line.

"Kay, are you going to ask old boy about what Dez trying to do?"

"I don't know. Papa said no. I still don't know why, but we will see."

We talked a few more minutes. After Nunu helped me decide on what I should wear, we hung up.

Spade still hadn't hit me back, but it was cool. I decided to come to his spot and if I ran into him, no matter if, he was with a bitch or not, I was going to step to him. Thanks to Cez I was able to get the location before I left California. The building was about 20minutes from my hotel. I pulled up the address on Google Maps, so I already knew what it looked like. It was located in Buckhead a popular area in Georgia. When I left the hotel, the sun was going down and by the time I pulled in front of the red brick building it was pitch black. It was three stories. The parking structure was on the side of the building. I pulled up and was stopped by a black husky dude standing about 6'3 with dreads. I rolled my window down and when he approached, I sneezed. Georgia weather was messing with my allergies. The guy chuckled.

"You are supposed to wait until I asked for the code." He shook his head. And directed me to move forward. It took a split second for me to catch on. Me sneezing was the code to get in. Well, that worked out.

The parking lot was close to full. The majority of cars were foreign, there were a few simple cars taking up parking too.

I parked between a white Range Rover and a black Maybach. I sat there for a minute, to freshen up. I applied my favorite body spray, a little perfume, and some red lipstick. Nunu helped me decide on wearing my black Levi's, I paired it with a black one sleeve sheer bodysuit. I wore black knee-high boots with a red Chanel belt to match my red Chanel purse. Because I wanted to look extra cute, I got a 24-inch curly strawberry-blonde weave installed the day before. Since I didn't know if I would be searched or not, I left my gun in my center console, but I had a razor blade stashed on the side of my hair and a box cutter in my bra. I tossed a piece of gum in my mouth.

When I climbed out of the rental, I was greeted by the cold chilly weather. I sneezed.

"Bless you, baby girl." A deep voice said. I turned and looked, but didn't see the person I was to thank. Therefore, I yelled my appreciation over my shoulder. I put on my runway model walk and headed for the black iron door across the parking lot. I figured the door would be locked, but I tried to open it, anyway. When it didn't open, I knocked.

"Is this your first time here?" It was the same voice that blessed me. I turned around.

"Oh, my God." I smiled big and so did he. It was Juice. Papa's friend's nephew and my old fling.

"Kay Money, what are you doing here?" He asked.

"Trying to have a little fun. And you?"

"I work here a few days out of the month, but tonight I came to try my luck." Juice was cute. He was average height for a guy, with a body of a nigga that worked out faithfully. His toasted-almond complexion was blemish free. When he smiled it was bright, but I noticed he had clear braces. He still looked good, though. I always found myself lost in Juice's big brown bedroom eyes.

"You are staring, can a nigga get a hug?" Without saying a word, I walked right into his arms. He rubbed his hands up and down my back. "I got a feeling you are going to be my good luck. Let's go take these niggas money." He kissed me on the top of my head. Juice had always been a smooth talker, and was gentle when he dealt with me. He was cool as fuck. Juice was doing him and so was I, neither of us, looking for nothing extra besides company and a good time. I was the first to pull away from our hug. My phone vibrated, so I took a minute to retrieve it. It was a text from Nunu asking if I made it. I replied with a yes. I had sent the address before I left. The next text had me laughing. I was going to beat her ass. She texted me asking if I ran into Juice. I didn't even reply. She was the most overprotective and sensitive of the crew.

"So, you really work here, or did Nunu send you?"

"Both." He grabbed my hand. "Let's go." We walked inside.

The Money House is what I called my spot. I had been in business for over five years and became rich in three. I didn't have to be a part of the dope game. The Money House made sure I ate and ate again. The only reason why I was still a part of the game was because it was a family business. Just like my daddy and brothers wouldn't leave me hanging, I couldn't leave them hanging. If it weren't for my little sister Hope and my right-hand, Jess, there was no way I could run my spot and play my position in the family business. Hope and Jess made sure my shit was running smoothly. Hope was in charge of the cash flow, and Jess in charge of making sure the money was washed clean. I'm a gambler and I love everything about it. Taking risk to get rich had always been a thing for me.

"Alright, babe. I'm about to go downstairs and eat." Jess said. We had been in my office for the last hour going over paperwork. I glared at her.

"My bad. It's hard to turn it on and off so quick." She admitted. We had just gotten done fucking at her house almost two hours ago, she must've still been in the moment calling me baby. I'm fairly sure muthafuckas knew we were fucking, but they never questioned me about my business and if they came at her, Jess would check their asses and then tell me so I could check them. Jess and I have been friends since high school. She was the new girl in school who was dirty, but she was far from scary. When the kids would diss her, she would try to beat their asses. Once, this nigga from the football field tried her. When she stepped to him, he slapped the shit out of her, knocking her glasses off. My brother didn't know what the fuck was going on. I ran off the football field so fast. I beat that nigga up. I fucked him up so bad that the coach kicked me off the team. I was suspended for a few days and when I came back to school Jess stepped to me asking me why I fought for her. I told her the truth. She was cool. We had two periods together, and we sat right next to each other. Both of us were smart, so in class there was always a friendly competition on who would finish first and get the best grade. We ended up becoming good friends when her pops started working for my pops. She came around to the functions, and she wasn't 'Dirty Jess' anymore. It was her senior year in high school when I realized how fine she was. I took her virginity. And she got pregnant. It wasn't the first time. Jess had been pregnant by me a few times. However, I wasn't trying to be her baby's daddy or her man. We agreed on abortions every time. In fact, she had a white boy that she was engaged to, but that didn't stop us from doing what we did.

"Bring me some wings and a coke." I told her. On the third level of my building, Miss Wanda cooked wings, shrimp, catfish, fries, and shit like that to sell to the gamblers. My guests could bring their own drinks, but we also had a bar on that floor too. There was a lounge area where a nigga could kick back and rest if needed or chill until they felt like gambling again.

"I got you." She walked out of my office.

I got up from my seat and stretched. I walked across the office and stood in front of my top-of-the-line security cameras. It showed the parking lot, and every room except the bathroom. It was so clear, it was like I was right there in the room.

206

"I know the fuck she ain't. She must think I am a joke." I fumed. There on the muthafucking camera was Kay's ass. She was standing at one of my dice tables with my worker Juice. He had just had her blow on his dice. Juice rolled them and then slapped her ass.

"I will beat this bitch's ass." I spat. Before I knew it, I was headed out of my office and to the third level of my spot. Kay's stupid ass had me fucked up.

When I made it to the table, her back was facing me. She didn't see when I pulled Juice away.

"I don't know how y'all know each other, but she is off limits." I whispered in his ear.

"She is like family." He responded.

"So why the fuck are you rubbing her ass?" I snapped. I could feel the veins in my neck threatening to burst out.

"Cause I didn't know she had a nigga." He responded. And that told me right there they were fucking. He could tell what I was thinking. "Spade, it ain't like that with us. I ain't seen her in a few years."

"So-" My words were cut off. Kay had walked up. If looks could whoop a bitch's ass, I swear shawty would've been beat the fuck up. I took a step toward her. I was all up in her face. I leaned into her ear. "You think I'm a muthafucking joke. I will hurt you." I looked into her eyes, and I could tell she was either in her feelings or nervous.

"Can we go somewhere to talk?" She asked.

"No, but you can leave." I told her. I was dead ass serious. Kay looked around as if she were trying to see if anyone was watching us. She was embarrassed. Feelings probably hurt, but I didn't give a fuck.

"I guess I deserve your ass to kiss. It's cool, Spade." Her voice cracked, and that shit touched me, but I didn't show any emotion. I had concluded Kay was with the bullshit. I was daring her to say anything to Juice. I would've snatched her ass up quick. Lucky for her, she didn't even look his way. She stormed off. Juice went to walk after her, but I grabbed him by his arm.

"She's family man. If anything happens to her, her Papa would have my head." He told me.

"Did you tell her to come out here? Y'all together? She told you about me and her?"

"Nah. Nunu told me she was coming here and asked me did I know about the spot. I told her I worked here, and she told me that Kay was coming and to make sure she was safe. I was already here when she called me. I stayed in the parking lot until she came. Kay didn't know." I gave him a head nod.

"Alright. I got her. Gone and do you." I wasn't about to let him go after her. I would have to kill both of their asses if they ended up fucking.

"You didn't see me calling you?" I spoke over her shoulder. She was sitting on the third level with a plate of catfish and fries in her face. I don't know how long she had the food, but she hadn't touched it. The glass in her hand was half-gone. I had one of my boys to follow her when she left. I wanted to make sure she made it back to the hotel safely, but her ass didn't even go back to her hotel. Kay didn't acknowledge me. I was cool with that. After snapping off on her in my spot, I was certain she was going to snap back on me. I took a seat on the empty stool next to her. She didn't even look my way.

"What are you doing in Georgia?" I asked her. She looked at me. Her eyes were low and red. She either was high or had been crying.

"Now, I'm minding my gotdamn business." She cut her eyes at me. Kay was so pretty. I loved the reddish blonde hair on her. I was mad as fuck at how she got at a nigga that night, I had to whoop on one of her niggas. I was done with her ass when she sent me on, but seeing her tonight reminded me of how much I fucked with her.

"Kay, what you come here for?" I asked again. The waitress came and sat another glass filled with brown in front of her. She picked it up and gulped down half of it. She then looked at me.

"I came because I couldn't stop thinking about you. I came to say I was sorry for how I acted." Damn. That shit touched me. She sounded sincere, but a part of me kept thinking she still had motives.

"You didn't come to get on my good side to try to get me to do business with your crew?" She frowned, looking at me like she didn't know what I was talking about, but then her face changed. She knew what I was talking about.

"Fuck, no. I don't care about that. I didn't even know if I was going to get at you about that. I came because I miss you and I want you. I never did no shit like this before. I don't know what kind of life you-" Her words were cut off when I put my lips on hers. I slid my tongue in her mouth and she and I shared a long, passionate kiss. The way our tongues slowly danced, I was convinced that this woman had a piece of me I had never given no one. The way I was feeling about Kay Spade and what I wanted with her was something deep. I hadn't even known her a full month and only spent time with her a handful of times, and the girl had me wanting to build with her. Kay was the first to break our kiss. I used my fingers to wipe the side of my mouth, never breaking our gaze.

"Come back to my hotel with me." She said. I gave her a half smile. Shaking my head no. Kay put one hand on her hip, batting her long lashes. Her sexy ass was a handful.

"Spade. Either you are coming back to my room, or I am going to your house. You choose."

"Fuck you thought, Kay Spade. You are in my city. I ain't about to have you in no room. We're going to my spot, so you pack your shit. You are staying with me." I told her.

"How long are you here for?" I asked as I am walking her to her car.

"Three days."

"Change that flight. I need you here for at least a week." She hit the alarm on her rental car and walked up to a red Mustang. I opened her door.

"Kay Spade, did you hear what I said?"

"Yes, Spade. I will change my flight. Now follow me, hurry up. I want some dick." She slid in the car and looked up at me, blowing me a kiss. I leaned down, planted a kiss on her lips and shut the door. Kay had me on some other shit. It was too good to be true. When I felt like that, something bad always happened. I shook off my thoughts and thought about something positive, like the million-dollar construction building in Inglewood, California I was considering.

When we made it to our destination, I was a few steps away from taking Kay down to my pad. The way she was walking in those knee-high boots made my dick extra hard. Kay was sexy as fuck. The only thing that stopped me from taking her down was the song Locked Up by Akon began to play, letting me know that my pops was calling me.

"Kay Spade. I'm about to go on the balcony and take this call from my pops." She looked up and gave me a head nod. "Can I get a quickie when I come back?" I asked as I eyed her with lust-filled eyes. Kay was so gotdamn sexy to me.

"You can have whatever you like, Daddy." She replied with a grin on her face. I gave her a reverse nod. I answered my phone.

"Sup, Pops?"

"Lucas is in Cali. What the fuck is he doing in California by himself?" My father snapped.

"Man, I don't know, did you call him?" I asked annoyed. I loved my pops, but he acted like me, and Sen had to monitor our brothers like they were some fucking babies. Yeah, they were younger than us, but shit them niggas were grown.

"Yeah, I called him. His dumb ass didn't answer. Black Sam told me he exchanged numbers with Dez who is a part of The BGB Crew. What the fuck did I tell y'all? My word is worth more than a dollar."

"Pops. Chill. You are taking your shit out on the wrong nigga. I know what you told me, and when have I ever went against your word? I don't know what your son got going on, but I will find out."

There were a few moments of silence.

"Alright, son. Thanks. I told Black Sam to tell that little nigga I said come home. If he don't, I'm cutting him off." After that, he hung up the phone. Ever since Tone was killed, my father put the burden on me and Sen to watch over our brothers to make sure they didn't fuck around and get locked up or killed. I took a deep breath and by the time I let it out, Kay was walking onto the balcony with me. I tensed up when she placed her hand on my back.

212

"You, ok?" Her voice was soft.

"No. My pops said that Dez was having a meeting with my brother. I don't know what you guys trying to do, but my brother ain't got no say in shit."

"Excuse me?" She stepped backward and looked at me like she was insulted.

"You heard what I said." I gawked at her. Now I was starting to see why Sen ain't trust no bitches.

"First off, I don't need your family to eat. With or without my crew, I'm eating. Nigga, I ain't no stupid bitch. I'm a business owner, and more. Didn't I tell your paranoid ass that I didn't come out here for that? Didn't I?" She was pissed, and I could tell. I also could tell that she was sincere.

"So you don't know why Dez is meeting with my brother? Would she go behind your aunt's back and try to do business even though your aunt shut it down?"

"Who's my aunt and what are you talking about?"

"My father told us that he used to mess with your aunt Jo back in the day. She got at him and said that if any member from The BGB Crew tried to proposition him for business, to shut it down. And she wanted y'all to know that she blocked it."

She stared in a daze.

"Aunt Jo." She whispered. "Humph." She shook her head. Kay looked at me.

"The BGB Crew choose not to do business with your family. If my aunt said no, then that is what it is. Look, I will sort this out when I get home."

"Which is a week from now." I walked up to her. She looked at me.

"If you keep thinking I'm on some sneaky shit then I will bounce ASAP. I'm not on none of that."

I pulled her into me and wrapped my arms around her waist.

"You ain't going nowhere. I apologize." I kissed her lips, slipping my tongue in her mouth.

"Spade I, I, ohhh I can't take it! This, Ah ah, this is torture."

Spade had me bent over on his couch, with one leg propped up. My titties were dangling over the edge, eager to be touched. I allowed him to fully undress and position me exactly how he wanted to.

"Fuck me, Spade." I tried to tell him, but he hushed me by sticking his wet fingers in and out of my pussy, and then in my mouth. I could taste my pre-cum and didn't mind sucking every inch of it off. That made me crave him even more.

Spade removed his fingers out of my mouth, grabbed a handful of my hair, pulling me up toward his chest and whispered in my ear.

"Shhhh. Trust me. I got you, ma. Let me handle this pussy how it deserves it. It's all about you tonight." His tongue slowly slithered from my neck up to my ears and back down again. He slid those same two fingers I had just sucked clean with my tongue, around my belly, and back between the folds of my pretty shaved kitty. Spade had my insides wetter than Lake Tahoe. I was dying to fuck every inch of him, but first I had to be obedient and allow him to have his way with me.

"Mmm... Spadeeee, you are making me hotter!" He felt me trembling from his warm touch. My leg got weaker. After releasing the grip on my hair, he wrapped his arm around my belly to help hold me up and keep me balanced. Both of my hands were now squeezing his arm. I was going crazy from his touch. A part of me wanted him to let me fall to the ground. I couldn't take that torture any longer, but at the same time my mind wanted him to keep holding me up while his large strong fingers fucked me good. I was about to explode, and he hadn't even undressed himself yet.

"Bab..eee! I'mmmm baeee.. mmmm."

I couldn't get a damn word out. I went from mumbling to moaning and back to deep, heavy breathing every time I felt the heat from his breath tickle the hairs on my neck. He made me crave for the dick. Somehow, he managed to grip my breast with the same arm I was squeezing, sending me out of my mind. Now I was a senseless finger fucked whipped, bitch.

"Your nipples hard like this for me, Kay?"

"Oh, babe. Don't stop." I pleaded.

"Answer me, Kay? Tell me it's hard for me." He rotated his fingers faster on my swollen clitoris.

"Ahh ah. Yes, babe. Yesss. This pussy is hungry for Ahhhhhhh. Shit, you about to make me, me, cummmm."

My body jerked, shook, and shivered. I surely wasn't holding myself up at all at this moment. I could feel Spade sucking the hell out of my skin on my shoulder with small bites as he slightly lifted me off the ground.

*'Who cums in the air?'* I thought to myself as I tried to catch my breath.

Spade turned me around, lifted up my limped body and carried me to the bathroom where a bubble bath awaited us. There were white candles and red rose petals throughout. He even had some rose petals in the bathtub.

"Aww, baby. Is all of this for me? I want you to get in, too. I want you to give me a bath."

"Shit. I like the whole setup but fuck, I want you to bathe me." I grumbled. I was worn the fuck out.

"Relax, Kay. I got you." Was his reply.

Spade lowered me into the tub and laid my head back on the edge. The water was nice and warm. He took a washcloth, soaped it up and began gently washing me all over, sending electric shocks through my body. *What the fuck was he doing to me?* I asked myself. I had never experienced this feeling before. No one has ever taken their time with me and catered to my body as he did. When he reached my breast and vagina, Spade gave them both an extra squeeze and massage. They were both overly sensitive to the touch in those areas.

"Baby, please take your clothes off. Get in with me."

I whined and begged, but Spade ignored me. He sat the small towel down, brought his hands up to my face and massaged my cheekbones while looking me in my eyes. I couldn't resist bringing my hands up to his handsome face, slightly pulling him in closer to me. I had to kiss him. I planted three soft kisses on him. The third time, I didn't move my head back. Spade parted his lips as I did mine. Together our tongues met, and danced to their very own rhythm. I could taste the alcohol on his breath from earlier. He roughly wrapped his hand around the back of my neck, pushing my face in closer to his as I sucked his tongue. Spade broke the kiss, stood up, grabbing both of my hands and bringing my wet dripping body close to his. He kissed me again and picked me up. I eagerly wrapped my legs around his waist. I felt my pussy rub against his belt buckle, and I couldn't help but to move my hips. His kisses were addictive, and I wanted more. Spade carried me into his bedroom, laid me out on the bed, and stood back to admire his future wife. Me!

He was in love with every curve on my body. I could tell.

I bit my lip as I watched him grip my legs and pull me to the edge of the bed, bend my legs back and had a face-off with my pussy.

I always got what I wanted, and right now, I wanted my cum sliding down his throat. The thought of it almost drove me crazy.

"Ah Ah, Ahhhhh. Ssssssss. Oh, baby!"

Spade kissed me everywhere but on my clit. I felt his sweet lips softly kissing me on the left thigh. I couldn't take it anymore! I smashed his face right in the center. His tongue slithered across my clit and then down to the crack of my ass.

He repeated that a few times before licking the kitty. I could feel his head moving side to side, and his tongue felt warm going in and out of me.

"Ummm mmmmm. Yes, babe. Just like that. Suck this pussy, baby. Oh oh ummmm. I-- never-- been-- wetter-- than

I am right now! You're so fucking good to this pussy. You want this cum, Spade?" I asked, on the verge of another eruption. I should have never asked. What he did with his tongue next made me think of a racecar in overdrive.

I tried to squirm away and push his head away from my center, but Spade locked both of my arms down by my hips. I allowed his tongue to work its magic freely, causing me to hit a high soprano note. Minutes later, just when I thought there was nothing left in me, I flowed like a river in his mouth.

"That's it baby girl, feed daddy." I heard in between slurps.

"Pleaseee, Spade. Let me go. I can't take anymore, baby." My body was shaking out of control, and I had no breath left in me.

Spade got up to give me a break, so I thought. He left out of the room and seconds later walked back into the bedroom with a lit blunt dangling from his lips. Damn, he was so sexy. I didn't think I could cum again, but I damn sure was about to have him feed me the dick on a platter.

I wanted to give Kay a break and allow her to catch her breath, but when she got up, she crawled back to the corner of the bed and started reaching for my belt. I hit the blunt a few more times, and took my shirt off while she wrestled with my jeans until she dropped them both to the ground, not giving me a chance to step out of them. Kay gripped my dick and began with nice and long strokes. Not once looking at me, she spoke directly to my dick.

"My pussy needs you. I will do whatever you want, but first I'm about to make you cum on my titties. Umm. You look tasty."

Kay had her legs bent back sitting on them, both hands were gripping my dick. She looked so beautiful, handling me the way she was. I took a couple hits again on the blunt before she opened her mouth and took me in. I slid in and out. Kay would sometimes gag but never stopping her steady pace.

"Ummm. You like fucking my face? Huh, this is what you been waiting for?"

She asked between jerking and slobbering me down. Kay removed her hands and now was on all four. She slightly tilted her head to the side, mouth wide-open, lips covering her teeth. She held her breath, suctioning me in, damn near down her throat.

"Fuck, Kay. Damn, ma."

I grabbed the back of her head and jammed my dick in and out of her mouth fast. I gave her so much pre-come that it surprised me that she wasn't choking.

"Ummmm, baby. You like that? I want to be your sex slave."

She jerked and spit on my dick and allowed me to tittie fuck her. Kay slapped my dick all over her titties, and then back down her throat. The rotation was mind blowing, but I didn't want to cum yet. That good pussy was calling me. Kay stood to kiss me. I lifted her leg up and broke into her walls. My hands gripped her ass as she rocked her hips with me.

"I love the way your dick feels inside of me. Ahhh. I'm in heaven, baby." She laid her head on my shoulder with her legs gripping around my waist rotating her hips. I helped glide my dick in and out of her until I felt too weak to hold out any longer.

"Don't put me down, baby. This feels so good. Umm. You're handling this pussy like a pro. That's it. Give that cum just like that, babeee. Yesssss, umm just like that." I could feel her pussy muscles squeezing me.

"Fuck, ma. I can't take this shit." I blurted out. After holding her up for a few more minutes, I pulled out of her, turned her around and positioned her on all four at the edge of the bed. I used the tip of my dick to massage her clit before ramming it back into her. Kay made her ass clap back on me with every death stroke I gave her.

"Yesssss!!!! Fuck me, baby. Fuck meeee. Pound me harder with that big cock. Fuck me harder, until I can't remember my name. Mmmmmm ahh ah mmm!" I fucked her a little more and in a few swift motions I turned her over, wrapped her legs around my neck, entering her again.

"This pussy making me weak, ma. Oh, you gonna throw shit back like that? I'm about to teach this pussy a lesson. I'm the boss in the bedroom."

"Yes you are, daddy. You're the boss, babeeee!" I crossed her legs, pushed her knees into her chest and switched gears. Kay's face contorted. I felt her punching at me, but I was about to drop my load into my future.

"Cum with me, Kay. You can do it, ma. Give all you have. Fuckkkkk."

I shook and shook until I released every drip into her. Weakly I fell onto the bed but to my surprise, Kay got up with a slight smirk on her face, crawled on top of me and brought my dick back to life as she sucked all our cum off my dick.

"Damn, bae. Ah fuck." She had my dick standing strong. Kay climbed on top and eased down on me. She was still warm, dripping wet and tight. She stood on her tippy- toes and bounced up and down. I almost lost it when she spread her ass cheeks, and leaned back while bouncing down hard on me. I had to gain some control. I reached out to grab her titties. Squeezing her nipples, I rotated them in my hands. It only made her ride me faster.

"That's right, baby. Ride this dick. It's all yours. You're my future." I squeezed her ass and smacked it. Kay rode me going 95 South until I came again.

She fell out on top of me, leaving my dick still inside of her pulsating. A couple of seconds later, I heard light snores coming from her.

A few words of 2Pac came to mind.

"All I need in this life of sin, is me and my girlfriend."

I pulled the covers up, wrapped my arms around her and lay there in silence until I was off to a deep sleep.

# Back in Cali

## Dez

"What's up, Black Sam?" I greeted, taking a seat on the empty patio chair next to them. Black Sam and the cute nigga next to him visited Bandz Strip Club that I owned with my cousins. It was perfect timing, too. I was trying to wait to see if Nunu or Kay got at the Jank's they fucked with, but I didn't trust they would come through. Especially since I found out that Kay dipped to the A and didn't even let me know she was going until she was already there. I didn't even trip, though. I wasn't about to let my momma or no one else stand in my way of hooking up with the Jank Boys. Doing business with them would take over the west and south. We'd be on our cartel tip, but my cousins acted like they were too stupid to understand that. To be honest, I was the one who got us where we are today. If I left it up to them, they would still be listening to Papa busting credit cards and setting niggas up by getting their whips stolen and other petty shit. I was the one that said let's stack first and splurge later. I'm the one that took the 26k we made off plastic and stepped to Vegas for some work. Vegas didn't like that a bitch could come to him without consignment, so he taxed me each time, but I didn't give a fuck. At the end of the day, my crew and I worked hard for ours. The dope game is how we copped the mansion, our business, whips, funded Uno's career, and more. The dope game is how we copped this strip club I'm sitting in right muthafucking now. I wasn't leaving the game until I was six feet under and even then, my legacy would live on through the name I made for myself in the streets.

"What's up, Dez. I see y'all remodeled. It looks good." Sam complimented. My waitress walked up and the young cutie that was with Black Sam slapped her on the ass. When the bitch giggled, I got mad.

"No touching on any staff unless you are paying." I said to him. Slowly he peeled his eyes from the waitress and looked at me. From my side view, I could see the waitress set down the bottle of Don Julio and Moët that I told her to bring over. Leaving the ice bucket and a few glasses, she scurried off.

"I don't take orders from nobody. I do what I want."

I burst into a fit of laughter. The seriousness on his face was too fucking funny. Of course, the nigga didn't know who I was. I may not whoop a nigga, but I would pull the trigger just as quick as the next street thug. I wasn't even mad at his disrespect. It was nothing.

"Man, get away from me." He said annoyed.

"Black Sam, check your boy before he gets fucked up." I stood up. He only looked at me. The young nigga was unfazed.

"Lo, this is the owner. Dez, this is Jank Lo who is my nephew." *Cute cocky muthafucka,* I thought. With a smirk on his face, Lo looked me up and down.

"It's always the cute bitches that gotta be all tough with the smart-ass mouths." He shook his head. Lo picked up the bottle from the table and popped the top. His rude ass put the bottle to his mouth and guzzled. When he was done, he burped.

"Man, sit your ass down." He ordered.

"Boy, fuck you. And since you think you the shit, let me see what that dick does." I went into my back pocket and tossed a card on the table. When I got to the exit of VIP, I looked back. Black Sam was making himself a drink and Lo was looking at me. I gave him the bird and he started laughing.

***

God is good, I said over a thousand times since I left Bandz. I don't even believe in God but the way I just so happened to run into a Jank boy, and the nigga called me not even an hour after I left the spot, I knew it was a blessing. Fuck what they thought. Homie called me. I normally don't answer NO CALLER ID calls, but I had a feeling it was him. Lo said he wanted to take me to dinner. I was all excited about him taking me out and for some reason I don't think he was trying to impress me. I had a feeling Black Sam told him who I was and what I was about, and dude wanted to talk business. Call it my gut intuition.

He told me he wanted to go to Lawry's Steakhouse. I was game, since I loved steak. I hadn't eaten all day, so I was going to fuck some food up. For dinner, I kept it cute and simple. I wore a pair of high-rise boot cut denim jeans, a tight fitted V-neck shirt and a pair of 6-inch red bottoms. My hair was in a high ponytail with a Chinese cut bang. I made sure to wear my gold hoops, diamond necklace, tennis bracelet, two diamond rings on each finger, and my Rolex watch. I ran to the west wing of the house to tell Nunu I was leaving. I could've called or texted, but I wanted her to tell me how I looked. Nunu's door was halfway opened, so I walked in. I knew she didn't have company because I wasn't alerted by the security camera, and I didn't see any unfamiliar cars in the driveway. Besides the night light, Nunu's room was dark. Her bed was unmade. There was a box of crackers on her nightstand and a 7-Up. When I heard her in the bathroom praying to the porcelain God, I knew the bitch must've had a hangover.

"What you drink?" I asked, standing by the bathroom door.

I frowned. She was still throwing up. Nunu couldn't respond. My girl was really sick. I walked over to her linen cabinet in the corner of her bathroom and grabbed a clean white washcloth to run some cold water on it. I went and stood by the door until Nunu got up. When she was done, she flushed the toilet and looked at me. Tears were running down her face. I walked over and handed her the towel.

"Did you take a BC podwer?" She nodded and forcefully wiped the tears from her eyes. "Why are you crying?" I asked. The way she looked at me was strange.

"Nothing, tired. Tired of getting drunk, tired of everything." She said, and walked to the room. I watched as she climbed in the bed and pulled the covers over her head.

"Get some rest, big head. I am about to go out to eat with my friend."

"Be careful and send me addresses." She demanded. I told her I will and that I would check on her. I then left to go meet

Lo. As I was walking out, I ran into Uno. We hadn't really seen each other in about a week. The couple of times we were around each other more than a minute, we barely talked. I couldn't believe she was mad because I handled Mina how I did. I loved my cousin, but I was not about to kiss her ass or apologize. I threw my head up and hit her with a what's up and kept pushing.

"Hey, girl." I heard her say. I noticed her voice was a little chirpier, but I didn't care. All I gave a fuck about at the moment was linking up with Lo.

"Hey, boo. How are you doing?" I asked, walking into Nunu's room. I sat on the chair next to her bed. The crackers and the soda were a give-away that she wasn't feeling any better than yesterday. Nunu believed that she had food poisoning.

"I'm good. Oh, my God. What is that you have on?" She tossed the covers off her, jumped from the bed, and ran straight to the bathroom. I know that bitch wasn't clowning my perfume.

"Ugh. I'm about to go to this meet and greet!" I yelled and hurried out the room. I had a weak stomach and if I stayed in there any longer, then I knew I would start throwing up myself.

I walked down the hallway and stopped to look in the full-length mirror on the wall. I was looking fine as fuck in my lime green bodysuit and white high top Air Force Ones. I wore an oversized black Prada bag and although it was night, I covered my eyes with a pair of large designer shades. I took my phone and snapped a picture. Before I left, I sent a group text letting my cousins know where I was going and, of course a picture of how I was looking. I had gotten a text earlier from a DJ inviting me to a meet and greet. He said that it was a private invite, and some big timers would be in the building. I asked Go to meet me there. Besides being my assistant, he was a friend.

The venue was at this place called Warehouse LA. The spot was extremely popular. Each night there was a different theme. I knew for sure Tuesday was hip-hop, Sunday brunch and reggae, and Saturday was a mixture of r& b and hip-hop. Tonight was Thursday, so I assumed the spot was rented to different promoters on this night. By passing the half-full parking lot, I pulled straight into valet.

"Okayyyy, bitch. Look at you with your fine ass." Go complimented. I didn't even know he was in the car behind me until I was on the sidewalk. I blushed at his compliment. Go was so extra.

"Thanks, you look cute too." I replied. He was dressed in a pair of Versace jeans, paired with a fitted T-shirt, and a pair of Prada boots. His blinged out designer belt set his outfit off right. The only jewelry was the two diamond studs in his ear, a pinky ring and a Cartier. Although he was dressed like a dude my guy still wore his Prada purse and his natural nails were in a French tip. The two of us hugged. Go took me by the hand, and we walked to the VIP line.

"What's up, Pretty Uno?" The security greeted. He was a short stocky Mexican dude. "He with you?" He asked, eying Go.

"Yes, and I'm taken." Go said.

"What your man got to do with me?" The security replied.

"Whatever." Go put his hand on his hip. "Put my number in your phone. Call me tomorrow around 12. I wanna go eat. And baby, I don't eat cheap shit." Go said.

I watched as the guard pulled out his phone and Go read off his number.

"So he your type?" I asked. Go was into niggas with money. Not the dope boys, either. He was dating executives and CEOs who cashed out on his ass.

"Girl, yeah. He's my type. That's Stevie. He's a concert promoter and event planner. I be thinking he work the door so he can flirt, but that ain't my business. His gay ass is paid." Go said. Leave it to his ass to know everything.

The venue was dimly lit with crimson and white lights to match the décor. In the center of the room were several round tables with gorgeous crimson and white centerpieces. Each table sat about six people. The female DJ was set up on a stage playing 'Soldier' by Destiny's Child. A disco ball reflected light on the dance floor creating a party vibe. A crowd of folks danced in that area while singing with the music. The DJ was rocking the house. I was definitely feeling the whole scene.

"Let's go move around. This is a meet and greet." Go said. "Uno, are you performing?" He asked.

"No." I didn't want to. I came to show my face and take a few pictures, but I wasn't performing.

"Okay, well, let me smell out the somebodies." He walked off, and I followed. We stopped by the bar and grabbed a drink. For the most part, we went around mingling, taking pictures, and drinking. I hadn't eaten since earlier, so I got tipsy pretty fast.

I had to go to the restroom. When I came out, Go was standing there with a bottle of water for me and a plate with crackers and cheese.

"Come on. I found a seat. The show is about to start." I took the water from Go and gulped it down. We made it to our seats just as the DJ announced...

"Let's give a round of an applause to our host Brazilian Doll."

"This bitch." Go said what I was thinking. When they called the hoe on stage, I wanted badly to look to see where the fuck Freda was. I knew she was there. I lied when I told my girls she texted me. She hadn't reached out, not once since she played me to the left for the hoe that was on stage.

Once the claps stopped, she talked. I blocked her out completely until that hoe announced some bullshit.

"When I added Cali as a place to have this beneficial event, I was doing it to help others. There are many people in this room that came to network with us. I saw this as an opportunity for artists, models, authors, producers, to sell themselves. I thank you all for coming. God said when you bless others, he will certainly bless you too. I was at a book signing a few days back and ran into my first love. We ended on not so good terms and I never had the courage to call her to apologize."

"This bitch is acting, with all that phony crying." Go whispered. He knew what went down, so of course he didn't like her fake ass.

"Let's go. I wonder if this bitch had the DJ to invite me." I said, as quiet as I could.

"Freda Harris, I love you. I don't care who knows." She announced.

I went to standup, but Go grabbed my arm. With tight teeth he said, "Bitch, if you let that bitch know you bothered, we will be fighting. Sit your ass down. They wanna play, let's play." I gave Go a look that said I wasn't with it, but I stayed sitting down. The first chance I got, I was out of there.

"Don't trip, friend. That bitch say the wrong thing, I will knock all this shit over." Go said. If he had too many drinks, I knew he would too.

# NUNU

## Later that night

I was next in line. My heart was threatening to jump out of my chest. I felt even sicker to my stomach than I did before I got to Target. I pulled my hat down on my head. I didn't want to be seen by no one. It would be just my luck, I knew the cashier. I didn't need anyone in my business. Some business I shouldn't even be a part of.

When it was my turn, I hurried and handed my three items directly to the cashier. She took them out of my hand. She didn't even look up at me. She rang up my three pregnancy test and gave me a total.

I swiped my card, told her to trash my receipt. I took the bag and tossed it in my oversized designer bag. I headed toward the exit.

"I can't believe I'm going through this again. Fuck, Nunu." I cursed myself. I prayed to God the entire ride over that I was just sick, but deep down I knew why.

My head was down when I was headed out of the store. I ran smack into a hard chest, causing me to step back a few feet.

"My bad." The deep voice said. I looked up at him. He was a young dude. Cute, too. My eyes landed on the chain hanging around his neck, and I had to blink twice. I couldn't take my eyes off the charm. Oh, my God. I hadn't seen that face in years. It brought back bad and vivid memories, and now I was feeling even sicker.

"You know him or something?" He held the picture of the dude up. Across his hand was RIP Tone. I felt dizzy. However, shook it quick. I had to get ready for whatever. I looked up at him.

He had a mean mug on his face. I could have kicked my own ass for leaving my gun in the car. "You know my brother?" He asked again.

"No. I ain't ever seen a piece like that. I would want one for my mother." I responded. His face softened.

"I knew that was you. I knew it!" The female voice yelled. I looked to my left, and it was Trish, she was standing in front of a basket that had Mina's son in it.

"What's up, Trish." I got ready to walk off.

"Don't what's up Trish me. Fuck you, Nunu. Fuck you BGB bitches." I stood there, staring at her. I knew she was hurt about her sister, but I didn't know who the fuck that bitch was coming at like that.

She grabbed her nephew out of the basket and ran out of the store. I looked back at dude, and he smirked before leaving behind Trish. I left out, too. I wasn't about to be up in the store like no chicken. I was outnumbered with no gun, but I was down for mine. I was glad I parked in the handicap park in front. I hit the locks on my ride and jumped in the car. I grabbed my pistol and looked out of all my windows to make sure no one was trying to creep. As I pulled out of the Target parking lot, I thought about how shit was about to get out of hand. What the fuck, I ran into Tone's brother and he was with Trish. The shit I was hit with outweighed my sickness.

I didn't want to go home, so I called Papa. I would tell him everything when I got there. He would know what to do.

"No. No. No." I panicked when I pulled up on my papa's block and saw the flashing lights. The fire trucks were further down the way, but I knew without a doubt they were at my papa's house. I drove as close as I could get. I threw my car in park. When I jumped out, I saw the paramedics pushing my papa on a gurney down the driveway. Tears clouded my vision. My heart ached. My papa, I couldn't lose him.

"What's going on?" I asked as I ran up to the truck.

"Nunu, he had a heart attack. He's still alive. Don't worry." His neighbor said. What the fuck did the bitch mean, not to worry?

"Can I ride with him?" I asked the paramedic.

"No. It's critical. We are taking him to Cedar." I watched as they put him in the back of the medic. I ran to my car.

"Why me?" I cried as I drove. It was hard for me to see because I was crying, but I couldn't stop. My papa. He was not just my granddaddy, but also the only father I had. People may judge his parenting skills, but that was their opinion on how he raised my mom and me. Papa was the perfect parent to me. I didn't care what anyone said. I needed him. I could not lose him.

On the way to the hospital, I called my Aunt Debra, Dez, Uno, and Kay. I needed them right then. I couldn't lose my papa.

Everyone was in a prayer circle. It was Nunu, Uno, Aunt Deb, and I. We were in the hospital with our heads bowed. While Debra was praying for Papa's healing and such, I was thinking about the few hours I spent with the young nigga named Lo Jank. Everything about him had a bitch mesmerized. Over dinner, he didn't waste no time getting down to business. He told me that Black Sam told him that me and my crew were the people to see in the streets. Told him that we are eating really well out here. Come to find out the nigga was out here trying to do business. He wanted to expand his organization. He told me he would front me two bricks on consignment. I laughed. I let him know straight up, my crew doesn't do consignment. We work for no one. I told him I was simply looking for a new connect. "My connect don't wanna see us eat. His bitch ass refuses to sell us over two bricks a month. And he is taxing stupid. I guess he can't stand to see bitches getting it and wants to limit what we got going. I wanna buy ten bricks. Can you handle that?"

He didn't show any emotion. While he was studying me, I glanced at the picture on his chain. It was a thick Cuban link. His charm was a diamond pendant and inside was a picture of a handsome dude. They looked just alike. "I see you looking at my chain. That's my brother. He was killed out here some time ago." I went to give my sympathy, but he cut me off. "I can get you ten bricks without a problem. The only thing is that you must cop from me. I will be your new connect. My bricks go for 38. If you are buying ten, I got you at 35 a brick." My next question was how soon I could get my shit. He told me he could have his mans out here in a few days, and he would call me. When he reached his hand out across the table, I was a little taken back by the gesture. He was old school. He wanted to shake on it. After the deal was sealed, we finished our meal and had a few drinks. "Now, let me see what that pussy do." He told me, and I smiled. Me and Lo went to his hotel and he fucked the dog shit out of me. When I say that little nigga fucked me all over that room, that is exactly what he did. Had a bitch spent. I didn't even realize I fell asleep until my phone rang back-to-back. I answered it and it was a hysterical Nunu telling me about Papa. I dressed in records time. During that time, I discovered Lo was gone. I didn't know where he went but I shot him a text letting him know that I was out and to hit me as soon as the cookies come in. I'm sure the nigga was hip to slang.

"In Jesus' name, Amen." Just as Auntie closed the prayer, my cellphone rang. I looked, and it was Lo.

"I'll be right back." I told them and walked off.

**** 

It had been a few days since Lo got at me and told me he couldn't do business with me. I was ready to go off, but he had better be glad I was in the hospital. Although I had walked to the other side, the way I was feeling I would have exploded and the entire hospital would've heard me. Through tight lips, I said, "Nigga we had a deal, we shook on it so, what the fuck you mean the deal is off?" I wanted to know. It wasn't even 72 hours since we made the deal and now the nigga was with the bullshit.

"I really ain't gotta explain, so I won't. Just know The Janks ain't doing business with The BGB at all." At first, I was thinking that maybe he heard something about my latest situation but when he mentioned The Janks wasn't doing

239

business with us, I had a feeling my momma had something to do with it. I was pissed. It wasn't even a need to get at her and trip because she wouldn't give a fuck. Kay, nor Nunu ever mentioned they got at The Janks. I was almost sure they decided not to. Probably because my mother or my papa said something in the past. I was trying my hardest not to dwell on it, but I did. I was tired of dealing with Vegas punk ass. I was going to have to figure something out. All I wanted was to be rich. My own family didn't even want to see me doing that. It ain't like I was no grimy bitch. I ate. We all ate. That's on everything I love.

I pulled up to the liquor store. I was on my way to check my trap. I needed a Swisher, so I could roll my blunt. I normally didn't hit the trap late nights, but I didn't go earlier like I was supposed to. When I pulled up to the store, I left the truck running and hopped out, making sure I hit the locks as I entered the store. I went straight to the counter and got what I came for, plus a pint of Silver Tequila Patron. Suddenly, I felt like sipping. When I stepped out the store, I looked across the street. Linda's fat ass stood in the alley looking like a big hungry hippo. She was by herself. Even if she wasn't, it wasn't going to stop me from stepping to her ass. I popped the locks on my ride and put my bag inside. I looked both ways before running across the busy street. I ran up on Linda, who walked fast into the alley. The bitch didn't even see me when she raised her blue jean dress and pissed.

"Now, what's the shit you was saying, fat hoe?" I asked, walking up. She looked up at me and I saw on her face that she was unbothered.

"Fuck you. Do I suppose to be scared?" She continued to piss.

"Nope." I walked up and she stood up.

"I know what you did. Everybody does and you going down."

Why did that bitch say that? I pulled the gun from the back of my waist and was up on her so quick.

Bam. Bam. Bam. I hit her over the head three times before the big bitch fell to her knees. I then pistol-whipped her. When she fell in her own piss, I stomped that bitch. I really wanted to kill her, but the damage I did; I believed would keep her mouth closed. With no fucks given, I made my way back to my ride, hopped in, and headed to the trap.

"It's a beautiful day." I said to Spade as we walked hand in hand into Roscoe's Chicken and Waffle. I'd just picked him up from the airport, and we were about to have lunch. A few days ago, when I got the news about Papa, I left right away. Spade asked if I was ok to fly alone, and I told him I was. I thought it was sweet how he wanted to up and leave to come with me, but I didn't allow him. That night after he fucked me into falling in love with him we talked. He told me all the things he had to handle concerning his business. So to know that he had things to do, I didn't want to get in the way of that. We talked every day using FaceTime. We even had phone sex a few times. I had fallen deep for Spade, and he admitted he was feeling the same about me.

"You are beautiful." He pulled me into his arms, and we shared a kiss in front of the eatery.

"Thanks, babe."

Being that it was the weekend, there were quite a few people outside waiting. It took about thirty minutes for us to be seated. We enjoyed our food and were both anxious to bounce. First, I was going to see Papa and then check on Nunu. She had been very distant lately. She wasn't herself, but I understood Papa was all she had left of her mother.

"I gotta use it right quick." I said to Spade. He gave me a head nod.

"I will be by the truck. I need to smoke." He replied.

When I came back out, he was peering at a black-on-black Jaguar. I walked up on him.

"What's up?" I reached for my waist and realized I had a dress on. My damn gun was in the truck.

"That Jag rolled past me twice." He said looking at it. The car was sitting at the end of the restaurant's driveway. A few seconds later, the car rolled off.

Neither one of us said anything. However, as soon as I got in the truck, I took my Glock from the glovebox. From the driver's seat, I handed my heat to Spade.

"Probably one of your niggas." He smirked.

"Whoever it is, you better shoot first and ask questions later." Spade looked over at me and smiled.

"That's my girl." We pulled off. I began to chop it up with Spade on how I wanted to try my hand at opening a soul food joint. No shade, but Roscoe's was so overrated. Back in the day, it was so good, but now it was just blah. Many places were like that. I wanted to open a spot. If Debra was with it, I wanted her to be the head chef. We stopped at a red light and he looked at me with admiration.

"Babes, go for it. All money in." He replied. The mug on Spade's face caused me to look to my right, and the same black Jag was on the side of us. The window rolled down. It surprised me to see that it was CB. Everything happened so fast. I heard gunshots. As my body was filled with heat, it jerked. It hurt so badly.

It was the Sunday before the end of the month. I went into the shop to go over inventory, the cash flow, and to go get my salesclerk and GM's opinions on a few pieces that I was thinking about ordering for the upcoming season. On Sundays, we opened from 12 to 3, so I made sure to go in after closing. I wasn't trying to be caught up with fans, I wanted to work. We ordered PF Chang's Chinese food, bottled water, sparkling sweet red wine, and worked. We even changed the store around a little. It was 8pm when I was headed out.

"I will be praying for your papa." My general manager announced. It had been a week and one day since Papa had the massive heart attack. I tried my best not to think about it. Papa was a remarkable grandfather.

"Thank you so much. Pray that we make the right choice." I requested. The doctors said that it was nothing else they could do. It was crazy because at his age he was more active than many of these young dudes out here. Nunu wanted him to fight. I loved Papa like crazy, but I agreed with Aunt Debra, Papa lived his life. Nunu just didn't want to let go. However, I understood.

The girls and I stepped outside into the night, and the first thing I saw was a vehicle that wasn't supposed to be parked in front of my building.

"Who is that?" My general manager asked when Freda got out and walked up on the curb and stood near the back end of her truck.

"Nobody." I answered.

"Look, I have pepper spray and I ain't afraid to use it." Warned my salesclerk. Freda cracked a smile and looked at me. I wanted to laugh, too. You could hear the nervousness in her voice, and she couldn't even pull the shit from her purse.

"Beautiful, can I talk to you for a minute?" Freda asked me.

"What about?" I wanted to know. I looked at the girls and told them it was cool for them to leave. It was just like Freda to invade my space. She walked up on me; the masculine smell of cologne tickled my nose. She was so damn cute, and she knew it. When she grabbed my hand, I snatched away.

"Uno, I came here to talk to you. I miss you, man." I looked at that bitch as if she was crazy.

"Get the fuck up out of here. Your wanna be foreign hoe must be gone back to where she came from. You whack as fuck." I snapped.

"I'm going to give you that because I know you mad and jealous and shit. Tone it down a notch." Freda snapped back.

I thought about it, I could stand there and check her ass, let her know that I wasn't jealous of no bitch, or I could simply walk away and leave the bitch where she stood. I had not talked to the hoe in weeks, and she got her nerve. Without saying a word, I headed to my car. I halted in my tracks.

"Fuck you BGB bitches!" A deep voice yelled. I looked toward the street. Before my eyes could focus on the vehicle, shots rang out.

Bocka. Bocka. Bocka. The shit was so close I could feel it in my chest. Ears ringing and all. Freda dove on me, making me fall to the ground. I hit the ground hard, hitting my head on the concrete. The pain was nonexistent. My adrenaline pumped. I reached for my waist, but Freda blocked me from getting to my gun.

"Watch out!" I screamed. I was trying to get to my gun. When I could finally pull my gun, the shooter or shooters were long gone.

"You good, you hit?" Freda asked in a panic.

"No." I stood up. My gun was in my hand. If they were to double back, I was going to blast their asses and I put that on Papa. I was going to hit something.

"Come on." She said grabbing my hand.

"Freda, I'm good." I walked a few feet away to my car. My tire was shot and my window. I had no choice but to hop in with Freda.

As we were driving, I was thinking about who could be coming for us, and the only person I could think about was Boom. This shit was all Dez's fault but regardless, I had her back. Now I didn't feel like calling my cousins to let them know. Nunu was already fucked up over Papa. If I called Kay and Dez they would call her, and I didn't want that. Not now at least.

247

Little Momma didn't know I knew, but I knew exactly who The BGB Crew was, and she was a part of it. Those bitches were about their paper. That was another reason why I wasn't trying to go there with Uno. If I fucked her, she was going to be mine, and her being mine meant she was going to have to walk away from the game. She would have to focus strictly on her music career and store. I didn't think she was ready for that. Uno was stuck on herself and used to having her way. Me, I wear the pants in the relationship. Of course, I would spoil my girl but what I say goes. Uno had too much going for herself, she had the potential to make it far, and I didn't want to see her losing that all over making dangerous moves. I have been there. Been in the game, but I was smart to get out before it cost me more than the five years, I did upstate. At 33, I was paid. On my way to becoming the next big magazine owner- black owned and more.

"You alright?" I asked her for the hundredth time, and her stubborn ass still didn't answer. Uno was sitting back in the seat. Shaking her leg with a scowl on her face. Little momma was on one. I shook my head.

"This shit is crazy." I said, more to myself than her.

"Hell, yeah. It's crazy but it's going to be even crazier when I find them muthafuckas and gun them down."

*'Oh now she wanna talk.'* I hopped on the 101-Highway going toward Hollywood.

"Where are we going? As a matter of fact, I need to go home." She said.

"We going to my house."

"No, I'm not. What I look like? Take me home!" She yelled. I was approaching an exit. I dipped in the first lane, cutting off another car and sped off the freeway. Across the street was a gas station. Horns blew as I pushed my way through traffic. She had me heated. Swerving into the station, I smashed on my brakes by the water and air machine. I put the truck in park and hopped out. She hopped out, too.

"Make this your last time putting me out your truck." She snapped. I grabbed her by the arm, pulling her back and pushed her against the backdoor. I wasn't rough, but I used just enough force to let her know I wasn't playing.

"What are you doing putting your hands on me?" She looked me up and down with a frown. I wanted to choke her ass out, but I chilled. I knew she was shaken up and still furious with me about Brazilian Doll. So, I was being easy.

"Uno, I need you to chill the fuck out. We just were shot at. We both could've been dead right now instead of being grateful you over here on some stupid shit. What the fuck you mad at me for?"

She sucked her teeth and crossed her arms. "Because I want you and you playing with me."

That right there, that confession, the way she looked at me had me.

"I want you, too. I apologize." I then leaned forward and gave her a sloppy kiss. The way she was moaning, I wanted to give it to her right there. I broke our kiss and looked into her eyes.

"Before we take it there, we need to talk."

"About your girl?"

"She is not my girl, but about that too." She gave me a head nod. I knew I was risking it even attempting to be with ole girl but with her playa ass, I really wanted her. Like I said, she was my crush.

Once we were back on the freeway, her phone rung. I turned the music down when she answered it.

"What's up, Dez?"

Silence. She sat up in her seat.

"Nooo." Uno screamed. "Oh, my God. Nooo…. My cousin. Please, God." She cried. I looked from the road at her. The way she was crying something bad had happened.

"Baby, what is the matter?"

"My cousin, she, she, my cousin, is dead." She sobbed.

The sickness and having to carry out the decision to let my papa go weighed heavy on me. Papa hadn't just suffered a heart attack, but a stroke. The machine was keeping him breathing, but the doctors said that if he were to come off the machine, then he wouldn't make it. Papa was in his 80s. He lived his life, but I still didn't want him to leave me. I cried every day, all day. Why did I have to make the decision to take my papa out of this world? Like I told Aunt Deb, if it was time for him to go, then I wouldn't have to do anything. If I wasn't at the hospital seeing him, then I was home asleep. I still hadn't taken the pregnancy test. I knew my body, and I knew that Sen had knocked me up. I hadn't talked to him since I told him that I was coming back to the hotel. It was the night of the shooting at The Black Out. I never showed back up, I changed my mind. I paid his ass back for how he treated me at the mall and shit. That was the last time I heard from him. I think I was holding off on taking the pregnancy test because it would confirm what I already knew, and a part of me wanted to abort the baby. I was feeling guilty about keeping Sen's child, a man I didn't even know, but I was quick to kill Break's baby. In addition, if I did confirm that I was pregnant, was I to tell the stranger? He did tell me after we had sex that he didn't want kids. Humph. I guess I had my answer. I cut my phone off.

I ended up falling asleep. When I got up, I took a hot shower and went to the kitchen to make soup. When I glanced at the surveillance, I didn't see any of my cousins' cars. We lived in a big ass mansion out it Pacific Palisades. My scary ass didn't like to be home but lately I've been appreciating it.

I decided to sit on my balcony. I sat there talking to my mother and asking her to give me signs. Man, I missed her. When I found out she was killed, it broke me down. For a long time, all I knew was that she was shot. A few years later, I found out that she was with a dude she was messing with and was killed by his enemies. Dude was still alive, but nobody knew where he was.

When I ended up in the bathroom with a pregnancy test in my hand, I knew it was a sign from my mother. I peed on two different sticks and sat the tests on the counter. My heart beat a mile a minute. I was now wishing one of my cousins were home with me. I was so scared to find out what I already knew. I walked back in my room. Just as I stepped out of the bathroom door, my other phone vibrated. I left my personal one downstairs. I kind of didn't want to be bothered unless it was business, plus I feared getting that call. Something was telling me that I was about to receive some bad news. My gut always had warnings. Slowly, I walked over to the phone. By the time I made it, it stopped ringing. My hand shook as I picked it up to see who was calling. When I saw it was the hospital, tears poured from my eyes. My papa was gone. I could feel it. I didn't answer, I hopped on my bed and cried.

Shortly after, I got a call from Aunt Deb.

"Hello." I answered, just above a whisper.

"He's gone." She informed.

# Dez

## A Few days later.

---

I just picked up some work when I got the call from Row telling me that I needed to get to Roscoe's Chicken and Waffle on Manchester and Main. The panic in his voice alerted me. At first, I thought something was wrong with his brother, and then he hit me with. "I'm almost there. Somebody called me and told me that Kay was shot. They just called. Just meet me there."

"What the fuck you mean? They said what?" I asked. My heart was thumping like a muthafucka. I was at least twenty minutes away. I couldn't wait that long. "What you mean she was shot? Is she ok?" I yelled.

"They said she is dead." I lost my breath. My hands were shaking so much. It was hard for me to control the vehicle. Tears poured from my eyes. I couldn't see good, but I was determined to get to my damn cousin. I was twenty minutes from the place, but I think I made it there in ten. There were a bunch of police, fire trucks, and people out. The tears continued to fall. I threw the vehicle in park and left it in the middle of the street. My knees buckled when I saw Kay's Escalade at the intersection. Yellow tape was around it. The moment I saw a white sheet covering a person in the driver's seat, I lost it. I took off toward her vehicle. Just as I approached the door, I saw her hand from under the sheet. My knees trembled uncontrollably.

When I woke up, I was in Row's truck. We were still at Roscoe's.

"I need to get to her. She's not dead." I cried.

"She's gone. They just put her in the coroner's van." I looked at him. Everything was a blur. This wasn't true. Kay wasn't dead. My cousin wasn't dead.

"Who in the fuck was with her? She ain't dead. That was somebody else." I cried.

"Call your people."

"Call them for what? She ain't dead?" By this time, two detectives walked our way. Although they were in plain clothes, it was obvious who they were. One detective introduced himself. I didn't want to hear anything. I covered my ears and cried.

I was calm enough to use my phone. The first person I called was Uno.

"She is dead. Kay is dead." I cried and I heard her scream. Row took the phone from me. I was too out of it to hear what he was telling Uno.

Every time I think about it, I tear up and before I know it, tears are running down my face. Not only was my cousin killed, but Papa had also died the same day. To make matters worse. I'm in jail. I got pulled over that night. There was a warrant for my arrest. Linda's bitch ass snitched on me. On top of that, I had a duffle bag filled with pure cocaine that the officers found. Now I had no bail. It was killing me to be away from my family while we were dealing with such tragedies.

I am my sister's keeper. It's been a few months since she's been gone and because her body hasn't been found, I still don't have the closure I need. Nevertheless, I'm making it. I'm staying strong for my nephew. He's all I got, and I plan on making sure he's forever straight, like my sister did me. The day I ran into Lucas at Club Slick was a blessing. Lucas Jank was my college buddy. We went to Georgia Tech together. He had a crush on me, but I had a boyfriend and he respected that. I lived on campus, but Lucas was from the A. He had his own place. Being that we had a few classes together, we studied together and after some time we would hang out. Once I was too tipsy and I slept with Lucas. I cheated on my boyfriend with him until he got a girl pregnant and dumped me. I felt it was Lucas' fault, and I stopped messing with him only to come back a month later, and he was with someone else. We went our separate ways. I graduated and came back to California. I hadn't seen or heard from him since.

When we ran into each other at Club Slick, I was down due to my sister. It felt like I had nobody, which I didn't. Our mother had been dead, and our father wasn't in the picture. My mom's best friend Linda tried to be there for us as much as she could, but she had let drugs destroy her some years ago, so she wasn't dependable or reliable. She helped me with the baby from time to time.

That night, Lucas asked me to wait for him. He was having a meeting with the owner. As soon as he left, I got a call from Linda. She was telling me that someone shot up my house. I ran to the office. I was in a complete mess. I was glad I left my nephew with Linda that night. Had we been home, I probably would've been dead. Or my nephew. My eyes watered just thinking about it.

"It was those BGB bitches. I swear I want all of them to go down." I said. Lucas didn't say anything on the ride to Linda's, he just let me vent. In the car that night, I promised I was going to get them. When I saw Nunu in the store, I wished I had the courage to beat her ass. I wished I had the courage to retaliate on them, but I didn't. I did have the courage to go to the police. There was a detective in particular I wanted to speak with. He was my client at the escort company where I worked. I told him how I thought The BGB Crew was responsible for my sister's disappearance. I told him the truth. Everything. I also told him about the trap spots and how my sister once told me they picked up drugs from a dude named Vegas. He claimed he was going to look into it.

A week later, Ronnie called, telling me that Linda was beaten into a bloody mess and left in the alley. They didn't think she was going to make it, but she pulled through. Linda made it. With the video footage from the store of Dez being at the crime scene and Linda's statement, they got her ass. I found out she had drugs on her, too. She was going to do some time, and I was happy about it. I hoped she died in jail. Boom's punk ass, too. Come to find out he shot up Uno's vehicle and was caught that same night. Beverly Hills PD picked him up. Another storeowner next door to Uno's shop was killed in her shop. A stray bullet hit her. She was found the next day.

Now, I wanted Nunu and Uno to go down. Kay was dead, and I didn't feel a damn thing about it. Karma is a bitch is all I can say.

"What are you doing in here?" I looked up and Lucas was standing at the door. I was sitting in his bedroom. I recently moved to Atlanta. There was nothing in Cali for me or my nephew. Lucas' family had a rental property that he allowed me and my nephew to stay in. The day we were leaving, there was a box on my porch. I was scared to open it. After Lucas confirmed it wasn't a bomb, I turned the box over and dumped out its contents. It was 100k. A card was in it that said God bless you and your nephew. I never found out who sent it, but I had a feeling. It was still fuck BGB. Money wouldn't bring my sister back.

I looked up at Lucas and smiled.

"Wishing my sister was here to see her son turn five." I shook my head. My nephew's birthday was in five days. Lucas took me by the hand, and I stood up. Lucas wrapped his arm around me, and I rested on his chest.

I thank God for Lucas. Although we weren't a couple, we fucked with each other heavy.

Lucas always made me feel better. When I gathered my belongings, he and I walked hand in hand out his room and into his backyard. He was having a BBQ and all his family was there. I was nervous. It would be my first time meeting them. When we stepped into the backyard, there were a sea of people. I spotted my nephew on the waterslide and smiled. He was happy playing with the other kids.

"Come on, shawty. You may as well get used to the family because you ain't going nowhere." Lucas said. I looked up at him, that big bright smile that I loved so much was plastered on his face. He winked at me. Like I said, we weren't official but what we had sure did feel like it.

260

Tupac's Life Goes On blared from the speakers of my shiny professionally waxed and polished burgundy Lincoln Navigator. I bobbed my head feeling the lyrics as I puffed my blunt. It was in the middle of the afternoon on a Tuesday, and here I was in Cali at the cemetery. I wasn't trying to get too fucked up because I needed to be in my right mind when I went to handle this business. Sitting at the graveyard where the lady I believed would be my wife was buried made it hard for me not to take gulps from the cognac bottle in my hand. It had been exactly one year and one month since my girl been gone, and that shit ached my heart the same as it did when she left me. It was my fault. I beat that niggas ass, and he came back blasting. He shot me in the arm and killed my girl. The amount of bullets that riddled her body, it seemed like he was trying to get her and not me. I hadn't talked to her peeps since the day before the funeral. Then the nigga CB was still in hiding, but I put that on my life, that I was killing that nigga whenever and wherever I saw him. I didn't give a fuck if it was at my son's graduation. Jess fucked around and had my seed. She wouldn't get an abortion this time. Her husband stayed with her too, but made her stop working for me. I didn't give a fuck.

"Fuck man, Kay Spade, you left me. Man." My voice cracked as I stared at her headstone. It was a picture of her smiling. Written underneath it said: Daughter. Sister. Cousin. BGB 4 Life. She was gone. My baby left me without even saying bye. This shit was fucking me up. I poured a shot of Conga in the grass for my wife. I kissed my two fingers and put them to her lips on the photo. Tears slid from my eyes.

261

"I will always love you." I stood up. It was heartbreaking because me leaving felt like I was leaving her again. Only if she knew she had a nigga shedding many tears this past year. I took my hand and rubbed it across my face. I stood there a few more seconds before I turned to leave.

"Hey." I spoke. Shocked to see that I was crept up on. Standing in front of me was Nunu and a little baby was in her hand covered by a blue blanket.

She gave me a faint smile.

"Thanks for coming." She told me and then made her way closer to where Kay was buried.

"That's your little baby?"

"Yup." She said without looking back at me.

"Congrats." I told her and walked off. I could sense she didn't want to be bothered.

"Wow Kay, no warning or nothing?" I said, as I made my way to sit on the green grass in front of my cousin's grave. "You knew your nigga was coming up here, you could've warned me. How about he would've asked to see my baby and saw Bryce looked just like his damn brother? You cold, but I still love you and fucking miss you, Kay." My voice cracked, and I cried.

When my cousin was killed, and my papa died on the same day, I was numb. It hurt worse than it ever did when my mom was taken away. I couldn't eat, I cried all day every day. I was sick. Then, Dez was arrested. All I saw was history repeating itself. We wanted to be hustlers like our mothers, and now our fate was about to end like theirs. With the advice of the lawyer, Dez jumped on a deal. Our attorney said if she took it to trial and lost, she was facing 14 years. If the FEDS picked up the case, she could do a minimum of 25 or more if they came up with something else. He also said that if the FEDS stepped in, then it could jeopardize all of our freedom. Dez took the deal and was serving 10 years. That was Uno and my cue to walk away from the game. I had my son, and she had her career.

The day I lost Papa and Kay was the day I asked my mother for a sign, a sign to let me know if I should give birth to a man's child who didn't want kids with me, and I wasn't in a relationship with. Four months ago, I gave birth to a handsome baby boy.

He was the spitting image of Sen. He didn't even inherit my eyes. For the last few months, I would wonder what Sen would do if he found out we had this beautiful little boy.

Would he want to be a part of his life? Would he be angry with me? It didn't matter that he didn't have a father. He was mine and I loved him. Plus, Gave was there.

I talked to Kay a little longer before my baby and I went to visit Aunt Deb.

Uno was out of town doing a show, so it was me and her. She still made a variety of our favorite dishes, but I didn't eat much. I was trying to drop this baby weight. And, I had an event I was attending in a couple of weeks.

"So, baby, what's on your mind?" She asked me. I played in my grits with my fork and looked up at her. Deb was holding a glass half filled with Jack in her hand.

I took a deep breath and let it out.

"I ran into a dude Kay was messing with at the cemetery today."

"Oh Lord, who died?"

"He was there to see her." Her face softened.

"He really liked her. I would've loved to see where things went with them. I miss her." Deb took a sip of her drink. I could tell she was getting choked up.

"So do I." There was a moment of silence. This shit was all bad. "Have you talk to Auntie?" I asked, referring to Kay's mom. Aunt Deb shook her head no.

"I've written her. I even tried to go see her, but she denied my visit. I know she blames herself." I thought about her at the funeral. She didn't shed a tear. The way she stared at Kay it was obvious, although she was there in the physical... mentally, she wasn't.

"Let's just keep her in prayer." I found myself saying.

"I'm praying for you, too. Praying that you find someone to love you, and you love them. I know we are some strong women, but that baby needs a father in his life. Have you reached out to his father?" Just like her slick ass to throw that in there. She was right, though.

I don't know why I was nervous. It wasn't like I hadn't kicked it with Gave over a hundred times. Tonight it was different. We were not just going out to grab something to eat or get drunk and fucking. We were going on an actual date. He had been feeling me for a minute and I knew it. I wasn't interested in nothing serious. Gave was handsome and very supportive. That was enough for now.

Gave was the head of our security at The Bandz. He was also the face of my driving service. I was the owner of a top dollar driving service. My clients were mostly independent artists, hood celebrities, and those who just needed a ride to show off for the day like a prom or something. Gave had been by my side the entire time I had been going through the nightmare. He was constantly checking on me, making sure that I was ok, bringing me food and such. He ended up being a good friend. When Gave found out I was pregnant, he asked me was it his. I told him it wasn't possible although we used protection, we hadn't had sex around that time. I kept it real, he wasn't my man and still isn't. I told him about my one-night stand- being sure to leave out that my baby's daddy was Sen Jank. He told me that he was there for me if I needed him, and he was. He was a real one. He and I had sex once when I was four months pregnant, and that was the last time. Tonight I was ready to give it up again.

I looked myself over in the mirror. I must say the no meat and eating in moderation along with working out 4x's a week did a bitch good. I shined like a rare gem in a captivating white floor-length formal dress with a curve hugging fit, plunging v-neckline, spaghetti straps, and sparkling sequins throughout. My hair was up in a cute high twisted top-knot bun with a swooped bang. My green eyes complimented the emerald, green clutch purse I was carrying. Although I only wore my diamond tennis bracelet, I was still blinging on my ears with diamond studs and my diamond Cartier watch. Taking a deep breath, I hurried down the stairs and opened the door for Gave.

"Gotdamn, Nutavia." I blushed at how he took me all in. Gave was one of the only people who called me by my government name. It was just something about the way he said it that made it feel like it was the best name in the world. "You look good as fuck. Damn." He continued to eye me.

"Thank you, handsome." I said looking up at him. Gave was about 6'3 and 290lbs of pure muscle. He ate clean, didn't drink, and worked out faithfully. His almond toasted skin was flawless. Gave was dressed in a black suit with designer loafers. He looked good himself. He always did though. Gave wasn't hood. He was one of those corporate like dudes and carried himself with class.

"Where's the baby?" He asked.

"With my aunt, remember?" He gave me a head nod.

"When did you take him?"

"She came and got him earlier." Gave always wanted to make sure that my son was straight. I appreciated it too, but I wasn't trying to allow him to get too close to my child, especially because I didn't know if our friendship would last.

"Can I get a hug?" He asked me. A kiss followed the hug.

Two hours later, we pulled up to a commercial building in downtown San Diego. His homeboy from Georgia had recently purchased the spot and was having his grand opening. They were also celebrating his brother being drafted into the NFL. I didn't ask what team. Sports wasn't my thing.

A lot of people had come out. Everyone was looking good. I had a feeling we were going to have a good time. I promised myself on the ride that I was going to loosen up and enjoy life. Tomorrow wasn't promised. Not even the next second.

The place was nice on the inside, whomever did the décor did a wonderful job. Everything was black and silver. There were blinged out centerpieces on the tables, accompanied by elegant menus and dinnerware. The DJ played music from the 90s. The crowd was diverse. Everyone was at least 21 and over and of all different races. I even saw Dr. Dre and Deion Sanders in the building. I was impressed.

"Wanna dance?" Gave asked me. I didn't even hesitate. I said I was coming to have fun.

"Yes." I smiled. Hand in hand, we made it to the dance floor. 'Overdose' by Jamie Fox was playing.

"Bro, I ain't trying to be funny but you better check that shit out. Add the months up. You said y'all didn't use protection. The baby was still new." The words of Spade played in my head. When he told me that shit a few weeks back, I paid it no mind. Old girl ain't have no baby by me is what I told him and that was that. I told her I didn't want no kids and plus she told me that she was getting the morning after pill. I didn't take Nunu as the type of bitch to lie. She hadn't even reached out to me, in fact she stood me up so I knew for a fact she would not have my baby. No one could convince me that she was that type of chick. I hoped she wasn't. I'd hurt her if she did some fuck shit like keeping my kid away. Ever since he told me, I had been thinking about it. However, that shit wasn't true.

Here I am standing over the balcony at the grand opening of my club and who the fuck I see on the dance floor with the homie Gave? Nunu's muthafucking ass. What a coincidence. Seeing those two on the dance floor, brought back memories. The day I took her phone in the hotel, right before we fucked, she was texting a nigga named Gave. I remembered the name because I had a homeboy with the same name, but never in a million years would I have thought that it was Gavin Dinero. Gave was from my hometown. We played ball together in high school. After school, he left and went to the military and relocated to Henderson, Nevada. That was the last I heard from him until my sister said she ran into him in Cali. She was out here visiting some nigga. She said she invited Gave to the grand opening, and I was pleased about that.

It slightly disturbed me, seeing him with Nunu. She wasn't my bitch but still, the pussy was good. I didn't like how the bitch curved me. We were supposed to hook up a second time, but she never showed up. That was the last I heard from her sexy ass.

I felt a pair of arms wrap around my waist. It wasn't nobody but Chanel, my fiancé of seven years. She rested her head on my back.

"Baby, you wanna go dance?" She knew damn well I didn't do no dancing. That was one thing that annoyed me. She always wanted to be noticed. She was bipolar, needy, and annoying but I was still with her.

I didn't even respond, and she caught on. I continued to watch Gave and Nunu dance. The more I watched them, the saltier I became. They had the nerve to be dancing off 'Overdose.' The music went off, and the host's soft voice blessed the mic. The host was my mom. Don't let the voice fool ya. Sarah Jank was a beast in a skirt. She thanked the guests for coming. "Dinner will be served shortly, but before we eat, I would like to acknowledge the man of the hour, Sincere Jank, my baby." Chanel came and stood on the side of me.

The spotlight shined on me. I raised my glass.

"My son isn't a man of many words, but later I will make sure he gets this mic and says a few words. Give it up for my baby though." She said and the crowd clapped. The entire time my eyes were on Nunu. To me, it seemed like she was nervous. She grabbed Gave's arm tight and with her other hand, she placed it on her chest. He whispered in her ear.

Right after they walked off the dance floor, I was about to go down there. I couldn't wait until she saw my face.

*Sincere Jank, Sincere Jank?* I knew my ears were deceiving me. There was no way I was at Sincere's grand opening. No fucking way. My heart was pounding like a lumberjack. I couldn't believe this. I wondered if Spade told him I had a baby. Oh, my God. I tightened my grip on Gave's arm. I put my other hand on my chest. *'I gotta call Kay'* came to mind and it crushed my spirits when I realized I couldn't call her.

"Are you ok?" Gave whispered in my ear and I nodded my head no. He ushered me off the dance floor and when we were on the sideline, he turned me toward him. I could see the worry on his face.

"What is the matter?" He asked me. I hit him with a fake smile.

"I need a drink." Was all I said. Something was telling me to be straight up with him, ask him was the person of the hour Sen Jank, but I just couldn't. I didn't want to face my reality or tell another soul that I had a baby by that man, and he had no idea he had a 4-month-old on earth. I was ready to go.

"You good, though?" He asked as we headed to the bar. I wanted to snatch my hand from his, for some stupid reason I didn't want Sen to think we were a couple. I knew that wouldn't be right. *Fuck, Nunu. You got yourself into some shit.*

"Yeah." We were now at one of the couple of bars that was in the place. I ordered me a double shot of Patron and a Corona.

Gave moved from my side, but I didn't bother to see why.

The flash coming from cameras were behind me and loud cheerful voices. Something was telling me not to look. I threw my finger up to the bartender, telling her I needed one more shot. I liked her. She was quick. I took that shit to the head and then turned up my beer. I turned, saw Gave he was smiling at whomever was behind me.

"The man of the hour. What's good, bro?" He said all happy and shit. I took a deep breath, let it out and then took another. I quickly turned back toward the bar.

I took another gulp of my beer.

*'Fuck it. I ain't never sacred.'* I turned around. Gave was standing next to Sen. A cameraman was snapping up their pictures. I was so muthafucking grateful for the four shots I took because a bitch was much calmer.

*'Gotdamn this man is fine. My fucking son looks just like him.'* I couldn't take my eyes off of him. His fine ass was draped in an all-white suit. We were matching. White loafers blessed his feet. He had designed cornrows going to the back. He was iced out from his ears on down to his wrist. I took my bottom lip into my mouth and smirked to myself, thinking, *This some shit right here.*

I stood there watching them take pictures. The two of them exchanged a few words before Gave looked in my direction. Then when I saw Sen, my pussy jumped. Two fine niggas gawked at me, but I think my pussy wanted Sen. I know her hot ass did.

273

I removed my eyes.

A light-skinned bitch wearing a black fitted dress that stopped just below her knees, cuffed her arm in Sen's. That's when I noticed the diamond ring on her finger. My eyes darted to his finger, but there was no ring. Either he didn't wear his wedding band or she was his fiancé.

I smiled big when the trio approached me. My focus was on Gave. I didn't look at Sen again until Gave introduced us. I peeped how he gave me the once over and put his cigar in his mouth. I guess his bitch did too because as soon as he reached his hand out to shake mine, she put hers out.

"I'm Chanel. His fiancé." She said. I looked at her hand for a second and then back at her. I gave her a head nod. I then turned to Gave.

"I'm going to the ladies room." I could tell he was uncomfortable by my actions, but I'm sure he saw how the hoe looked me up and down. I wasn't about to shake her hand, I don't give a fuck whose party it was. I walked off.

As soon as I got in the restroom, I texted my Aunt Deb and Uno in a group chat.

**Nunu:** Why this party is for Sen? He is here. He is Gave's friend. I'm so nervous.

**Auntie:** This is a sign.

**Uno:** I believe so too, Auntie.

Everyone wanted me to tell this man about his baby.

**Auntie:** If he doesn't want to be a part of the baby's life then that's his decision, but at least tell him.

I replied with an ok.

"Girl, you are wearing that dress." I looked from my phone toward the voice, and my heart stopped again. It was the host, Sen's mom.

"Thank you." I replied.

"You are welcome, beautiful." With that, she walked out the restroom.

**Nunu:** He has a fiancé. Was the last thing I texted before leaving back out of the restroom.

## A little while later…

## SEN

I couldn't keep my eyes off of Nunu. She was looking good in that dress she was wearing. She was already slim thick, but the baby I heard she had, had her body right. More ass, hips, and titties. And those fucking green eyes. That girl was dangerous. I didn't feel bad at all thinking about fucking my boy's chick. My dick jumped thinking about how wet and tight her pussy was. *Calm down, boy. We will be back in that soon.*

I wanted to get an eye on her. For the last two hours, I had been trying to figure out how I was going to get her alone. If I could figure out how I was going to get her to the 3$^{RD}$ level of the club and into my office, I swear I was going to fuck the shit out of her.

Gave was keeping her close. You could tell he was digging her. Chanel's clingy ass was getting on my nerves, as always, too damn clingy.

"One of your brothers has just arrived." My mother said. I couldn't wait to see Spade's face when he saw who was here.

"Aye, ma." I took her by her hand before she walked off. Standing from my seat, I whispered in her ear.

She looked up at me and smirked.

"Who is she?" I asked my mom to make Chanel leave. Chanel talked a lot of shit and acted a fool with me every chance she got, but when my mom told her something that shit went.

"Gave's chick and me have a little history, and you know." Her mouth formed in an O. She gave me a head nod. I loved my momma. She always had my back. However, I knew she was going to talk shit later.

My bro was going to be mad that I was going to be late for my bro's celebration. I was way in Los Angeles, two hours from the event and I ain't even handled the business I came for yet.

*They need to burn this bitch down.* I shook my head. The building looked like an old dirty ass shack. Compared to the other buildings on the block. I was surprised the city still allowed it. I just pulled in front of Club Slick to meet with the owner. I met with the nigga over a year ago. I acted like I wanted to buy the club, but in actuality I was trying to find out if he ever saw my brother. I knew it was a slim chance that he would remember being that it was a year ago, and many people came in and out that muthafucka but I came to Cali to see if I could get one step closer to who killed my brother. I remembered my brother mentioning if he ever went to Cali he wanted to visit the spot. That nigga loved strippers. I guess it was the spot back then because it sure in the hell wasn't now. Dude looked at me with a straight face and said he ain't ever seen him. I showed him a few pictures just to make sure, and he said no. Now he wanted to meet.

Me and Tone share the same mother and father. He was my everything, my protector, and my best friend. When I found out he was killed, I vowed to find out who committed the murder. It seemed like my brothers and father had put it on the back burner. Black Sam wasn't even no help.

"You can park there." Some old ass nigga said.

"Nigga, I'm parked." I told him with a mean mug. He shook his head. I continued on my stride because who was going to stop me?

The place smelled like funky ass cigarettes and ass. I frowned my face. Standing at the bar, I flagged the bartender down. The same chick was working the last time I came. With a small smile, she walked up to me.

"Hey, handsome." She spoke and I tossed my head up to reply. "What can I get you?"

"I'm here to see the owner. He is expecting me." She gave me the side eye. I watched as she walked away. She picked up her cellphone and made a call. A few minutes later, she came back.

"How is Trish? She told me she was moving out to Atlanta with you. I was the bartender the night you guys reunited."

"She is doing good. I will let her know you asked about her." I remembered that night when Trish ran to the office to tell me about her sister. Ole girl was trying to calm her down. She seemed genuinely concerned.

"Can you give her my number? Let her know I will be moving out there to get a new start and I would love to see her." I told her I would. I put the number in my phone and she let me know that I could go to the back.

\*\*\*

279

"I remember you coming here asking me did I know your brother. Well, first you acted like you wanted to buy the building." He started as soon as I took a seat in the black chair in front of his desk.

"Nigga, don't play with me. I ain't with all that beating around the bush."

"Look, I am about to shut this place down. I'm leaving California. I am willing to sell this spot for 60k with that comes some information that may be helpful. It's about your brother." I jumped from my seat and grabbed him by his shirt collar.

"Nigga, don't play with me."

"Get your punk ass hands off me. You got five seconds and I'll shoot your dick off, little nigga." When I looked down, the nigga had a gun pointed at my dick. I held him a few more seconds and then let him go. Sitting back down, I gawked at him.

"Deal?" He asked. I nodded my head yeah. I didn't want the building but the info, however, I would take both since it came with it.

"Yeah."

"Bring the money tomorrow. My flight leaves at two o'clock. I ain't worried about you running your mouth. I don't plan on coming back to Cali but just in case I do, I ask that you don't reveal where you got this info."

"I will see you tomorrow." I stood up and walked out.

We had dinner and gave a shout out to my brother who made it to the NFL but didn't show up to my fucking event. I knew it was his punk ass momma that convinced him not to come. My brother was the son of a cop bitch, that's what my dad called her. All these years she was bitter that my father didn't chose her and her son, so she did whatever she could to keep him away from us. This was one of those times. I loved my brother. I love all of my siblings, but I truly felt I was done with it. Shit, he probably was done with us, that's why he didn't show up. Lucas' ass hadn't made it either. He hit me an hour ago to say that he was on his way from Los Angeles. I don't know what the fuck for, and I didn't even bother to ask.

"So, tell me how in the fuck did this happen? Gave and Nunu?" Spade said to me. We are standing looking over the rail at the guests below.

I took a gulp from my cognac filled glass and shook my head.

"Shit if I know. You keep that nigga occupied. I'm about to go find out what she is on."

He took a pull from the blunt we had been sharing.

"I was surprised she spoke to me the way she tried to act like she didn't know you." Spade laughed. I didn't find shit funny. Besides, when Gave first so-called introduced us, she hadn't looked my way.

"Where is your woman?" He asked.

"My momma sent her home." I snickered and he laughed with a shake of the head. My mother convinced Chanel to go home and let the men enjoy their night. She tried to stay by saying Hope, my little sister was still there but my mother told her whatever she told her, and her ass kissed me goodbye and told me she would see me at home. I knew I wouldn't hear the end of it, but for now I didn't care. I was on a mission.

"Ask her about that baby." Spade called behind me. I ignored him.

***

Chanel was gone, Spade had Gave occupied, and I saw Nunu's fine ass walk to the exit that led to the large balcony that overlooked the entire city. It was beautiful out, but not as beautiful as she was. Standing on the far right alone, I spotted Nunu with a cigar in her hand staring into the night. I took a minute to take her all in. Her body was everything. The way her body looked in that dress had a nigga's dick hard. I don't know what it was. Was it that she curved me and stood me up? Was it that her pussy was just that good? Or was it that deep down I knew her little gangsta ass was a bitch I preferred to have on my arm rather than Chanel's stuck up, bipolar needy ass? No matter how much I wanted Nunu, something was still telling me to stay away.

Her sweet perfume delighted my nose.

"What's up, stranger?" I spoke, walking up behind her. I was so close, I could've planted a kiss on the back of her neck if I wanted to.

"Hey, Sen." She said, still looking straight ahead.

"That's it, no hug or nothing." I asked. She turned around and when she looked at me, those green eyes had me lost.

"Why would I hug you, we are both here with someone. I'm not sure about you, but I don't feel like explaining to my date that me and his friend had a one-night stand. You know."

I didn't like how she was calling Gave her date no more than I liked how she was trying to curve me again. Because I'm Sen, I pulled her into a hug, and I could feel her body relax. I then kissed her on the forehead.

"Don't do that." She said just above a whisper, pulling back. She turned back around. Her shoulders rose and then she dropped them indicating she was taking a deep breath.

"I ain't forgot about you standing me up. I should take you to the bathroom and fuck your little ass."

It was so hard for me to look at his fine ass. I swear our son was the spitting image of him. Not to mention sexy as fuck, and he wasn't being mean. The way he was looking at me had me feeling like he desired me over whoever the stuck-up bitch was that was with him earlier.

"It seems like you're in a committed relationship."

"I'm not." My back was still turned as I spoke.

"Well, you got a bitch. Go deal with her. I swear if she comes out here on some bullshit, I will beat her ass." I turned to look at him, and he had that same crooked smile as our son.

"Look, woman." He walked up in my face. He was so close, if Gave would've seen us he would've been questioning what was up. I know for sure if his bitch knew how close her man was, she would've flipped, and then I would've beat her ass.

"What?" I put the cigar in my mouth.

"You are making my dick hard." The way he said it, I had to chuckle. He really acted pressed, and I liked it.

"What, Sincere?" I called him by his government name.

"I will be here until Monday. I wanna see you tomorrow. You owe me for standing me up. Make it happen."

"Wh-"I got ready to speak, but he cut me off.

"Be quiet. I don't wanna hear none of that smart mouth shit. Now put your number in my phone." He removed it from his pants pocket and put it in my hand.

*'Fuck it.'* I thought as I keyed in my number.

"That's a good girl." He took his phone back.

"Is that it?"

"I'm not playing. Don't make me come find you." He pulled me in for another hug. It felt so good being in his arms. I could've stayed there. "I never got a chance to tell you, but I'm sorry about your cousin."

I cleared my throat.

"Thanks." I told him.

I watched as he strolled off.

"Sincere." I found myself calling him by his government name again.

"What's up, Nutavia."

He smirked. I wondered how he knew my name.

"Congrats. This is a nice place."

"Thanks, shawty. I'll see you tomorrow." He left.


***


When that Negro told me he wanted to see me the next day, he didn't mention his ass would still be in San Diego.

"So, am I supposed to really drive out there? Almost two hours away?" I said to Uno. She and Freda were sitting in the living room. They were such a cute couple. I loved them together. Freda was just what she needed to slow her ass down. She was incredibly supportive, too.

"If it's worth it, go." Freda added. Uno excused herself to the restroom.

I didn't say anything. My phone went off, and I walked across the room to pick it up.

**Uno:** I really think you should tell him about your son.

I read the text and put the phone back down.

Thirty minutes went by and Uno came down the stairs with the last of her luggage. She, Freda, and Go were traveling overseas. My girl was going on tour. She signed to Freda's new label, and she was making it happen for her. If I didn't have Bryce, I would've been out there too.

"I'm so happy for you, but sad you are leaving me."

I told her, giving her a hug.

"Thanks, cousin. I'm going to stop by to see Aunt Deb and my nephew."

"You just saw them yesterday." I teased.

"So. Hater." She said and the three of us laughed. Uno loved my son like he was hers. If something ever happened to me, I knew she would take care of him.

***

"Gave, let me call you back." I said into the Bluetooth. Per my navigation, I was five minutes away.

"All right, baby. Be safe." He said. I promised I would and hung up. I lied and told Gave that I was visiting Dez.

After two hours of driving, I still didn't know the real reason I was at Sen's hotel. Was it to fuck his fine ass or to tell him we had a son together? I pulled into the valet of the 5-star hotel and climbed out the car. It was spring in Cali, so I dressed accordingly. I wore a burnt orange bodysuit and heels. I wasn't sure if I was going to hook up with Sen, but just in case I did I had Uno wash and flat iron my hair. Go beat my face earlier. I made sure to wear my bling. I was looking too cute and smelled even better.

I never responded to Sen's text when he sent the address. That was a good thing. If he wasn't here, then that meant whatever I came to do wasn't meant to be.

"Thanks." I climbed out of the car. I took the ticket from the valet and headed to suite 14009. I hoped I didn't need a keycard.

"What the fuck you want?" Is how I greeted the caller. It was Lucas' punk ass.

"Don't be mad, bro. I had a very important meeting."

"Where are you?"

"I'm at the airport. I gotta get back, so I can go see Dad. Sen, you won't believe this shit." He said.

"So you out here but didn't come to my shit." I was salty. As brothers, we were supposed to always support each other. I already washed my hands with his punk ass.

"I swear this meeting was important. It's about Tone. I gotta go see Daddy first. I swear. I love you. I'll see you when I get back." He said anxiously.

I didn't bother to ask him what about Tone. I was almost sure what it was. If he was going to see our pops, then he wanted to run it by him first.

"I will be there tomorrow. No more talking over the phone. Tell Dad I said hi."

"Alright, bro." Lucas hung up. Losing Tone fucked with all of us. No matter if we had different mothers, the Jank boys were close. Tone and Lucas had the same mother and father. He took it the hardest. He used to always say that he was going to get at whoever was responsible for his brother's death, and I believed that's what he did. I had a feeling shit was about to get ugly.

After I hung up with him, I started to call Spade. But changed my mind. I didn't want to get to assuming shit, so I waited until Lucas told me/us what was up. If my brother did have a lead about who killed Tone and Boy Boy, I hoped he let me pull the trigger. I think then I would finally get over the guilt of letting my brothers go to Cali alone. If I was there, I bet they wouldn't have been killed and robbed.

Light knocks on the door pulled me from my thoughts. I smiled, thinking about who was at the door. It was like I could feel her presence on the other side of the door. I even believed I smelled her sweet perfume. Nunu didn't respond to my text, but deep down I knew she would come.

"Who's there?" I asked.

"Open the door and find out." I couldn't help but to chuckle at her smart-ass mouth.

I opened the door and there Miss Nunu stood, looking real fuckable.

Baby was dressed comfortable in his lounging clothes when he opened the door. Sen was in a wife beater showing off his tattooed filled arms and a pair of basketball shorts. The way he was looking at me, I just knew that he was going to pull me in the inside and fuck me crazy but nope.

"Come in, have a seat. Let's talk." He extended his hand for me to enter, and I was hesitant to enter.

*'Let's talk?'* That made me nervous. What in the fuck, did he want to talk about? Did he know something?

Reluctantly, I walked in and stood by the door.

"I said, have a seat." He requested.

"So, I came all the way out here to sit and talk?" I responded. I was trying to read him.

"What you are saying is, you came to get some dick, and you ready to get right to it?" He smirked.

'Was I saying that?'

"Whatever, Sincere." I looked at him and rolled my eyes. Walking over to the sofa in the room, I asked. "When did you get so considerate? If I can remember correctly, you were a mean asshole. Who told me in my face that he didn't trust me. Choked me and demanded I give you the password to my phone." That was the night I fucked him, and we made our son. I flopped on the sofa.

"That is the same night you gave me the pussy. Let me find out you like that toxic shit."

"Real muthafucking funny." I spat.

He laughed. I stared at my gotdamn baby's daddy.

"Would you like a drink, mean ass woman? You too cute to be like that."

"Yes, whiskey, if you have it. If not-"

He asked me was Jameson good. I told him it was, and I would like it on the rocks. Sen handed me my glass.

"I apologize for how I handled you." He sat next to me. "I wanna keep it real. After we fucked, I thought about you countless times. Something was telling me to stay away from your fine ass, but I couldn't stop thinking about the smart mouth chick with the fire pussy. And those fucking pretty ass green eyes. I thought about you a lot. After you stood me up, I thought about you. I wanted to find you and fuck you up for how you dissed me."

"Ain't no chick ever stood me up, but you did. And even then, you've run across my mind more than I would like."

"Should I take that as a compliment?" I asked. This nigga didn't know he was turning me on more and more. I wanted him bad. I took a sip from my cup. This nigga was too close.

His confession, his sex appeal, him being the man that gave me my first child all played a part in my pussy being wet and wanting him to fuck me right there.

"You look good, Miss Nunu. My brother told me you had a baby. That baby got your body right. Are you still with the father?"

*'This nigga setting me up? Oh, so that's why he wanted to talk.'*

"Why? I didn't come to talk about my personal life." I was now annoyed.

"Cool." He stood up, walked over to the bar, and picked up a bottle of Patron. My heart was beating a mile a minute as I watched him make his drink. Something was telling me this nigga knew something or assumed something. Why else would he ask me about my child?

"I know you asked me to stay out of your business." He looked at me. I hoped he didn't see the nervousness on my face. "Did you ever finish that book you were writing?"

I was shocked that he remembered. When he took my phone the night we had sex and demanded that I gave him my password, he saw my word app open.

"No. So much has happened since then."

"Finish that book. You can do it. We gotta use all of our gifts. You ain't creative for nothing. Look, I know life happens and sometimes we gotta put shit on the back burner, but for how long? Tomorrow ain't promised to no one. Your book

294

is just another inheritance for your kid. How old is your baby, anyway?"

"I didn't come to talk about my child, and thanks for the words of encouragement. Tell me about your fiancé."

His stare made me uncomfortable but if I looked away, it would show guilt. I gawked back.

"Chanel and I been together for a little over 7 years. I'm not in love with her, but I love her. I am still with her because I guess I'm familiar with her. I don't feel like learning another woman, letting her get close only to realize she's just as crazy as Chanel or worst."

He basically told me in my face there isn't a chance, but I don't care. Or do I?

"So you would rather be unhappy. Why not be single? I didn't take you for a punk." He raised an eyebrow.

"Watch your mouth."

"Grow some balls. Nigga, you scared to be single."

"You talk too much." He said taking my drink from my hand and leaning in to kiss me.

When I say Sincere fucked me all over that hotel, that nigga gave it to me. On top of that, the dick is so big it should have its own zip code. Got a bitch walking strange. We had sex so long in so many crazy positions that my legs were stretched out and doubled over to the point where it hurt, but I didn't feel it in the heat of the moment. When we finished, it left me with 'dead legs' that wobbled when I stood up and tried to walk. The last time we had sex, I thought I needed a walker for senior citizens. Being that it had been so long, I knew that this nigga was going to have me out here hobbling like a wounded deer.

I opened my eyes and Sincere was standing over me. He was butt naked. My middle was still sore, but my pussy jumped at the sight before me. The man had the body of a god.

"What's up, sleeping beauty?"

"Hey." I replied.

"Your phone been going off like crazy. Let your people know you are ok."

"I will."

I pulled the sheet over me as I sat up. I looked over at the digital clock on the nightstand and it was almost 8 o'clock at night, which meant I had been with Sen for some long hours. Damn.

"Handle your business and let's go eat. I'm about to shower." He said, walking off. I gave him a head nod.

I had a dozen calls and text messages. Gave wanted to know if I was ok. Uno and Aunt Deb group chatted and had a full-blown conversation with each other about me telling Sen I gave birth to his seed. It pissed me off. I decided not to tell him.

**Nunu:** He has a woman; he doesn't plan on leaving her because he is comfortable with her.

**Uno:** How do you feel about that? You didn't just go out there to fuck, you like him. Admit it.

**Nunu:** No, I came to fuck. I do not want this man.

**Uno:** You could've fucked Gave. You like your baby's daddy. Just admit it.

**Aunt Deb:** It's your choice. But I really think you should tell the man he has a child. And you like that nigga. I know you do. But seriously, tell him. All this ain't by chance.

By the time Sen made it from the shower, I was fully dressed. He walked back into the room in only his boxers. This man was so fine. He had always been cute to me, but his maturity made him sexier.

"You ain't going to shower?" He asked, eyeing me.

"No, I'm about to go." The text between my aunt and Uno had me in my feelings. Had me questioning myself. Why in the fuck did I come out here? Was it really just for the dick, or was it to tell this man the truth? Because I couldn't figure it out, I was ready to go.

"I said we are about to go eat. Go take a shower and then re-dress, unless you wanna go out smelling like sex."

"I don't want to." I whined.

He took in his bottom lip and shook his head.

"You fine as fuck. We ain't gotta go out, I will order us dinner. But you ain't leaving."

How could I argue with his sexy ass? *Fuck it,* I thought heading to the shower.

## Two Days Later.

### Jo

---

I was lying in my bed reading a Thuggish Love by author Apryl Cox when the CO approached my cell. It was in the middle of the night so for Jackson to approach me, I knew it was something I needed to address right away. I sat my book down and walked over to the bars.

"Bubbles." She said, referring to another inmate. "Said to check this book out." She handed a copy of "Not Even The Lord Was Fucking With Me" by Aleta Williams. I took the book from her and when she walked away, I climbed back in my bed. Opening the book up, I retrieved the cellphone from it. Two seconds later, an incoming call came in.

"Yo." I answered. I was a little anxious, hoping it wasn't no bad news about Dez. I knew my child could handle herself, but I couldn't sleep or focus most of the time knowing she was behind bars. I had people watching out for her, though. I hadn't talked to her since she has been down, but she was still my child and wasn't nobody going to fuck with mine.

"Judah Jank." Is how he greeted me back. Hearing his voice made a bitch's heart skip a few beats. I haven't heard his voice in forever. When I reached out to him telling him not to do business with The BGB was by way of kite. He replied in the same manner. To hear his voice brought so many memories. He sounded so good.

"Thank you." I said. I was thanking him for honoring my wishes.

Silence. He cleared his throat.

"Jo. I hate to be calling for this, but you know how I feel about my kids. Your niece, Nutavia aka Nunu was the last with my son Tone the night he was killed. They left together. She must pay for his death."

The news he delivered was a blow to my chest. Knocking all the wind out of me. My eyes watered thinking about how my girls were out there without their mothers, or even Papa to have their backs. However, my crew and I weren't the Queen Pins for nothing.

"I don't know what the fuck you are talking about, but I don't take threats lightly. You touch mine and it's war. I'm not playing fair, either."

He chuckled.

"War it is." With that, he hung up the phone. I could've screamed. What the fuck happened? Nunu killed his son. Fuck!

I had to get this handled.

As I sit in my room staring at my son who I held in my arms as he slept, my heart was saddened. I began to feel selfish. I spent two days with his father, and neither of them knew about the other. It was fucked up. I wanted to bring up to him that I had a son, and he was the father, but I didn't have the courage.

Sen and I agreed on not talking about our personal lives and enjoying the moment. He was so different from a year ago when I first ran into his arrogant ass. I asked him did he like me before and was just playing hard to get. After all, he did diss me and choke me, before he fucked me. He said he had always thought I was attractive, but something was telling him that he needed to stay away from me. I thought it was funny. I was a cold bitch back then, and I did have plans on getting Sen hooked on the pussy and never dealing with him again. Which I did. I stood his ass up.

The day and a half I spent with him, we fucked, ate, watched movies and talked about a lot of stuff mostly business since we agreed we wouldn't discuss our personal lives. I didn't know what we were doing, but I liked it. Deep down, I wanted to see him again. After he fucked me to sleep, I woke up and he was gone. Something told me he left me without saying goodbye, but I didn't want to believe I got dissed. I texted him and my text went undelivered. After an hour, I left with the confirmation I needed. He did not need to know about my son.

After I was sure Papa man was asleep, I laid him in his crib. I stood there for a second, looking over him to make sure he wouldn't wake up. His little butt was a faker. As long as I was holding him, he was sleeping well but as soon I put him down, he would lift his peanut head up. Instead of going to my room to shower, I used my son's shower in his baby room. When I came out the shower, he was still sleeping. I didn't even bother to go get dressed. With only a towel, I took a seat in the rocking chair next to his bed and fell asleep.

"I can't, get it, help-" I tried to scream, but the pressure that was applied to my neck wouldn't allow the words to escape. In my dream, I was fighting Sen. The nigga was trying to kill me. I tried to wake up, but my eyes wouldn't open.

"You scandalous ass, bitch. I knew I couldn't trust you." My eyes widened. It was Sen. He was really standing over me, choking me. I clawed at his hand, but there was no use. The way he was staring at me, he hated me from the depths of his soul. He wasn't the same man I laid up with just days prior. He was going to kill me.

Waaaawww wawwwwwaaa.... My son's crying at the top of his lungs woke me from my sleep.

Sitting at the head of the round table, it was me and Spade. Lucas told me to meet him, and his ass was late as always. I took the blunt from behind my ear and with the lighter that was sitting on the table, I blazed. I was ready to hear what the fuck Lucas had to say so I could get the fuck on. I needed to get back to California. That bitch Nunu had me 38 hot. I was so mad, I wanted to kill that hoe. I had plans on popping up on her, too. I put that on my dead brother.

"Do you know what this is about?" Spade asked.

I did, but sadly, that isn't what I was thinking about. I was thinking how that bitch Nunu was hiding, I had a whole fucking son.

"You know I was with that bitch Nunu." I said to Spade. I got up, crossed the room and went to the cabinet where we kept the liquor and pulled a bottle of 1738 from it. I grabbed two glasses and walked back to my seat. I set the glasses down and poured two shots.

"What's wrong, bro? You seem tense. What she do?" Spade asked. He took the semi-filled glass in front of him. Still eyeing me, he took a sip.

I took a deep breath and let it out. I hit the blunt and passed it to Spade. I stared at my brother. Besides my momma, I shared shit with him that I wouldn't share with anyone else. He would always have my best interest at heart. I started. "Fucked the bitch into a coma. While she slept, I got to thinking. Thinking about what you said and how she got defensive when I mentioned her baby." Spade gave me that knowing look. He shook his head.

"Nigga, what happened?" He asked.

"I got a hold of her phone. Went through the shit. Her people were asking her did she tell me about the baby. I couldn't even read it anymore, so I screenshot her text and airdropped them to me."

"What you do? What they say? The baby yours, bro?"

"I left before she woke up. I didn't want to kill her ass. Leave the kid without a mother. I had to go. Now after reading all the messages I'm ready to hop on the next thing smoking and murder that bitch. I got a son, and that bitch didn't think to tell me." I was ready to explode all over again.

"What Sarah say?" He asked referring to my momma. He knew I told her everything. She had my back.

"I ain't told her yet."

"What you going to do?"

"Kill her." I said, just as Lucas walked into the room.

"Kill who? This bitch that got your baby?" Spade asked in a surprised way.

"Bro, just do the right thing." Spade said. We then looked at Lucas. The nigga was dressed in army attire from head to toe. Lucas walked in with a large envelope and an old

304

videotape. He sat at the table, reached over, and grabbed the bottle of the 1738.

"I'm late because I was trying to find a VCR player. But look." He slid over the large envelope. "Guess what bitches responsible for our brothers getting smoked." His face-hardened. He looked at Spade. He referred to Tone and our God-brother.

Spade grabbed the envelope and opened it.

"The BGB bitches had something to do with it. I am killing that bitch. That's why that hoe was looking spooked that day in the store when she saw my chain. Those bitches were bold. Wanna do business. I can't wait." Lucas argued.

When he said The BGB were responsible, I looked at Spade. He had a surprised look on his face. I was hesitant. I didn't even want to see what he was looking at. I sucked that shit up and slid the envelope over taking all the contents inside.

Nunu. Smoke was coming from my ears, and all I could see was red. I was heated.

"You were fucking with one of the bitches." I looked up, and Lucas was looking at Spade. He shook his head. I saw Spade tense up. At any given second, that nigga was going to jump over the table and beat his ass. I hoped Lucas would shut the fuck up. "I know you didn't know, bro. Don't trip, though. She's dead and Daddy put a hit on the rest of those bitches."

Without saying a word, I walked out of the meeting and jumped in the car slamming the door risking breaking my windows. With an increased heart rate and shaky hands, I peered out of the parking lot. "I knew that bitch was on some grimy shit." I growled. That bitch hit me with betrayal back-to-back. I must say that she was gangsta with that shit, too. She was even bold enough to flirt, fuck me, have my baby, and not tell me. She did all of that knowing she had something to do with my brother's death. When Tone was killed, I knew my pops blamed me. I blamed myself. If it wasn't for me trying to prove to Chanel that I wanted her, I would've gone on that trip with him. I felt powerless when I learned of his death. Not having any clues and such made me feel like I failed my family. Nunu was going to pay for this. No matter how I was feeling her, all that shit was dead the moment she kept my child from me, and it was revealed that she was the culprit behind my brother's death.

I pulled up to the iron gate that lead to my mother's million-dollar home. I pressed my palm on the security system and moments later, I was granted entrance. Driving down the long driveway, I mashed on my brakes behind my mother's Bentley. Leaving the car running and all, I hopped out and headed to her door.

Before I could make it the last step, my mother swung the door open. The all black she was wearing, she was dressed for the occasion. Sarah was a real one. In actuality, she was the mastermind behind The Jank Empire, but she allowed her husband to take the credit.

"Ma." I said as I walked past her into the house.

"You found out, huh?" She said. I turned around and she was shutting the door. I looked at her as if she had two heads.

"You knew?" I asked her.

"No, your father called. He has declared war on The BGB. A war that we can't have." She shook her head and made her way across the living room. I followed her into the foyer.

"Ma, The BGB bitches are responsible for Tone and Boy Boy's death. What you mean we can't have war, shit it ain't even going to be war. The bitch in jail, we have killed. One already dead. It ain't hard to find that rapper hoe. And Nunu. I paused. I know how to locate her."

"Look, son. Jojo called me." I gave her a quizzed look.

"Jojo is one of The BGB's chick's mother. The one that's in jail. She is also your father's ex-mistress. Not to mention we did business with their crew for years." She paused.

"I'm listening."

"Well, I owe her. When the Fancy and Fine crew went down, they could've taken me with them. They owed me no loyalty, since they never knew I was the HBIC. They only owed your father their loyalty. It's fucked up what happened to Tone and Boy Boy. They were my sons, too."

"You don't owe them bitches shit."

"If she had opened her mouth like the FEDS wanted her to, their kids wouldn't have had to grow up without them. I would have been taken away from you, and we would have loss everything. I can't let your father touch those girls. I won't do it. I'm too loyal for that. I told him to call it off." My mother was sounding very stupid right now. I wanted to shake some sense in her, but she probably would have shot my ass.

"If they had killed me, would you have let it slide?"

"I wouldn't have nothing to live for. She still has the power to destroy us all. Trust me. We have to let this go." She turned her back on me. I could tell this was much for her. I really wanted to understand her logic, but I couldn't.

"Nunu is a snake bitch. She don't deserve to live." She turned and looked at me.

"Is she the same Nunu you sneaked off with?" I didn't keep much of anything from my mother. When I asked her to get rid of Chanel, I told her why. When I asked her to, I was staying in Cali a few extra days and I told her why.

"She is the same Nunu I fucked last year. The same hoe that didn't tell me she got pregnant and had my baby. It's a boy. I just found out, and it was by going through her phone."

She stared at me long and hard before walking away, claiming she needed a drink.

"I will not allow you to take my grandbaby's mother from him, but if that bitch plays with you seeing your child, she will have to see me." She stated when she walked back into the room with her drink in hand. "Bring her to me."

"What about Lucas, Dad, and my brothers?"

"Bring her to me. Let me handle all of that." I didn't know what to say, so I turned and walked out.

"Chanel, I need you to listen to me."

"I'm listening, Ma."

"No, stop what you are doing and listen, dammit."

"Ma. I can hear you. I'm trying to make sure I don't forget anything important."

I stood at the top of the stairs eavesdropping, trying to figure out what was going on. Normally, I didn't do shit like that, but the urgency in both of their voices along with the small suitcase by the door had me suspicious.

"Sit your gotdamn ass down now. As a matter of fact, answer this FaceTime." Her mother demanded. I heard the FaceTime alert and Chanel answered.

"Yes."

"I know your mind is made up. Nevertheless, I want you to hear me out. Look at me when I'm talking to you. That man is in his early 20s. He was just drafted into the NFL. From what you told me, he has a few women he deals with, including you. Chanel, do you really think that young man is going to give you what you want?"

"Unlike Sarah, his mother raised him with morals. He will take care of our child. He loves me."

That was all I needed to hear before I dragged into the room. Chanel paced the floor. The last thing she said before I made my presence known was, "He's nothing like Sen."

I drew my gun.

"You got three minutes to get the fuck out my house." Chanel's eyes were threatening to jump from her head.

"Oh, my God. Please don't shoot me." She pleaded.

"Two." I wasn't playing with her ass. That bitch had better be glad I didn't want her, or I would've killed her ass. "Chanel, get the fuck out!"

"Just go, baby. Go." Her mother ordered in a panic. Chanel took off out of the room and I followed. She grabbed the luggage by the door, and bounced. The bitch didn't even look back, or even try to explain. It was good though. I was tempted to shoot the tires out on the G wagon I purchased for her, but I let the bitch go. Javier could have her. Both of them were dead to me.

In fact, I pulled my phone from my pocket to call Spade.

"What's up?" He answered. "Is it important?" The way he asked and by the sound of his voice, I could tell something bothered him.

"Who you ready to kill?" I asked him. Spade wasn't like me. It took a lot for him to fly off the handle, as for me, I tripped off petty shit.

"Jess and her punk ass white boy. She's talking about them moving to Oregon. She's taking my son to dirty ass Oregon. She's crazy. She keeps testing me, and I'm going to call my sister."

Spade had a son by a white chick that already had a man. From what I hear, her man had always accused the two but of course, Jess denied it. It wasn't until she got pregnant with Spade's child that she had to come out with the truth. Her man couldn't have kids. So, she couldn't put the baby on him. Even if she tried, he would've known, nephew don't look like he has a speck of white in him. All nigga.

"You over there now?" I asked.

"Nah, she here picking him up. Talking about they're moving in three months."

"Alright, Spade, damn. I won't move. I'll tell my husband and pray he don't leave me because I am putting your feelings before his."

"Good." Was all Spade said. I heard her call him an asshole and I smirked. I don't know why he just wouldn't be with her. He liked her enough.

"Sen, where you at? What's up?"

"You'll never believe this shit."

"What?"

"Chanel and our baby brother are fucking. Plus she's pregnant."

"Word." He replied.

"Nigga, why it sound like you knew?"

"Yeah. He pulled up on me last night. He said that's why he didn't show up to the grand opening. He felt like he was further sticking the knife in your back."

"Fuck out of here."

"Cold part. He bounced last night. Said he don't want the baby or her."

I was blown away by it all. Here it was, I was over here ready to kill a bitch who ain't told me I got a seed and this nigga was leaving his. I'm questioning if he's really a Jank. My father's blood didn't rock like that.

"You know what. I'm cool. I wanted to go over there and get in his ass. It's the principle."

"You don't love her, and you were looking for a way out. I know it's a cold thing, but you got what you wanted."

There was a moment of pause. I did want to get rid of Chanel, but I was comfortable. The pussy was good, and she would do anything for me that I asked.

"I'm flying to Cali tomorrow." I announced.

"I'm going with you." Spade replied. I told him about my moms calling off the war. He wasn't feeling it, but he respected my mother's order. After all, she was really the leader, plus she was the mother figure he never had. While Spade's mother ran the streets, looking for love, my mother was there for him. He stayed with us more than he did with her. When Spade was 16, she left and moved to England with her man. Spade ended up living with his granny, but still was with us most of the time.

"Alright. I'll text you with details later."

"Alright. Have you talked to Lucas?"

"Nope. I'll go check on him, though." When Lucas learned the war was over, he was angry. He knew better than to go against her. He knew how she got down and plus he respected her a lot. "My momma probably turning in her grave knowing I won't handle the person responsible for her son's death." Lucas' mom died 4 years ago from lung cancer. She and my mom were cool. She was a fool in the streets, but my momma was crazier, harder, and most respected.

"Ok." He sighed. "When you going to tell him she has your child?"

I asked my mom not to mention it. I didn't want Lucas to believe that's the main reason she was still alive.

"No. I haven't told him maybe tonight."

"What the fuck, Nutavia? Where the fuck are you?" It baffled me how my aunt got at me. I had to look at the phone. *Was this really my Aunt Jo coming at me like that?*

"Leaving my office." I told her as I put the baby in his car seat. "What's going on? Are you ok? Did something happen to Dez?"

"Are you strapped?" She asked, causing me to stop what I was doing.

"Auntie, what's up?"

"I have been calling you for the last two days and your shit has been going to voicemail." The urgency in her voice had me nervous.

"I turned my phone off. I needed time alone just with my thoughts." I explained. I think Sen leaving me at the hotel and not reaching out to me had me in my feelings, I felt alone. Gave would've been there if I had reached out to him, but I didn't want to be bothered with him. Like I said, my baby's daddy had me in my feelings.

"Where is my sister?" She asked.

"Aunt Deb is in Jamaica with her boyfriend."

"That's why she ain't answering. Look, I gotta go. However, you keep this number. When I call, you pick up. I need you and the baby to get out of town ASAP. Call Uno and tell her not to come back until I give the ok."

"What is going on?" I hurried and ran to my desk and grabbed both of my Glocks.

"The BGB Crew is responsible for Tone Jank's death. You remember leaving the club with him five years ago and setting him up? The Janks found out and guess what? Their father declared war. Let me get this shit handled. Leave tonight."

I couldn't even speak. Tone was a Jank? I killed my baby's uncle.

I couldn't even grasp that. I looked over at my son and all I knew was I had to protect him. Hearing that I was the cause of Tone Jank and his folk's death, I concluded that is why I had the dream of Sen killing me. I dropped my cellphone, but didn't bother to pick it up. An eerie feeling came over me like I was being watched. I took my child out of the car seat and cradled him in my arm as if I was holding a football. In my free hand, was my gun. I hurried and made my way out of the rear exit.

*Fuck*! Was all I could think. They got me.

Boca…. Boca… Boca….

A bullet hit me. I tried to take off running, never letting my son go. I eventually fell to the ground. My baby screamed out crying. I lifted my arm trying to fire back, but I was too weak. A figure appeared over me.

When I pulled up to the office, I was glad to see that Nunu's car was parked in its designated spot. She hadn't been fucking with me since I took her to the party. I wasn't feeling that shit. For a long time, I wanted her badly. She was sexy, a hard worker, dedicated to the hustle, and a good person to be around. Her vibe was cool as fuck. In addition, the pussy was excellent. I was even willing to play daddy to her son. Although he should've been mine in the first place, I was willing to step up and be what both of them needed. She had yet to tell me who her baby's daddy was. I took it that, she slipped up with a lame and was too ashamed to say. Either way, I didn't care. Nunu was the type of chick I wanted on my team, but when she wasn't sending mixed vibes, she was acting like she was cool on a nigga. I tried not to push her because I didn't want to come off as thirsty, plus she was dealing with shit. Tonight, though, I wanted to know where we stood. If there was no us, I would throw up the deuces and stop tripping over it.

I parked and was ready to hop out of the car when I got an incoming call. It was my mom. I instantly became alarmed. My mom stayed in New York, which was a three-hour time difference. My dash read 8:32 pm, which meant it was 11:32pm her time. My parents went to bed at 6 pm. So, what could they be calling for?

"Hello." I answered.

"Hi, this is Cathy Jean. Your parents' neighbor." The rhythm of my heartbeat was beating like a drum. "Your mom wanted me to call, she's pretty shaken up. She says that she needs you to come home."

My heart dropped to the pit of my stomach.

"What's going on? Where are my parents?" My eyes darted to the side door of the office. Nunu walked off holding her baby in her arm. I saw her gun in the other. Before Cathy's words could register in my head, "Your father passed in his sleep." I heard gunshots and Nunu fell to the ground. I scooted down in my seat as my hand went for my glovebox. I grabbed my gun. A male figure stood over her with his gun pointed at her.

He fired off another round. Boca...

I bust back at him and shattered my window, hitting the target in the back of his dome. I watched his body drop to the concrete pavement. I hopped out of the car and ran to Nunu. The nigga I shot was face down. I bent down and turned him over. It was Black Sam. I looked back at Nunu. Tears trickled down her face as she struggled to breathe. Cherry-red blood covered her entire shirt.

"Don't panic." I told her. She gave me a slight head nod. I attempted to grab her, but stopped and went for the crying baby instead. I checked him to make sure he wasn't hit. A sigh of relief escaped my mouth when I only noticed a knot on his forehead. Cradling the baby in my arms, I told Nunu I would be right back.

"I'm going to get help." After retrieving my phone, I ran back to Nunu, and placed a call to 9-1-1. The baby screamed to the top of his voice. I could tell Nunu was trying to be calm. Looking at her with all the blood all over her shirt, a heaving chest, and silent tears proved she was a soldier. She fought for her life.

"You going to be alright." I calmly told her.

"I don't wanna die." She said in a low but audible tone.

"You won't. I got you." I assured, and prayed I wasn't lying to her.

# Lucas

## Next day

---

I looked over at Trish in my passenger seat asleep. Her nephew was in the backseat looking out of the window. We had just arrived in California. After eating, I was going to meet Black Sam at his spot. I had been calling, but the nigga didn't answer. I told his ass that I had a new burner phone and to answer any unknown calls, but he didn't do the shit. He probably didn't want to risk what we had going on. I paid him to take out Nunu. Sarah said she didn't want her dead because she owed the Fancy & Fine Crew for a favor, they did for her and because Nunu was the FF Crew's family, we had to call off the war. Even with the seriousness on her face I still figured she was bullshitting, wasn't no way she wanted me to let a bitch live who was responsible for my blood brother's death. I didn't expect Sen nor Spade to take action because they were riding with Sarah. It was cool because I just knew my dad had my back. However, when my father called, and she put him on speaker, and he said out of his own mouth that the war was over, my heart dropped. Tears fell from my eyes because it was at that moment that no one was showing loyalty for my brother. His own fucking father was turning a blind eye on his son's murderer. I knew them and if I didn't obey their orders, it could cost me my life. I acted like everything was cool, but in the back of my head I was on some revenge shit. That old bitch Sarah knew it, too. She warned me that I'd better squash it and let it go. *Yeah right, bitch,* I thought as I looked at her and gave a head nod. When I left the meeting, I went straight to Trish and told her what was up. The BGB bitches killed both of ours, and we gon' murk them hoes. I also told her we would have to bail after we did it, and she was down with that, too. Trish was right by my side when I ran up in our spot and stole the 500

320

racks that was there from our last business transaction. I hit up my lawyer and told him to get my money in my accounts that were out of the country. Of course, he was blessed with a big lump sum. Being a Jank had its benefits.

Besides Trish and Black Sam, no one knew that I was done with my family, and I wasn't fucking obeying their orders. Tone was my brother. Fuck them. I didn't even have to ask Black Sam, he offered to body Nunu and the rest of their people for 200k. I wired 100k to him that same day and was giving him the rest once I knew the job was done.

"Baby, we should be pulling up in the next twenty minutes." I said, touching Trish on her leg. She shifted in her sleep before sitting up. She looked in the backseat at her nephew.

"Boy, you still up?" She asked her nephew.

"I'm sleepy, Auntie." He said.

"Well, go to sleep." Trish chuckled.

"Tee Tee, every time I close my eyes, I see mommy and she is crying. It makes me sad."

Trish looked at me, and I looked from the road at her.

"It's just a nightmare, little man. Mommy is happy in heaven." I told him. There were a few moments of silence. My eyes bucked. I was about to crash. I smashed on my brakes trying to prevent from hitting a black truck that blocked me off.

"Oh, my God!" Trish screamed. I stopped just in time. I went to look at Little Man when the doors of the black truck flew open, and four niggas jumped out with AK's. Quick on my toes, I threw the car in reverse.

Boom… the impact from hitting something stopped us. And without a fuck given, the niggas with the AK's shot up the car. I swear to God I wish the first bullet would've killed me how badly that shit hurt and just like that it stopped. The pain vanished.

"You know I hate you right now, bitch." I sneered as I gawked at Nunu. She laid in the hospital bed after the almost fatal shooting. She took one slug to the stomach and one in each shoulder. Lucky for her punk ass, Black Sam wasn't a straight shooter. She only was hit three times. There was one bullet in Nunu's neck. The doctors were scared to remove it due to fear that it might move and end up killing her.

At the sound of my voice, her eyes popped open. She looked at me with pure hate in her eyes. I had to give it to her, though. Even in her condition, she was still shit-talking.

"You should've finished me off because I swear to God, I'm coming for you and everything you love." She threatened. Tears fell from her eyes. "Bitch ass niggas came for me when I had my baby in my arms." She was so mad, her eyes turned redder than a tomato. I was sure she was about to set her machines off. She really needed to calm the fuck down.

I hated that bitch. I hated her for killing my brother, I hated her for keeping my son away from me and I hated that her tears tugged at my heart. Fuck her. It would always be fuck her. The only reason she was still alive was that I feared my momma more than I feared any man walking.

Nunu's hands moved from under the sheet and on her lap was a .38 revolver.

"The only reason I won't shoot now is that my son needs me. Remember, no witness, no case. Fuck you. I swear you should've killed me." Her voice cracked.

I walked up on her, and she raised the gun. For a bitch to be shot up, she still talked shit and was ready for whatever.

"You keep saying your son. Bitch, that's my son. You kept my son away from me because you a grimy ass hoe. That's why you are alive. Because of my momma and my son." I was now standing over her. "Pull the trigger, bitch. I double dare you." I was so mad I could feel my veins popping from my neck.

"Son. Step out, please." The sound of my mother's voice in the hospital room further proved that lady had pull. Gav was the reason I knew where Nunu was. I called him after I pulled up to her spot and saw the yellow tape and police. How did my mother know? Sarah Jank knew everything.

"Sincere Jank, please allow me to talk to my grandbaby's mother."

The sweltering hot sun brightly shined as I stood in the door way dressed in a pair of super short shorts and a halter-top. I watched as Sen walked toward the house carrying our son in his arms. Every time they were together, it warmed my heart. My baby deserved to have both parents in his life. If it wasn't for the special women I had in my life, my baby would've been missing out on a good father.

The day Sarah requested Sen to step out of my hospital room, so she could talk with me, I learned that Lucas hired Black Sam to take me out after his family told them to stand down. Sarah was like, "Your family is the reason I'm here today. The reason I was able to raise my own son. And now the reason I will get to spoil my grandson." She stared at me. I gave no reaction. I knew they knew about the baby. I saw the screen shots in my phone that Sen took. It was the messages between Aunt Deb, Uno and I. It hurt that he tried to have me killed. Sen's mom continued.

"I'm going to tell you like I told your Aunt Jo. Just like her, I can make shit shake and unless it is, a federal agency involved and depending on the situation, my word is bond. I never sent anyone after you." Tears ran down my face because I was mad. All I could think about was how they came for me, not only trying to take me out but my son too. Sarah said. "I'll give you some time, but know that our bloodline will never walk this earth without being a part of our life. A blood test first." With that, she walked out of the door.

I broke down crying. This shit was overwhelming. All of it. Your past is not a past. That shit always resurfaces and reminds you of it.

Sen walked into the room. I could feel him staring at me. I didn't have any energy to fight, although I wanted to ask him what the hell was he looking at.

"Stop crying. You're stronger than that. Let me know when your aunt gets the baby." He said. Shocking me that he gave me a compliment. The baby was with child protective services. Aunt Deb and Uno were landing today and I couldn't wait. I needed my family. First, they needed to go get my son. Since I had no other family to claim my son, I had to wait for my family to fly in. Uno and my aunt were out of the country. Uno was on tour in London and my aunt in Jamaica. My incident made the breaking news. I assumed that's how Sen found out. He reached out to Gav. Gav also told him what hospital I was transported to and where my aunt stayed. I wanted to call New York and cuss his ass out. However, it all worked out. I guess.

Aunt Jo did confirm what Sarah said. She put the hit on Lucas. Apparently, she knew more and had more pull than I thought behind those walls.

After a few weeks of meditating and praying, I finally put on my big girl panties and texted Sen to meet me at my aunts. I wasn't surprised that his mother was with him. We did the DNA test, and it confirmed what I already knew. My son was his. The first thing Sen did was ask me to change the baby's name to Sincere King Jank, Jr. I even put his name on the birth certificate. I was cool with all of that. I wanted my baby to have what I didn't, both parents in his life who loved him.

"You don't think you're showing a little too much?" Sen asked as he stepped on the porch." Without giving eye contact, I replied.

"I'm on my private property. I'm good not to mention grown." I reached for the baby but he didn't hand him over. I looked up at him and the way his eyes pierced mine, sent chills all through my body.

"What?"

"It's been three months and you still haven't invited me inside. I'll invite myself." He turned sideways and walked inside. I had wanted to invite him, but I was scared he would decline. Yes, the beef was over and he was now a part of his son's life, but it still didn't change the fact that I was the reason his blood brother was dead, and it was me who pulled the trigger on their other brother. No, I never admitted it but who's stupid? I was the last person they were seen leaving with. Plus, whoever they got their information from let it be known that I was close with Break, a known jack-boy.

"Where's his room?" Sen was standing at my stairs, looking back at me. Without responding, I climbed the stairs and he followed. After placing the baby in his bed, I took off his shoes. When I turned around, Sen was staring at me. He made me so nervous. The way he would stare at me made me feel as if all he saw was a person who was responsible for his brothers' murders. I knew he hated me, but tolerated me because I had his son. I would never confess anything to Sen because I was too afraid of how harsh his rejection would be, but I wanted us to be friends if nothing else.

"What are you doing for his birthday?" He asked. My baby was turning one.

"Go to the cemetery to see my mom. My aunt will probably cook and of course a big cake." I looked up at him, and he was staring at me again. Like a coward, I looked away and at the baby.

Every time I looked at Nutavia I couldn't help but feel like I was looking into the eyes of a poisonous snake. From the very first day, that she tried to push up on me, my gut was telling me to leave her ass alone. Not thinking clearly, I allowed my desire for the forbidden to corrupt my mind. Every time I saw her, it was a battle. Sometimes I couldn't stand to look at her, and other times I wanted to fuck her real good and tell her I wanted to give the family shit a try with her. The shit was crazy. A grimy bitch had part of my heart, and she didn't even know.

"Let me know what day your family will celebrate, so I can let my mom know. His birthday is on the same day that Tone was killed." She looked up at me with wide eyes. I didn't say it to make her feel uncomfortable, but it was the truth. I continued. "She wanna throw a big party for them both." I wasn't asking her, but telling her.

For a minute, she only stared. At first, I thought I was tripping when I saw her eyes water. She gave me a reverse nod and turned around to walk off. When I pulled her back to me, she kept her head down. Her shoulders shivered.

"What's the matter?" I asked, turning her around to face me. NuNu buried her head into my chest. I wrapped my arms tightly around her and allowed her to cry. As I rubbed, her gently on her back, I wanted to tell her that everything was gonna be OK. It was at the tip of my tongue to tell her that I forgave her, but I couldn't because she never apologized or admitted it.

It was as if she read my mind. Nunu looked into my eyes. "I'm sorry for the pain I caused your family, especially you. I'm sorry for everything." She burst into a loud sob.

"I really am sorry. So sorry." It was at that moment I forgave her. I trusted her. I believed her. It felt like the weight of the world was lifted off my shoulder. I forgave my baby's mother for her past and maybe now we can create a future, who knows.

"I forgive you, Nutavia." I wanted to kiss her on the top of her forehead, but she gave me those lips. Without giving it a second thought, I picked her up and carried her out of our son's room to the first open door. I walked over and tossed her on the bed. I had to have her. By the way, she laid there with sexy eyes and her bottom lip in her mouth. She wanted me, too. I could move on from the past as long as there were no fuck-ups moving forward.

# UNO

Freda was my everything. The love of my life. Never in a million years could you have told me that on this day, I would be marring the woman of my dreams.

The day that Freda came to my boutique to talk about the drama between her and that Brazilian Doll bitch who, I might add, is no longer in the picture by the way.

The day Freda showed up at the shop, I didn't want anything else to do with her. I was done. My ego was bruised. I never had a female make me feel insecure, like I wasn't good enough. I was used to being desired by damn near every chick. So, for Freda to come along with her nonchalant attitude and not giving me the attention I desired, I didn't know how to handle it.

But God works in mysterious ways because if Boom's punk ass did not shoot up my ride trying to retaliate for Dez killing Mina, I probably wouldn't be marrying the love of my life today. I would have never gotten in the car with her on that day.

Since that day, which was a while ago, Freda had been by my side every step of the way. She was there through the deaths of Papa and Kay. Dez went to jail and Nunu was almost killed. She was there through my crying spells, the anger, the attitudes, and the fear of ending up in jail like my mom.

One night we were laid in her bed. We were eating ice cream and watching the reunion of The Bad Girls Club. Freda made a move on me, and I accepted. She fucked me into a coma. I had already felt like I was falling in love with her, but after her thunder tongue blessed my clit, and she hit it from the back with her strap-on dildo, I was in love. God, I only desired her.

The next morning, I woke up to breakfast in bed. We ate together. That's when she explained to me that Brazilian Doll was her ex. An ex that she was in love with, but they cut ties after Brazilian broken her heart. Freda said Brazilian Doll was too ashamed to make their relationship public. She told her being gay would be bad for her image. They were living together. One day, Freda came home to find a Dear John Letter. Some shit about needing to follow her dream and needing time to find herself. When she ran into her at the event, Freda admitted that she had mixed emotions, and she needed closure. She could've saved the part about them fucking. She said she tried to understand her, but Brazilian Doll was still the self-centered fake bitch that she wanted no parts of. Freda claimed the time she spent with me made her miss the small things. Like me being a real bitch. Freda said she and Brazilian Doll were having dinner. Freda excused herself to go to the restroom and left her there. That's when she popped up at the shop.

A few months after our first sexual encounter, Freda told me she started a label, and she wanted me to be a part of it. However, I had to walk away from The BGB. I didn't even have to think about my answer. I was done with the game and ready to focus on my career. Things had been going well.

Freda proposed to me last Sunday. On today, which is exactly one week later we will be married in her mom's backyard. Besides, my aunt, Nunu, and my nephew aka Baby Sen, I will have no family there. Well, I guess you can

332

call Big Sen family because he is coming with Nunu and the baby.

"Here, baby." My aunt said as she walked into the room and handed me a cellphone. I looked up at her before speaking into the phone.

"Hello." I smiled when I heard my mom's voice.

"I wish I was there. I wish you the best. I love you. I'm so glad you found love. I'm glad you made it." I could hear the tears in my mom's voice.

I cried. I loved my mom.

Although she left at a young age, she was my idol. I tried so hard to be like her if not better. Freda helped me realize that being me was more than enough. Following my heart would not only keep me free, but also set me free.

"Thank you, Momma." I said into the phone. We talked a bit before I handed my aunt back the phone. I have to get ready for my wife.

I love my cousins, but I'm cool on them. I'm not feeling how they walked away from the game without consulting with me. I knew I would forgive them one day, but as of now, I ain't fucking with them. I heard Nunu hooked up with Sen and Uno married that funny-looking hoe. I wished them the best.

Anyway, I gotta get ready for my visit. My bitch Lydia was coming to see me. I know you're thinking I'm scandalous for going behind Uno. Wrong, I had her first. We just kept it on the low. Charge it to the game. Everybody was out doing them. I was going to do me, too.

**The End**